Lonna Enox Publications

Lonnaenox.org

UNTOLD AGONY

By

Lonna Enox

Copyright 2018

Lonna Enox

ALL RIGHTS RESERVED

First Printing November 2018

ISBN: 978-0-9977424-7-3

Library Of Congress Control Number: 2016920089

UNTOLD AGONY

BY

LONNA ENOX

Joy!

Hope you enjoy!

Lonna Enox

To My Grandparents

Lonnie and Ellen Hill and Willie and Winnie Scantling

Who all lived to past 80 and 90 and made it seem so easy

ACKNOWLEDGEMENTS

My husband, Ron Tucker, patiently continues to save me—and my computer—from disaster. He tirelessly tramps through the New Mexico sandy hills and wilderness areas, listens to my ideas, cooks meals when my nose is buried in a chapter I can't leave, and is truly my partner.

My children—Monica, Marissa, and Nathan—believe I can do this even when I am sure I can't. They continue to be proud of me, and make me proud.

My kitties, Elsa Grace and Trixie Rose, provide inspiration for Flash and Van.

My Editor and friend, Dr. Sandra Shannon, of St. Louis, Missouri, has patiently worked with me through this novel in spite of moments with challenges for both her family and mine.

My sweet aunt, Etolia Scantling, calls just when I need a "hug" via the telephone, and is president of my Stockton, California, fan club.

My pastor, Ret. Detective Troy Grant, walks me through crime scenes and gives me advice on legal situations.

My former colleagues and former students send me notes and unknowingly lend me insight into my stories.

"There is no greater agony than bearing an untold story inside you."

Maya Angelou

Prologue

"*Forgive me, Father, for I have sinned,*" the voice whispered. "*I've done something horrible. No . . . don't say anything. I . . . I don't have time. I promised to take a letter to the sheriff. I accepted the money. But I didn't do it. So I sent it—*"

The man gasped, a rattle sounding from deep inside.

"*My son,*" *the young priest began, but the man grabbed his arm with surprising strength.*

"*I promised her, Father. She trusted me.*" *He gasped deeply, the rattle echoing in his chest. "I should have…" He gurgled and gasped, his eyes rolling back.*

The young priest began the final rites. The man grew so still that the priest thought he'd gone unconscious. But in a final burst of resolve, the eyes reopened and the man grabbed the priest's arm. He gripped it with surprising strength—a deadly desperation—and gasped a string of almost intelligible words, "Reed. Sheriff. Teacher. Murd…" The man's body stiffened and then gradually relaxed. He uttered a final gurgle and then a long, tired sigh.

The young priest completed the rites as sirens wailed in the distance and remained there with the body, leaning forward a bit to shelter it from the full impact of the rain while he whispered prayers for this troubled soul.

The first responders waited respectfully until the priest rose. Anyone could see they didn't need to hurry. Still, when the priest stepped back, they rushed forward to perform the standard procedures to ensure they were correct.

A policeman reached out with his hand and guided the priest a few steps down the sidewalk. "I need you to answer some questions, Father," he said, almost apologetically.

"*Shall we step inside?*" *the priest asked.*

The police officer looked at the other officers setting up lights and taping the area. "Can we sit in the back of my patrol car instead?" he asked. "I need to make an initial report, and then the detectives will visit you later for details." He opened the door to the back of the patrol car.

The air smelled sour in the back seat, but the priest settled thankfully and found a damp handkerchief in his jacket pocket to wipe his brow. More vehicles had arrived, and people had set up lights so that the whole area resembled a gruesome movie set. *I'm watching too much television*, he thought.

He watched the police officer talking into a cell phone, punctuating his comments with a finger pointing in different areas.

The young priest blew his nose and breathed shallowly through his mouth to clear his nose of the sour smells of someone's body odor—or worse—vomit. He'd finished his first year here in this small New Mexico town, and this was the first incident of this sort here for him. But growing up in Chicago, he had witnessed much worse. He bowed his head to pray.

The door opened once more and he jerked his head up. An older cop, probably a detective since he wore a bolo tie at the neck of a drenched shirt and jacket, slid into the seat beside him and slammed the door shut.

"Father Joseph," he said and held out his hand. "A sad place to be tonight."

"Ah, yes." The priest turned to the familiar face and shook his hand.

"What can you tell me?" the policeman asked.

The priest shrugged apologetically. "You realize that I can't—"

"I know you can't repeat anything he said in confession." The detective waited, a pen hovering above a small pad. "We know his name and some details from his wallet. Can you tell us anything you might have seen?"

"I had been watching television when I heard a pounding on the door. My housekeeper doesn't live in, so I slid into my jacket and hurried to open it. This man was hurt, out of breath as if he'd been running, and he was already soaked. I reached toward him, and he began to back away, looking over his shoulder. Then he began to run . . . stagger more like it . . . and I followed him, begging him to come inside and let me call for help."

"Did he—"

"Of course, you realize that anything he said would be a confession and I cannot repeat it."

The detective sighed. "I know. But had you ever seen him before? Did you know him?"

"I'm new here, you know. Since my predecessor died several months earlier, I have not yet learned the names of many parishioners. I have no idea if he is a member of this church."

"Did he ask—"

"I can't say."

"Did you see anyone else? Maybe someone who was shooting? A car that sped away?"

The young priest shook his head.

"Very well. I may be back to verify facts another time." The detective nodded to him and reached for the door.

"A pick-up truck. I saw it idling at the curb before it took off down that street." The priest waved toward the right. "But I don't know the license or even the color and make. I'm sorry I can't help you."

Later that night, the young priest prayed for the soul who had passed, as well as for the person whose trust the young man had betrayed.

Chapter 1

"Quiet! Hey, everybody—"

I cupped my hands around my mouth but not quickly enough. Reed had heard me, from the grin he shot my way, and wasn't impressed with my leadership skills.

"Are all the Lions here?" he called. "Raise your hands."

Several wiggly Cub Scouts raised their hands.

"Tigers? Wolves? Bears? Webelos?"

Hands flew up and waved as he listed off the various Cub groups.

"Now, parents and other guests, unless you're helping down here on the gym floor, you need to find a seat in the bleachers. You can cheer each one along, but please wait until the winners of the derby are announced before you come down to congratulate your child. When all Cubs have raced, Ms. Janes will be snapping photos. You'll be given the opportunity to order photos from Ms. Janes at that time. And remember, Scouts are good sports. No booing or jeering the other troops."

Sofie chose that moment to toss her water bottle. Reed glanced over just as Teri thrust Sofie in my direction. "Here, Sorrel, let me chase down the bottle," she whispered.

"I'll get the bottle." I gave my goddaughter a kiss on the top of her head before I interrupted the errant bottle's escape and handed it to Teri. When I stepped back, Reed cleared his throat. Teri then took her tiny one and the diaper bag back up in the bleachers, turning to whisper, "Good Luck!" to the twins.

"Lions line up with Ms. Janes. Other Scouts sit with your leaders in this section of the bleachers," he said.

I assembled a wiggly group of small Lion Cubs into the semblance of a line before we walked across the gym floor to the race track. Admiring their tiny racers as they held them up for me to see, I clicked photos.

Four hours and two bottles of cold water later, I snapped the last photos of the champions from each den. "Are we finished?" I asked Jose. "Oh, wait, I need to get the names—"

"I can do the captions if you want, Sorrel. I know all of them. If you'll download the photos to my email, I'll take care of the rest. I'm going straight from here to the paper to write up the article anyway."

"I would love to do that! And I owe you—"

"Don't let her offer to cook dinner!"

I looked back at Reed. "How rude!"

The twins patted my shoulder in passing. "It's okay, Aunt Sorrel. We all know you can't cook. But we like hot dogs anyway."

I made a face and growled at the twins as they ran off laughing. "Your uncle Reed is a bad influence on you two," I called after them.

Reed walked by carrying a box. "I'm starved. Run by the paper long enough to do what you must. I'll pick you up there and we can grab something to eat. I have about thirty more minutes to sort trophies and ribbons for the different troops."

"Don't you have to go in to the office?"

"I took today off for the Pinewood Derby."

My stomach growled and Reed laughed.

"That's a yes?"

I made a face and turned to leave. "Give me about thirty minutes."

It took closer to an hour before I'd checked each photo and chosen the best ones for the newspaper. Finally satisfied, I emailed them to Jose, gathered up my camera bag, waved to the newspaper office in general, and headed down the hall toward the front door.

"Sorrel?" a gravelly voice called from behind the door to my right. The secretary's desk was empty, so I stepped to the door and peeked inside.

Randall Byrd, editor of the paper, sat behind a well-used wooden desk. He motioned me inside, draining a coffee cup in a single gulp. "The Scout photos ready?"

"I've written the dens and pack names, as well as city. Jose is identifying the Scouts by name as we speak. Did you have something else you wanted? My schedule is a bit crowded—"

"No, we're good—unless something comes up. At this time, there's always news from the state legislature—and school news, of course."

"Good! With Teri home with Sofie, I'm shorthanded at the shop. In fact, I should be there now, but Reed asked me to lunch."

He smiled, his eyes straying back to his computer. "Thanks for the morning!"

Mr. Byrd's behavior seemed out of character a bit. Or maybe I was just tired and my "radar" was slightly off.

Reed was leaning against my Jeep Liberty, his phone against his ear, when I stepped outside. He ended the call instantly when he saw me. "I'm parked right over there," he called and pointed three vehicles down.

"I can follow you," I told him as I approached.

"Nah. I'll bring you back here. Do you have a preference about the food?"

"No. But I'm hungry."

He grinned but wisely didn't comment. He held the door open for me and closed it when I'd settled inside. Once he'd climbed into the driver's side and started the engine, he looked over and winked. "I called an order into Pizza Madhouse, and it should be waiting on us. Figured you might be as hungry as I am."

6

"I could eat a cow—and I hope to never see a tiger, bear, wolf . . . whatever critter again!"

"Then I can have the pepperoni off your slices?"

"Just keep your hands off my pizza!"

We chatted about the morning and other news as we drove to Pizza Madhouse. Reed had been a city policeman when I moved to Saddle Gap. He'd only joined the sheriff's department a few months ago. He and I had also only begun dating about that same time — officially, at least, but still casually. But our relationship had begun almost two years ago, when I moved here from Houston and opened a gift shop in a little house that had been left to me by my mom's aunt.

I'm also an aspiring wildlife photographer. Because both the shop and my photography are fledgling careers, I work part time for the local newspaper as a news reporter and photographer. And the fact that I'd been a television crime reporter for a large station in Houston, Texas, before moving here helped me snatch the job. My being in witness protection when I first arrived in Saddle Gap added yet another dimension to my complicated life.

But when Reed and I met at the scene of a murder, *complication* was like calling the Mexican food here hot instead of roasting. In spite of these drawbacks, and several others, our relationship had progressed gradually . . . though not smoothly. Still, a few months ago, we agreed to expand our friendship. Both of us had previous failed marriages, as well as busy work schedules, so describing us as cautious is a huge understatement.

"You must be hungrier than I thought since you're so quiet. Have you eaten your fingernails?"

I raised my hand to show him. "Check for yourself! "

He parked in a spot right in front of Pizza Madhouse, laughing. "You're tired, I imagine. I know I am. Events like this one would be a terrific birth control advertisement. And, in case I didn't say it earlier, I do appreciate your volunteering to help out."

"You know I love it, Reed, not to mention the fact that I'm getting paid for the photography. The paycheck, however small, helps the shop during these slow seasons."

Neither of us wasted time talking at first. Instead, we both filled our mouths with the hot pizza and washed it down with iced tea. It was only after I'd licked the sauce off my fingers that Reed spoke. "They will be starting on the barn next week."

"Oh! I meant to ask you about that. Which style did you choose?"

"The same style of the one that burned. They kept showing me those big red barns that you see in movies and magazines, but they look ridiculous beside the old ranch house. I think an aluminum one will suit my needs. If someday I decide to get a herd of milk cows or something, maybe I'll consider something bigger."

"What does Madonna say?"

He grinned. "Plenty. She's female, you know, even though she's a dog. But I'm making an enclosed area inside with a dog door for her. She's agreed to give it a try . . . at night anyway. She and those worthless pups spend their days on the front porch guarding that old house from varmints."

Everyone listening to Reed might not notice the affection in his voice. But I did. "It's their home," I said. "She's grateful to have someone to share it with her."

"Typical female interpretation, Red," Reed drawled. "You females always make it sound like you are protecting the home front."

"We are protecting our homes while our males go out and work . . . or chase other females . . . "

"Wrong again! We're simply helping you ladies be stewards of your time so you have more time to bedazzle us poor males into obeying your every whim in our weak moments!"

Reed couldn't control the grin that spread over his face at the sound of my giggles.

"What a phony, Chris Reed," I gasped, wiping tears. "You're just a whining softie. Now tell me about the barn."

We finally arrived back at my Jeep after stuffing ourselves with ice cream cones on top of the pizza.

"I'll never fit in your barn if I keep hanging around you," I complained when he held the door of his truck. I waddled as I walked toward my Jeep for effect.

Reed took the key out of my hand, stowed me inside, and leaned in to give me a peck on the cheek before shutting the door. "More to love is what my mama always said."

His eyes danced as he interrupted my gasp. "I've got a letter to read at the office. Got the sheriff in an uproar." He walked to his truck, opened the door, and called, "If you come up with something edible later, I may bring it over and tell you about it."

"How can you even mention food? I may never eat again!"

He didn't answer, his laughter echoing as he climbed inside the truck. He had a nice laugh.

Chapter 2

I didn't have time to satisfy my curiosity about the latest crime in our small community, for immediately after opening the door connecting my living quarters to the shop, I sensed catastrophe hovering overhead.

Usually when I'm out of the shop, Teri fills in. However, since giving birth to her daughter, Sofie, and corralling seven-year-old twin sons, Teri can no longer come into the shop to work. Yet somehow she continues to create her line of beauty and facial care products at home and finds time to help decorate the shop for special events. When I do need extra help, she has an endless supply of cousins, sisters-in-law, and aunts who are happy to step in. Sometimes that is advantageous; other times, it borders on disaster.

When I stepped into the shop, I knew we had one of "those days." A local young woman holding a bawling baby bounced and swayed as she argued with Teri's aunt Josephina. Behind her, an older couple turned toward the front door as if to leave.

I stepped around the counter and hurried toward the older couple. "How may I help you?" I stuck out my hand to shake first her hand, then his. "I'm Sorrel Janes, owner and wildlife photographer."

The lady motioned toward a packet of Sandhill Cranes notecards. "Did you take these photos?" she asked.

"Yes. I took them at the annual Sandhill Crane Festival at Bosque del Apache near Socorro, New Mexico."

"They are gorgeous! I don't write letters much anymore, but these would be unique mementos from our trip." She turned toward the wall opposite us. "I assume those are your photographs on the walls also?"

I felt a soft nudge. "Yes, they are," I answered as I turned slightly. "May I help?" I asked Aunt Josephina.

"Raquel wishes to put something in layaway. I told her we do not do that, but she says she knows people who have done so."

I turned to the couple. "Do you have more questions?"

They smiled. "No. We just need to decide how many we will buy."

"Music to my ears!"

I motioned to Aunt Josephina to stay with them and turned toward the young bargain hunter.

After both parties left us a half hour later, Aunt Josephina sighed. "I could use something to drink!"

"Would you settle for peppermint tea?" I asked, plugging in the small electric kettle that I kept in the tiny office area. "Or a cup of strong instant coffee? Why don't you close the shop while I get them and join me in my quarters? It's actually a little after time."

"Coffee," she said. "And I'll happily lock up here. That gal was a challenge!"

By the time we settled on my elderly sofa with a cup of coffee and a plate of cookies Aunt Josephina had whisked from a tin she'd brought, I felt the tension seeping out of my shoulders. "It's been a long day," I told her.

"How did the *muchachitos* do with their little cars?" she asked.

"They won first and second place in their troop," I said, "but they didn't win at the district level. They took fourth and fifth."

She smiled. "That would be a disappointment for Jose. Jose needed Reed to help him and the twins. They always worked on projects together and are still just boys themselves."

I nodded, then continued casually. "I guess Reed had a busy night last night."

"*Dios mio.*" Aunt Josephina leaned toward me. "That poor man. And the young Father—he must be so upset."

"What happened?"

"Some man came in the night. He had been shot! And when he pounded on the church door, he left blood."

"Do you know him?"

"I haven't heard his name, but he was Anglo. I don't know much more, but he was bleeding and then he died. He talked to the priest . . . but, of course, the Father cannot say."

We moved on to talking about her day in the shop before she left to cook the evening meal for her family.

I spent a few minutes checking for messages in the office but remembered Reed had warned that he'd be stopping by for dinner. So I returned to my kitchen, placed pork chops on my small electric grill, and baked a couple of potatoes in the microwave. Finally, I emptied a small package of frozen broccoli into my electric steamer. No time to prepare a dessert, but the sherbet in the freezer and the leftover cookies Aunt Josephina had given me would do.

"So what do you have to say about this dinner, Christopher Reed?" I asked. My cats, Flash and Van, awoke and meowed before settling back to finish their nap.

Reed arrived just as everything finished cooking. *I'll never do that again*, I thought, arranging the plates on the kitchen table before I opened the door. "Just in time!" I sang out.

Reed sniffed. "Smells great! I'll just wash up first."

I watched him disappear into the bathroom. Something bad hovered. He hadn't made a single smart remark about my cooking. I'd wait to probe until he'd eaten.

Although Reed asked about my afternoon, he didn't comment on anything I reported. Instead, he ate the meal almost mechanically and declined dessert. He'd only spoken a sentence or two during the entire meal. I sensed that his latest murder scene weighed heavily upon him, understandably. It was best if I waited until he broached the subject.

"Why don't you relax while I clear these up," I told him when he offered to help. "I'll put on some coffee. You sit." By the time I'd stored the remaining food in the refrigerator, he was already settled in the old overstuffed chair with Flash on his knee, his head back, and his eyes closed. I washed dishes, reminding myself that I needed to keep my hands busy until he was ready to talk.

"Coffee?" I finally asked after he'd had a brief nap.

Reed jerked awake and straightened up, startling Flash. She leapt off and skittered across the kitchen to her food dish. "Thanks." He accepted the mug and settled it on a coaster beside him.

"Bad?" I sat down on the sofa cushion near him and sipped cautiously.

"Yeah." He sighed then reached for his mug and sipped.

"Someone you know?"

"Kind of. Actually, I knew his dad instead of him, but I've seen him around. His dad was a senior football player when I was a kid just starting to play on the peewee team. Mama took me to some of his games, and he became my idol. He was one of the best quarterbacks Saddle Gap has ever had. Nice guy. He won a scholarship to the university, and people thought he'd play professionally. But he had some sort of injury during his last year at the university, so he came home to coach in his high school. In fact, he was my coach and he was really great. He always warned us to keep our grades up in case our dreams changed. He also reminded us that football wasn't all there was."

I leaned forward and took his free hand in mine. He held it tight, his mind still in the dark place he'd gone. Finally, I asked, "Did you notify the parents yourself?"

"No, they'd done that this morning. But I went over to see them . . . you know . . . to work the investigation. They just sat there, you know, like zombies or something. I've seen it before, of course, but I kept thinking of how strong and happy and confident Coach—now this grieving parent—had always been. I wanted to be like him, you know. That guy wasn't there today . . . just a ghost that sort of looked like him . . . only like he'd grown old overnight. It almost makes a guy

13

never to want to have kids." He stopped talking, took another sip of coffee before setting it back down. Then he just sat there, his hand gripping mine while he grieved the losses both recent and long ago.

I heard my aunt's old clock chime an hour note. Chris jerked, released my hand, and stood awkwardly. "I'm lousy company tonight, Sorrel."

I stood as well. "No, you're not. Besides, you know me. There are plenty of times when I've been lousy company. I am surprised, though, that you haven't given me a food rating."

He didn't react. Instead, he gazed ahead, seeing things he'd never wanted to see and trying to get past that gut reaction. "I'm never surprised at the horrible things people will do to each other. I think what surprises me is how they deal with the misery they leave behind."

"They don't," I told him. "We deal with it. You by finding them and making them answer for their crimes, and me by reporting it so that society can breathe easier knowing they're locked up." Then I corrected myself, "Well, I did report it. Every time I feel a little bored and think I'd like to get back to the career I'd thought I wanted, something like this reminds me."

Reed pulled back and stood. "Time to get back to it. Sheriff wants me to meet with the homicide detectives and some others working the case." He stretched, took a few steps toward the door, then stopped and turned back. "I can't believe you cooked—and I could eat it! Are you Sorrel? Or has some creature stepped inside—"

"Watch it, cowboy!" I warned.

He chuckled feebly.

"It's okay, Reed," I reminded him. "We have to smile or cry, you know."

He started to turn, then roughly pulled me into a hug. "I know you know, Sorrel. I feel so sad . . . and now I'm starting to get mad."

"Good!" I leaned up and kissed him. "That's a good luck kiss. You have to get a little mad, you well know. I remember a seasoned reporter who told me, 'Embrace the agony. It powers you along.'"

Chapter 3

"Miss Sorrel! We've been wondering when you'd be stopping by!"

I grinned at the group gathered in the front waiting room, not reminding them that I come by Casa de Oro, the senior care center at least once every week. "I came to see the beauty pageant. I'm the official photographer, remember? Let me sign in here at the front desk, and then you can take me to the pageant area." I looked at the three ladies on the sofa. "Are all of you competing?"

"No, not I! I wanted to give the others a chance." The speaker, Sarah, ignored the laughter and comments from several of the others seated nearby. "I'm using my time practicing for the talent show instead."

I pinned the visitor's badge I'd just received onto my shirt and walked over to greet each of the boisterous crew. "I see beauty and talent everywhere I look," I told them and snapped some candid shots to support my statement. "You still have a couple of months until the talent show. I expect to see you all competing."

Ruben, the self-proclaimed grouch, grunted. "You should be out taking photos of the latest murder we heard about on television instead of snapping pictures here," he said. "I can't believe everyone is thinking of a beauty queen when that boy is dead."

"You knew him?" I asked.

"Sure. All of us old-timers did. He did yard work here from the time when he was just a kid in school. He didn't need to work, he said, but his daddy and mama wanted him to learn the value of work." Ruben looked around. "He always was a polite kid. I can't believe someone killed him."

Several others nodded.

"He's almost grown," someone muttered. "Kids grow up and change."

"He didn't change," Ruben insisted. "He really cared. The police need to care enough about him to look into it, not just look into it a day or two." Ruben glared at those around him, as if daring them to argue.

"Probably just in the wrong place at the wrong time," someone called out.

"Right!" Ruben spat out. "Murder is always being in the wrong place at the wrong time. Otherwise, no one would be murdered."

Cindy, obviously the group peacemaker, tutted. "They try. Maybe they're doing more than you think. We have to be patient. I'm sure they're working night and day like those policemen do on television."

Ruben grunted but seemed a little calmer. "I still say one of our young men getting killed matters more than this silly pageant. Nobody wants to see a bunch of dried-up old bodies like us performing."

"Speak for yourself!" snapped Louisa. "I didn't really know that kid—only saw him when he came around and worked outside. I'm sorry and hope they find the murderer, but we can't do anything about it. We've just got to live our lives and try to get as much pleasure as we can. I was Piñata Festival Queen three years in a row, remember?"

"How could we forget? Everybody else dropped out." Ruben struggled to his feet and shuffled about with an exaggerated swing of his hips.

"You're going to fall, you old fool!" Sarah called. "A broken hip would ruin your love life!"

"Little she knows!" hooted Ralph from his favorite chair near the window.

I sneaked out amid the jeers and laughter, happy to escape during a lighter moment.

I'd never have thought this center would become my favorite place to visit when I first came to recruit crafts for my shop. Since then, my whole outlook has taken a full 180-degree turnaround. Besides the smiles they always bring, these seniors also make me aware of aging and its challenges. Other than Aunt Rose, I'd not been around older relatives much. My visits here remind me that all too often the oldest members of our society become invisible.

The lunch room had been transformed into a makeshift pageant room. Chairs were arranged into rows with an aisle down the middle. A backdrop of tall potted palms lined the back of the stage area, disguising the serving line. Wall hangings featuring silhouettes of Twenties' era flappers were scattered down both walls. A few tables across the back of the room held various potted plants. I stopped to admire one. A card tucked into the back read, "In sympathy."

One of the volunteers bustling by noticed the card also. She whisked it out and into her pocket. "We make do with what we can," she whispered and rolled her eyes.

I snapped photos about the room, mostly checking the lighting, and then settled to wait with family and friends. Staff maneuvered the people in walkers and wheel chairs to their seats before the ambulatory residents arrived. Small cakes, cookies, and a punch bowl filled with weak lemonade were placed on the small table at the back.

When everyone had settled into seats, someone started a cassette player and the promenade began. A local radio announcer introduced each contestant, interspersing humorous as well as serious facts about each.

As beauty pageants go, this one moved much more quickly than usual. The talent portion had been waived, leaving only the opening promenade, individual walks up front, and a short question/answer portion.

In spite of the earlier teasing, members of the audience clapped and cheered for each contestant and called compliments as they paraded past. Ralph managed a few whistles. After the pageant director crowned the winner and gave flowers to her and the two runners-up, everyone cheered for them as they strolled to a separate table at the back where they would enjoy refreshments and greet guests. Their fellow contestants would be seated at a table nearby.

I took several candid shots of the tables, promised to bring the photos out in a couple of days, and congratulated the participants.

"You're all winners," I told them.

"I'll drop a photo at the newspaper," I told the director as I passed her on my way out. "Is someone writing up the story?"

"Yes. Thanks for being here, Sorrel. Your photos always make them feel so special."

"They are special," I told her. "They're just young people in old bodies."

Once in the Jeep, I picked up my copy of the newspaper I'd ignored this morning and scanned the article about the murder. The accompanying photo, a shot of the Catholic Church in the background, had an overlay of a clean-cut young man, Brent Brownley. It was obviously a professional photo and might have been taken a few years earlier.

I glanced over the article and read a brief summary of his murder and requests for information. The reporter mentioned that Brent had graduated from the local high school and a junior college. He'd volunteered with a couple of local charities, coached a soccer team, and worked at a local bank. Just as Ruben had said, he seemed to be a good young man. The article concluded with a meager listing of survivors: his parents and a few cousins. The reporter also noted that his father had been a local football legend and was a retired coach.

I stared at the photo. Although I'd reported on numerous crimes as a television reporter in Houston and realized that crimes are committed by people from a variety of backgrounds, something just felt odd. Had I met this young man in life, I doubted I'd ever suspect him of anything more than what I saw. My gut reaction told me there was a more complicated story here.

Of course, he might have been a perfectly innocent man who had been caught in the wrong place at the wrong time. The information about him here clearly indicated an ordinary young man who had just begun his life. He'd contributed to his community, grown up here, and eventually would have married a local girl and settled down. More than likely, just as one of the seniors had suggested, he'd been a victim of random violence, again noting the conservative clothing and

19

kind-looking face. In fact, he looked a bit like my former husband, Kevin.

I'd been so immersed in thought that I'd not heard the impatient tapping against my car window. But the car door being swung open immediately got my attention.

"You should have locked your car, Sorrel," an aggravatingly familiar voice scolded.

"You could have announced your presence," I popped back. "You're lucky I didn't—"

"Have your hearing aids on? I tapped until I wore my hand out!"

I glared at Reed. "Why are you here, Deputy?" Then I looked closer at his face. "You've been up all night. Why aren't you in bed?"

"I tried to catch a quick nap, but you know how it is. The scene just keeps running through my head like a cheap movie. My mind knows my eyes have missed something, so it doesn't want to turn itself off. I finally gave up, took a shower, and am on my way to eat something. Figured the gal who can eat constantly and still look like she's not eaten in years might want to join me."

"Only if I drive. You're too tired!"

"I can't leave the truck here. Follow me to the station and I'll leave it there. Maybe I won't run over anyone in a couple of blocks!"

"I'm not counting on that," I hollered. His laughter even sounded tired.

Chapter 4

Reed swore he felt refreshed when we sat down to lunch. Actually, he did look better, especially after our iced tea arrived. He further argued that during his career in law enforcement, he'd often spent long hours without sleep, sustained by adrenaline, countless cups of coffee, and the compulsion to solve a case. So I dropped that line of conversation and pursued a different course of snooping.

"The residents at the Casa de Oro were buzzing about your murder case." I bit into the edge of my taco and leaned over my plate so the juice wouldn't drip on my blouse.

Reed grunted. "Murder isn't a daily thing here like it is in the big cities."

I swallowed. "They said he'd worked on the grounds there when he was younger and now still stopped by to run errands, etc."

"They did? Any of them say anything about him?"

"I'm not sure. One of the men, Ruben, mentioned him when he was complaining that we didn't need to worry with a beauty pageant when this kid needed his murder solved. Apparently, this young man continued to stop by on his time off to visit. Anyway, Ruben always grumbles about the activities—and then never misses them. He surely knew this young man, but I'm not sure if he actually remembers him."

"Probably not." Reed motioned toward the guacamole in a tiny dish beside my plate. "You planning to eat that?"

"Keep your eyes on your own lunch. I love guacamole!" I scooped a hefty bite with a chip and crammed the whole thing into my mouth.

Reed chuckled. "It has always been a mystery how you can eat like you do and stay so skinny."

"Good genes. And exercise."

We concentrated on clearing our plates for the next several minutes. When Reed had eaten the last forkful of refried beans, he continued with our conversation. "It wouldn't hurt to talk to this guy, I guess. Maybe later. Unfortunately, the priest isn't talking as he regards anything the young man said as confession."

"Did he know him?"

"No. The priest is new—only been here a couple of months—and said he didn't recognize this guy. So he apparently hadn't been to confession or to services regularly—at least, not recently."

"They have a front page spread in the paper, but most of it is about his father. You don't think this is some grudge against his dad, do you?"

"Not likely, Sorrel. Coach has been retired since—"

"Hey, Deputy! You already solved that murder?"

We both recognized that voice, and neither of us smiled.

Reed sighed. He muttered something I probably didn't want to hear, then glanced up. "Hi, Mr. Mayor. No, it's early days yet. You'll need to talk to the sheriff."

"Well, seeing as how you're on a date . . . "

"Just grabbing a bite. And you? Coffee break?" Reed motioned toward our waitress.

The mayor glanced around the room after the waitress left and lowered his voice almost to a hiss. "We should be giving this one special attention. For Coach's sake!"

Reed pushed his chair back from the table, reached in his pocket, and pulled a bill out. "You need to talk to the sheriff, Pete!" he said. "I'm just the deputy, as you know. Besides, the call came in last night and we're still collecting evidence. Sheriff sent me off to eat, and I'm due back to relieve someone else." He dropped the tip on the table and stood. I stood as well.

"I'm Sorrel Janes," I said, leaning and offering my hand across the table. "I'm a news photographer with the paper."

"I know who you are," he said, still staring at Reed. He ignored my hand, so I dropped it. "I expect an update soon."

Reed grunted. "The sheriff didn't give you one, so you thought you'd harass me." He cupped my elbow and guided me a couple of steps in front of him. "No comment," he said as we walked away.

"I'll be talking to the sheriff," the mayor's imperious voice called after us.

"You do that," Reed replied without a backward glance. He handed our bill to the man at the cash register and pulled his credit card from his wallet. "Great food as always," Reed told him. "Thanks."

As we walked to my Jeep, I thought about how I liked his hand lightly touching my waist. He walked around to his side, ignoring the mayor and his entourage assembling on the sidewalk behind us. The mayor had followed us outside and stood before a crowd gathering in the lot. His voice, pompous and elevated, he burst into a litany of complaints about law enforcement. However, he didn't get the reaction he sought, although I noticed that Reed's lips tightened.

"Obviously, there's history between you two," I commented as I started the Jeep. Reed grunted and I pulled out onto the street. I wisely dropped the subject. Maybe we'd revisit it some other day.

We stopped at the light at the corner before Reed spoke. "I have an appointment with the parents. It isn't going to be easy. Coach was terrific with us athletes. We'd do anything to please him. He was a big part of my life in high school. And not only my life, but most of us guys. You might say he was our hero." His voice dropped, almost as if he were speaking to himself. "Sometimes it's easier when it isn't your own kid, I guess."

I turned onto Main Street, then continued toward the sheriff's office. Reed paused but I didn't think he expected an answer. He continued, as if talking to himself. "They only have this one kid. He must have been a surprise, except that Coach's wife was much younger. In fact, she was in my graduating class, although I didn't really know her well and I've only seen her a few times since. Funny how most people sort of faded into the background around Coach.

He'd been signed by a professional team right before he graduated from college. Only played a couple of years before he was injured. Everyone had predicted fame and success for him. It must have been devastating to see the dream vanish."

I could hear the emotion in his voice and I felt his pain. Reed had lost his own father by then, and Coach must have been a hero to him.

When I parked behind his truck, Reed continued speaking as if we hadn't ridden in silence for the last several minutes. "I've often wondered how he ended up here, in a small New Mexico town, coaching high school football," he said. "No one talked about it. But however it happened, there was no mistaking that he had that special touch, that charisma."

I reached over and slipped my hand in his. He squeezed it then leaned over and kissed me lightly. "Do you want me to go with you?" I asked.

"No. I think he'd prefer me to be alone. But I hope you'll agree to terrorize me with dinner tonight. Frozen TV dinners or sandwiches are fine."

"Fine with me. I have some work to finish . . . photos for the paper, etc. Would seven or so be okay? That way, you could catch a nap."

He smiled. Then he climbed out, but he didn't immediately close the door.

"Something wrong?" I asked.

He shook his head. "I guess I'm starting to get accustomed to your bad cooking," he said. "Or maybe I just like having you listen to me at the end of a hard shift while those pesky cats transfer hair to my uniform."

"I don't mind going with you, Reed."

"I know you don't, Sorrel. But he would mind. Sometimes us guys just find it hard to . . . you know."

"Yes, I do."

I couldn't resist touching his cheek. "I'm running by the paper. Won't be home until later this afternoon."

"I'll call before I come."

Reed watched me leave. I knew the next few hours would be hard for him. As I turned out onto the highway, I reached for my cell and pushed automatic dial. Teri picked up right away.

"Teri, I think I'm going to need your Tia's help."

"Ah. Reed coming for a special dinner?"

"Just dinner. But he doesn't need one of my meals. I have to stop by the paper with photos and write some short captions for them."

"I'll let her know. When will you need it?"

"By this evening. Probably six or later."

Chapter 5

"Great job on the Casa de Oro Senior Care Center article, Sorrel!" I stopped and looked over my shoulder. I'd thought Mr. Byrd had left earlier.

"Thank you, sir. Visiting there is always the highlight of the day." Praise from Randall Byrd was always genuine and welcome. I'd worked for news editors who considered themselves elevated high above journalists. Others raved effusively, then claimed all the credit. "They are a fun bunch," I added.

"Do you have a minute?" Mr. Byrd always formed this command as a question.

"Yes, I do." I walked through the door he held open into his office. His desk dominated the room, but he also had matching dark brown leather chairs in a corner with a tall lamp and a decorative wood art piece above.

"Would you like something to drink?" he asked.

"No, thanks."

It occurred to me, as I slid into the same chair I always chose, that we news people are creatures of habit. Next time, I'd sit in the opposite chair and accept a bottle of cold water.

Mr. Byrd sat in the other chair. "I think I would even have enjoyed that beauty pageant."

"Most of the male residents complained, but they all attended," I said. "Even the man who is essentially blind sat by me and requested descriptions."

He laughed. "His imagination and your descriptions were likely better than reality. That's often how it is, isn't it?"

I didn't want to appear impatient, but I had planned to work in the store tackling invoices and other paperwork. So, I opened my mouth, but he spoke instead. "I'm glad we have happy things to report besides the sad ones."

I nodded and waited.

"I know you've heard about the latest tragic death . . . a murder . . . of Brent Brownley."

I heard the sadness when he pronounced the name. "Personal friend of yours?"

"My godson." He stared at a landscape painting on the wall before he continued. "His father grew up in my neighborhood and was a great friend with my younger brother. They played football together and accepted scholarships to UNM in Albuquerque. When my brother died in a car accident on graduation night, Joe was the only survivor. I remember him promising my parents he'd be playing every game for Robbie. He never neglected to stop by our house on holidays and Sunday afternoons. He essentially stepped in for Robbie. He even named his son Robert Brent."

He cleared his throat in the pause that followed. "He received several offers after he graduated from UNM, but he came back here and revived the struggling football program. He is much loved."

I waited. Finally, he looked over at me and said, "I would like for you to write the story."

"I'm your photographer, Mr. Byrd."

"Photographer now. Award-winning crime journalist/television anchor previously."

I smiled gently. "That's why I prefer photographing critters now. Even with killing and sometimes eating each other, they seem kinder. Does that sound weird?"

I'd hoped to lighten the moment, but he only sighed. "I'm a professional and I can write it. It's just . . . " I watched him struggle for a moment.

"How about you let one of your staff write the obituary? Or maybe one of the other coaches or teachers who work with him would talk to your reporter?"

Then I mentally kicked myself even as I heard my voice continuing. "I wouldn't mind talking to some of his athletes . . . maybe putting a personal touch. A smaller story . . . human interest?"

He brightened a bit—only a bit—and smiled sadly. "I knew I could count on you to help, Sorrel."

"Well, I have the sale in two days so—"

"Then you need to get going on the story. I'll need it before 10:00 am to include it in the special edition we're running."

"I thought I'd just add photos of other athletes and write captions beneath them," I protested weakly.

He didn't hear me—or simply ignored me. "Take as much room as you need."

A light tap on his door interrupted any further protests from me, although he hadn't heard any I'd made so far anyway. He rose and hurried to the door.

"Joe. Helen. Such a sad time." He gathered the small blonde into a gentle hug, then stepped back for them to enter the office. I rose and walked toward them.

"This is one of our photojournalists, Sorrel Janes," Mr. Byrd told them. "We were just talking about how to handle Brent's story."

"I am sorry for your loss," I murmured. Coach nodded impatiently and didn't reply. His wife put a hand on my arm and squeezed gently.

"I'll just let myself out," I told Mr. Byrd and started around the trio to the door.

"I'll want to see the story before it goes into print," Coach almost barked.

I paused and looked to Mr. Byrd. He turned to his friend. "I always approve the stories ahead of time, Joe. Ms. Janes is an experienced professional who has suffered tragedy of her own. She will not disappoint you and Helen."

I took the reprieve he'd provided, nodded to both, and murmured goodbye before escaping. *Why did I open my big mouth?*, I wondered as I hurried to the Jeep and climbed inside. Didn't I have enough to do without tiptoeing around grieving parents—especially when the father's grief had already escalated to the anger stage?

As I pulled away, my cell phone tweeted. I stopped and checked it. The text was from Mr. Byrd:

I'll handle the parents. See you in the morning—before 10 if possible.

I groaned. "This is why I left this business!" I complained to the empty vehicle. "Why am I letting myself be drawn back into it? Why didn't I just say no?"

I moved the gear to drive, turned left out of the parking lot, and headed to Teri and Jose's house. Teri would save me from my big mouth once again. She knew everyone—and almost everything—that happened in this town.

The only thought that hovered above me as I drove concerned Coach. His reaction not only felt 'off', but almost weird.

When I pulled up in front of Teri's house, I reminded myself that we all react differently to tragedy. Maybe I was being insensitive just now. I hopped out but the little voice inside my head whispered, *"Weird is the right word. And the only insensitive one in that office was Coach!"*

Chapter 6

I have always overbooked myself. Sometimes I can accomplish it all. Other times I find myself in impossible situations. As I logged into my office computer later that day, I repeated to myself all the reasons I should have said no to doing this article for Mr. Byrd. Instead, I called Teri.

"I'm taking food over," she said when I explained my promise to Mr. Byrd. "You can go along and help me carry it."

"I'm cooking for Reed tonight. Besides, the parents met me at the paper office," I said. "They wouldn't be comfortable with—"

"Not Coach's house," she interrupted. "I'm going to the athletes' gathering. Mateo Dominguez, owner of the Ford dealership, has offered his place for everyone to meet. Everyone—athletes and cheerleaders and pep club—will be there. Coach will likely stop by sometime as well. In fact, I'm sure Reed has been invited also."

"Teri, you're a treasure! I don't know how—"

"Oh, I'll think of a way! Wait—"

Loud squabbling had arisen in the background, and I waited while she negotiated a peaceful settlement. Then she returned as if she'd never left. "Until Jose and I get it loaded."

I heard Jose's voice, so I waited to reply. Then Teri returned. "Jose says he'll load and take the food—most of it anyway. You can drive by and we'll take the rest. Mom is here already, and she'll stay with the kids."

"I'll call Reed and tell him his life won't be in peril from my cooking tonight."

She giggled.

By the time we parked toward the back of the parking lot, Teri had filled me in on the team and Coach and had even provided me with a handwritten list of names and short details about them. Jose stood near the door, watching for us, and came over to remove the bags Teri carried.

"Teri!" The cry sounded strange coming from the group of plump "mom" types, but the squeals were those common in any high school gym.

"Cheerleaders," I muttered.

Jose laughed. "Yep!" he said proudly. "Teri was always the one at the top of the pyramid."

He left to take the food to the long tables along the front of the dealership, while I pulled out my camera and focused on snapping some casual shots. At first glance, you might have thought it was a class reunion. But a closer look at the faces and eyes reminded me that, in spite of the pleasure in seeing each other, the teammates and their families were respectful of the sorrow that not only they but also their friends and the family felt.

I was accustomed to maneuvering among strangers, recording comments, and gathering snippets of information that I'd use later for a story. But this time was different. Maybe it was the camera lens mirroring the sadness in the eyes or the shutter capturing compassionate shadows lingering around gentle smiles. Saddle Gap had changed me, as subtly and quietly as the Southwest skies had crept into my heart. For a moment, I struggled with separating my heart for the people I'd grown to know and admire—not strangers—to my job of reporting the facts of their tragedy.

But it was also a reunion of sorts. I noticed smiles appearing as people recounted the same old stories they could all recite in their sleep, munching on plates piled high with food, exchanging hugs and updates on their own jobs and families, and expressing horror for the recent tragedy. I'd worn a small microphone to record some of the statements, even though I'd not use many. When I snapped a photo, I introduced myself and the recorder picked up their names and how they had known the family. It was really the only information I would need, and Teri could help me out should I miss someone.

When the noise level reached the roof and the dishes were almost empty, Coach stepped up to a mike and called for attention, his hand on his wife's elbow urging her along with him. As the voices hushed obediently, he waited a moment, looking down and obviously gathering his emotions. When he spoke, his voice held the experienced ring of a coach settling his team down before a game.

"My wife and I appreciate all of you kids (laughter made him pause) planning this event tonight. In spite of the tragic circumstances, it has been wonderful to see all of you together." He stopped and surveyed the room with eyes tired but dry. "We should do this again in times not so sad."

He then continued recounting the times they had played together as a team and reached victorious highs in their lives. When those highs seemed like lows, they had all overcome them as a team. As his voice grew more animated, his audience followed him, almost spellbound as he recounted dozens of stories of the challenges and victories they'd shared together. Any moment, I expected the cheerleaders to break out in chants.

Sorrel, I silently chided myself, *you should be relieved this isn't the sad wake you expected.*

I moved the camera over the crowd slowly, capturing faces, snapping hugs and smiles. Then my lens settled on Coach's wife. She was dressed just as well as she'd been when I'd seen her at the paper. Her hair hardly moved and her make-up looked as fresh as if she'd only just put it on. Only I knew she was a carbon copy of earlier today, although the suit had been replaced by gray slacks and a navy jacket. She stood so stiffly that I watched closely to catch her chest move with a breath. Just before I snapped the photo, she looked into my camera lens.

Throughout my years as a television crime reporter, I'd witnessed that look countless times. She might have been sending me a personal message as she stared into my lens, but I doubted that she saw me at all. Instead she stared, her eyes filled with the misery of having lost not only her child but also a part of herself. She must be thinking of the grandchildren she would never know, the man he would have become, the Christmases that would no longer be filled with exclamations of joy, and the hugs forever gone.

I snapped the photo and lowered my camera. Still she stared at me. Then I knew she saw me and she recognized me. Her body tensed with anger, horror, and purpose. *Find who did this to my child!* she screamed at me with her silent eyes. I'd seen those eyes countless times, and I'd thought to escape them when I moved here and opened my gift shop. Her eyes held me powerless, sending messages I could only hear.

"Sorrel?"

I felt Teri's hand on my shoulder. Coach's wife turned away, and I expelled the breath I'd been holding. I tried—and almost succeeded—in pushing away the guilt that flooded me for the respite I felt from her tragedy. "Yes?"

"I want to introduce you to the other girls who were on my squad. Would you take a photo of us?" Teri drug me along as she chattered, filling me in on each girl with stories I'd most likely have to ask her to repeat. I obediently snapped photos on request and recorded names afterward.

Their husbands gathered around Coach in a huddle near the food tables. I chose a long shot with a wide lens and snapped several photos. Most kept their heads down, but a couple looked up unexpectedly just before I took the photo. Coach kept his face down and spoke softly. Through the lens, I could see the rigid muscles in his neck bulge.

Finally, Coach and his wife began moving through the room in a sort of final farewell of hugs, amid more tears from the women and awkward backslaps or handshakes from the men. Coach had retained his composure throughout the evening, although his eyes and tight lips hinted at the strain and tight control as he guided his wife along with a big paw on her elbow.

When they approached Jose, Teri, and me near the door, Coach glared at me before turning to Jose. "I told Randy Byrd this was a private get-together tonight. What's she doing here?"

"Sorrel is a personal friend of ours," Jose said. "Mr. Byrd asked her to write a piece for the paper tomorrow . . . sort of a human-interest thing . . . so we invited her along. You can trust her, Coach . . . she's suffered her own tragedy—"

"We don't need any outsider—"

"And her tragedy sent her to Saddle Gap. She owns that new gift shop out on the highway. Rose—you remember Rose?—was a sort of an adoptive grandmother to her. You can trust her, Coach."

Coach kept his eyes on Jose. I noticed his wife had kept her eyes downcast, but she shot a telltale glance at me as Jose spoke. I made a mental note that she would be a source for the story that we had not yet heard. "I want to read it before they print it!" he finally snapped.

"You need to speak to Mr. Byrd about that, Coach," Jose replied. "He's the editor. I'll have him call you."

Jose and Teri hugged the couple and led them to the door. Then we noticed that the room had emptied of all but the three of us. We began clearing up.

It was almost an hour later when Jose walked me to the Jeep and held my door. "Don't mind Coach, Sorrel," he said. "He's a great guy."

"I'm sure he is," I told him. "I could see the affection all of you guys have for him. It must be devastating for both of them right now. I promise to be as sensitive as I can when I write the story."

Uncharacteristically, Jose gave me a hug. "Thanks, Sorrel. I appreciate it. Coach was almost a father to many of us, and—"

"She will be as gentle as she can while still doing her job, Jose," Teri interrupted.

I gathered my thoughts as I started the drive home, but I was soon interrupted by a phone call from Reed.

"What are you doing?"

I told him about my evening.

I heard him sigh. "I would have liked to have been there, but there's—"

"He understood, Reed. In fact, he probably is relieved that it's someone he knows who is working on the investigation."

Reed didn't answer right away. Then he said slowly, "It's complicated, Sorrel. It's one case I wish I could give to someone else."

After we hung up, that statement came back and settled into my mind.

Chapter 7

Reed's call woke me after far too short a night and went to message while I was still reaching for the phone. I punched the button with my eyes closed.

Reed's voice sounded exhausted. "Sorrel? When you get this, call me. I've had Coach on the phone late last night and early this morning. Call me on my cell."

I squinted at my bedside clock. Six o'clock? I'd not been in bed long enough to even warm the sheets. I pulled the blanket over my head and snuggled down. What could Reed have learned from Coach that he couldn't wait to tell me? I wiggled again to get more comfortable, dislodging both cats. Even if Reed had uncovered some juicy details, they wouldn't have fit in this piece. Hadn't Mr. Byrd requested a family-friendly article with a touch of nostalgia? I doubted anything Reed had uncovered at the crime scene would have been family friendly.

I closed my eyes just as Flash stepped into the curve of my legs and snuggled against them. I could feel the vibration of her purring. Darn! An additional hour would have been welcome, but it wasn't going to happen. Reed's message had aroused my curiosity.

I stifled a yawn and climbed out of bed amid Flash's protests. Reed could wait until I took a shower, at least. But first I padded into the kitchen to fill cat dishes and start a pot of coffee. Then I texted Reed: Pot brewing. Showering.

He must have been close by. By the time I padded barefoot into the kitchen in jeans and tee shirt with my damp hair hanging down my back, I peeked out the window and glimpsed his pickup truck beside my Jeep. I unlocked the door, stuck my head out, and whistled. Reed's head jerked up. Had he been dozing or just reading something? I motioned for him to come in.

As he stepped inside, I handed him a steaming cup of coffee. "Now this is service!" he exclaimed. "Am I in the right place?"

"Cherish it," I popped back. "You just looked pathetic out there. Forgot where you live?"

Reed took a gulp and made his way to the overstuffed chair he favored, easing down with a sigh. I looked at him closely. "Haven't you slept the past few days?"

"Hardly." Van followed him and settled on his lap. Reed took a sip of his coffee, stroking the big cat's solitary ear. "Heard you were at the wake last night."

"Coach call you?" I asked. "He didn't appreciate my presence, but Jose explained why I was there. I don't think it sat well with him." I sat on the sofa and settled my cup on a coaster. "Both he and his wife put up a good front, but I could see they were devastated—and rightly so. I'm surprised they came."

"They are a team . . . always."

We drank in silence for a few moments. Then I asked, "Do you want something to eat?"

"No. I drove through McDonald's on the way." He continued to stroke Van, who obliged with his gravelly purr.

"Fast food will harden your arteries!" I scolded. When he didn't rise to the bait, I continued on another tack. "You look exhausted. You should go home and sleep. You mentioned spending hours with Coach." I knew curiosity seeped into my voice, but he didn't seem inclined to share much. "Did he give you anything to work with?"

Reed didn't immediately answer, but he sat up straighter. I could almost hear the wheels in his brain turning. When he finally spoke, I could hear the frustration in his voice. "It doesn't make sense. Who would want to harm this kid? According to his parents, he's never been involved in anything the least bit illegal as far as anyone knows. He was quiet, always helping out, went to church occasionally, made good grades. They had a list of people who knew him if I wanted to interview them. So I did that. Still have a few I haven't spoken with. No one so far has had anything negative to say about him."

"Maybe it was just a random thing?" I offered.

"I don't think so."

"Why?"

He sighed. "No concrete reason. At least, not yet. It's frustrating when you sense something is right there, but you can't see it." Then he looked straight in my eyes and said, "Most parents would be after me to spend every waking moment until I find who did this to their child. And Coach? He's worse than most. Until tonight."

"It's his only child. Maybe—"

"He shouldn't be trying to have me stop. I shouldn't be saying this to anyone else, Sorrel, but I get the feeling he doesn't want to know. Or he does know and, for some reason, doesn't want me to find it."

"If he suspects someone, why wouldn't he tell you? I would!"

"So would I." Reed stared down at his hands. "If it weren't so weird, I'd think they're covering for someone. But that's impossible. Why would they do that? This is their child!"

"Did you tell him that?"

Reed grunted. "You don't tell Coach much. But I did remind him that a motivation for Brent's death—whether by accident, his own hand, or someone else—would help us."

"Did that help?"

"Hardly! He ignored the cause of death question. In fact, he glanced around and said something about the family must 'heal.' It was weird." He sighed. "He said he wanted this cleared up so the family could move on. When I asked the typical questions like why he wasn't home, etc., I got stonewalled by silence."

"Well, maybe that's the only way he and his wife can face the horror."

"It wouldn't be mine." He turned and grabbed my hand, almost hurting me in his intensity. "If my child were dumped somewhere to die, I'd have law enforcement on speed dial, hounding them until they found who did it! I'd be out there myself. Who cares about the family moving on? My flesh and blood, Sorrel. How about you?"

I pulled my hand away and cupped his face in mine. "We'd not rest until we knew!" I whispered. "What can I do to help you, Reed? He may not be our child, but any kid deserves that."

Reed leaned forward, pulled me into a tight hug, kissed me gently, and then pulled back. "Sorry. Guess I'm a little . . . close to this one. Coach hasn't ever lost anything much—or anyone—that I can remember. Losing isn't in his vocabulary. I guess I have to consider that he is holding himself so tightly right now that he needs to hold in his sorrow."

I rose, reached for my coffee cup, and nodded toward Reed's cup, but he shook his head. "Thanks, but I need to get home and try to catch a nap. Coach, like any parent, is anxious for answers, even if he is keeping a strong front. It doesn't help that I know him so well."

"Or that he knows you so well."

"I wasn't his favorite, Sorrel. In my memories, Coach was mostly all business—and he expected you to be the same way. I told you that my dad died and Mom and I were on the ranch until she sold it. When I got a job after school and couldn't play football my senior year, Coach didn't take it well. He even tried to make Mom give him custody so I could live with him."

I gasped. "Did she do that?"

"She would never have done that. She told him that he was single, and so was she. So what was the difference?" He smiled at the memory.

"So he wasn't married then?"

"Divorced. He married again the summer after I graduated." He stared into his cup but didn't take a drink. "She was so much younger that it made quite a stir. This is a little town, you know."

I didn't say anything, but my reaction must have been visible because Reed grimaced. "It didn't go over well at first, but a winning team soothes most anything."

"When was the son born?"

Reed stood and put on his hat. "Do the math."

"Was he a good player?"

"He played." Reed reached over to pat Van. "We can't all be stars. He was in Honor Society and Drama Club, a quiet young man. A parent should be happy with that."

But he wasn't, I thought. "And the mother?" I asked.

"He was her pride and joy as the old cliché goes."

"But not his father's. That's a heavy burden for a young man. Often leads to a troubled teen."

Reed didn't immediately comment. Finally, he said, "Most of us do a few things we're not proud of in those teen years. But as I said, I never heard anything this kid did wrong. But I haven't really kept up with Coach, so it is unfair for me to imply he wasn't a good dad. But whether or not Coach is hiding something, his kid's death should have him demanding that I do more than my best. That's the way he is. He's acting weird."

He opened the door, then turned back. "I'll sleep, you sell, and maybe we can share dinner tonight? I'll call."

"Wait." I walked over and gathered him into a hug. I could feel the tension in his shoulders, then a light shudder as his arms wrapped around me, first returning the hug before patting me.

"Thanks, Sorrel, for listening to my sentimental musings," he whispered. "High school wasn't the easiest times, and this has unfortunately transported me back to those days."

"They aren't the easiest times for most of us." I sighed. "You've never seen my prom photos—or worse, heard my stories."

He gave me a squeeze, then released me. "I had this maiden English teacher—a really hard teacher—who would have had the perfect literary quote for this moment."

I smiled. "We all had one of those!"

Reed chuckled. "I'll be in touch." He winked. "And I'll take a raincheck on those prom stories!"

I watched until Reed had driven away, not yet comfortable with the emotions he stirred but liking them nonetheless. But I had a business to care for now, and he had a murder to solve.

As if on cue, my cell phone rang. "Sorrel Janes," I answered.

"Sorrel? Randall Byrd here. I'm leaving the office and don't have a lot of time. But can I stop by your place?

"I'm putting the finishing touches on the article now, sir."

"Wait on your article, Sorrel. I need another favor."

"I have a full schedule, sir, so I can't take on anything extra just now. I was up late last night working on the article, and I have the big sale at the store tomorrow."

"I know you've been working more for us than usual. But I want to talk to you about something else. I just need a small favor. And before you ask, I'd like to discuss it with you in person."

"How about 8:00 tomorrow morning? The sale will not be started, but people will be here to set up so I will be available."

"That would work," he said. "Thank you. I know this is a bad time, but I really think you're the one to do this."

Lonna Enox

Chapter 8

For the five-hour "Thanks for Supporting Our First Year in Business!" sale, I had advertised a 9:00 opening and a 2:00 pm ending. Besides the cut prices, I had arranged a taco truck and lemonade stand—one taco and one glass of lemonade free for customers when they showed their register tape—along with live music out beside my gazebo.

"I should have said no to a last-minute article for the paper," I grumbled. I pushed the Send button. Good, bad, or mediocre—at least the thing was finished.

When Randall Byrd tapped at my office door, I shut down the computer screen and waved him inside.

"Busy place out here," he said.

The taco truck had already pulled into a parking slot at the end of the lot, and the local 4-H group were busily decorating the lemonade stand they had constructed in the shade of large umbrellas.

"I'm getting hungry just smelling that taco meat," Mr. Byrd added.

"Me too! The mariachi band will be here in a half hour, just before the doors open. I'm trying to keep my mind busy so my stomach doesn't growl."

"Let me know if that works! It's just . . . "

When he didn't continue, I finally gestured toward a chair. "Sit down. And you're sure about the coffee?"

"No coffee." I pulled a seat facing him and waited for him to continue. About the time I decided we were going to meditate instead of talk, he spoke. "How's your progress on the article?"

"I just sent it. Hope it's acceptable. With all of this going on—"

"I'm not here to pressure you about it, Sorrel. I trust you have used your usual tact and finesse. And I do apologize for interrupting you in an obviously crazy time."

"It's just a sale. And Teri is out there directing everything. I'm hiding out in here anyway."

He attempted a smile. It better resembled a grimace. Something was very wrong, or maybe he just was wrestling with his own grief. I hoped it was the latter of the two.

"I focused on the positives as much as possible in writing the article," I said. "People shared so many stories about Coach and his family at the gathering last night, but finding anything about the son was a challenge. So I researched a site that has high school yearbooks and found a few more facts about him. But he wasn't as outgoing as I'd have expected."

"It's hard to grow up in the shadow of a hero."

"Yes, I suppose it is. But I'm excited about what I discovered from an unlikely source. Apparently, he had worked for a yard mowing company for much of his high school years. One of the places that contracted them is the nursing home! It seems he was really popular with them. And he volunteered to help some older people in the community. People have shared some wonderful stories, which helped me present him in a different way from the one we had seen."

Randall Byrd didn't immediately react. Finally, he said, "I'm glad, Sorrel. I imagine his mother would love to hear it."

"And Coach?"

"I know people react to grief differently. Guess I should have expected him to be rabid to find the perpetrators. But I hadn't expected him to pressure me to relegate the story to a standard notice on the obituary page."

Mr. Byrd seemed unusually evasive. He hadn't looked at me as he spoke, and his hands didn't seem to know where to rest.

"So why are you here?" I asked, but I suspected I knew the answer.

"We won't be publishing the story."

"Why not? You haven't even read it yet. It's a good article, Mr. Byrd. I took great care to be as objective as possible while—"

"It has nothing to do with you, Sorrel. The paper will just not be doing anything more than a standard obituary." He rose and turned toward the door, still not making eye contact.

"I know he's a friend—"

"It isn't just that, Sorrel."

"Money," I whispered.

"Advertisement is what keeps the paper in business. No matter how many papers we sell, it's the advertisements that pay the bills."

"But . . . I don't understand."

He reached for the door knob, then half-turned to me. "I will pay you for your time, Sorrel. Were it my choice, the article would run. But I also answer to others, and they are more sympathetic toward Coach's situation than they think I am."

He gazed at the wall behind me for a moment, and I could see the struggle behind his professional face. "You have been in this business long enough to understand—as do I—that some battles are left unfought. The funeral on Monday will apparently be private, for friends and family by invitation."

He stepped out, not looking back, only raising his hand slightly in farewell. "Mrs. Byrd and I will not be attending the services—it is invitation only. I imagine she'll be out here later. You will, of course, still be paid for your excellent work. Good luck with the sale," he said and closed the door.

I felt frozen to the spot. This was something I had never expected to hear from Randall Byrd.

Another tap came and the door opened. Mr. Byrd leaned back inside my office. "I meant to wait until after this sale, but I can see your emotions in your face. There's a different story to write on this, Sorrel. We aren't holding up any white flags. We just want whoever is behind this to think we are. So we're circling our ponies until this cools a bit."

"I thought--"

"I know. It's what we want people to think—that it's a simple crime. And they particularly do not want any reporters poking into things. But you're too savvy for me to worry about you. You can be discreet. And you're a darn good investigator. Start poking around behind the scenes when you can. Like I said, I'll reimburse you for your time." He winked.

"Yes, sir."

"But first, you'd better step into your store. People are lining up to come inside and there's not a parking space anywhere!"

"You can say that again!" Teri called. I could see a line forming at the front door when I glanced through the glass.

"You're right," I exclaimed. "Gotta get out there and help!"

Chapter 9

"Whew! I'm exhausted!" I smiled at my helpers hours later.

I'd carried the last of the unsold merchandise into the shop, with the help of Teri's various relatives. We had spent several hours outdoors. The New Mexican sun had been merciless, even in late spring. "I'm glad we're closed next week. And I can't thank all of you enough! I'll make out checks and have Teri deliver them."

"No, no, senorita! We made very good money ourselves with the food. Helping you put things away is a simple way to thank you for the opportunity." Teri's Uncle Ramon held his hand out to shake mine. "We will not accept money."

"Wait! You also helped Teri inside here while I worked out there."

But I was talking to his back. He walked through the front door and joined several others in the taco truck that waited in the parking lot. Still others climbed into the remaining pick-up truck and formed a caravan as they pulled out onto the highway.

"They enjoyed every minute, you know."

I jumped and squealed. "Reed!" I threw up my hands. "You shouldn't creep up on people like that. I didn't know you were here? Where's your truck?"

His wide grin tempted me to either laugh or smack him. He must have realized that because he quickly explained. "I used the department vehicle today. When I returned to the station, mine had a flat tire. So I caught a ride this far, hoping to charm a certain photographer into taking me home. Teri sent me back into your living space—do you call that an apartment?—to wait for you and I fell asleep on the couch."

"She never said a word."

"You were busy, from the looks of things, and so was she. Her aunt even waited on customers with the baby on her shoulder! Looked like half of Saddle Gap had squeezed into your shop. I don't know how you managed it, but those ladies acted like they had discovered treasures they'd never seen before."

I couldn't be cross. "We did have a steady flow of customers," I admitted. "By the looks of the displays, the consignees will be busily working on replacements the next few weeks."

I picked up an embroidered tea towel and placed it back on the display above it.

"I'm considering closing for a week to restock and change the displays," I chattered. "At first I thought of doing that before the sale since I figured people wouldn't buy knitted scarves and sweaters. But bargain hunters will buy them during a sale. But I think I should stay open if I can."

Reed grunted assent as he leaned against the small counter I used for checking out items. He had slept, because I could see the creases from lying on my couch on his face. But he still looked really tired. "I'm convinced you females would buy most anything if it were on sale," he said.

I laughed. "We had a large number of males here too, you know."

"Married, I'm sure," he said, then yawned.

"Long night?" I asked.

"Long story," he said. "Your news story done?"

"Long story," I replied.

"Sounds like we need to find a tall glass of iced tea and—"

"No burritos!"

"Steak," he continued. "Bart's. Could I beg a ride to my place so I can feed the critters and run through the shower?"

I resisted the "as long as you don't fall" wisecrack. Anything besides tacos or burritos sounded terrific. But he truly needed to rest.

I picked up my purse and keys and walked to the store front. "I'll lock up here and follow you on through my living quarters," I said. He held up a hand as he walked away.

A quarter of an hour later, Madonna, his small rescue dog, had quite a lot to say when we drove up to the older ranch he'd bought. "Women! Always bossing me around," Reed muttered. Then he smiled. "You can pick me up in an hour, unless you find me passed out alongside the road trying to hitch a ride." He leaned over and kissed me on the cheek. "I promise to scrape these whiskers off first."

"You need to sleep, Reed. We can talk tomorrow."

"I told you I took a nap. Besides, I promised dinner."

"I could make dinner—"

"I'm hungry, not suicidal!" He ducked as I raised my hand. Then he grinned. "I may find you a challenge, motor mouth, and contrary dinner partner," he said, "but I am never bored or disappointed having dinner with you . . . when someone else cooks!"

He ducked his head, ducked my mock punch, and then slid out the door. His laughter erased the exhaustion.

"I'll pick you up in a couple of hours then. Catch a nap if you can," I called after him.

My cellphone rang as I drove away. A quick glance showed the nursing home's number, so I answered it.

"Hello?"

"Ms. Janes?"

"Speaking."

"I'm Margaret Hall, the social worker here at the Casa de Oro. We've met a few times when you've come to collect items from the craft room?"

"Yes, I remember you."

"I'd like to visit with you about a matter I'd prefer not to discuss on the phone. Would you be able to drop by?"

"I'm busy just—"

"Oh, not tonight!" she interrupted. "I know you've been involved in the big sale. Our residents have talked of nothing else for quite a long time. I'll be at the center tomorrow afternoon. Could you possibly stop by sometime after two?"

I mentally ticked off a list of must-dos and should-dos for tomorrow. "Would three o'clock work?" I asked.

"Yes, it would. I work until four tomorrow. My office is in that short hall on the left when you first step in the door."

"Very well. Then I'll see you tomorrow at three."

"Thank you. I know you must be exhausted."

"I need to come out anyway. I know everyone will want to hear how their items sold."

After she thanked me again and we hung up, I pulled back out onto the shortcut route to the store from Reed's house.

Once back at the store, I gave the cats a snack before showering and repairing the damage of the day. The couple of hours flew, and soon I was headed back his direction.

Reed must have been waiting by the door. He'd obviously rested a bit and changed. I'd showered, slid into a sundress and sandals, and twisted my damp hair into a low knot on the back of my neck.

"Wow! You clean up really good!" he said when he opened the door.

"Well," I said.

"Well what?"

"Clean up well."

Chris screwed up his face in mock horror. "Please don't tell me you are my Senior English teacher reincarnated!"

"Let me grab my purse and I'll let you check my ID."

Christopher Reed can always could make me laugh. Then it hit me! There was a vehicle in his driveway. "Hey! Where did you get that beauty?"

"Magic!" he drawled.

"Jose!" I said.

"Yep! I'm following you home and we're taking it. I'm supposed to be trying it out."

"I won't argue with that. And speaking of new trucks, I hope you can afford me. I'm starved." I glanced sideways at his tired face. "Are you working tonight?"

"Nope. Not unless I get called out."

He flipped on his blinker and turned onto the highway. "But don't get quiet on me. I'm becoming accustomed to your smart mouth." He shot me a quick grin, but I could see it droop. He'd spent hours working on a crime scene that not only had been horrific but had also been close to his own heart. I reached over and tugged his hand into mine.

"We'll find him," I said.

"We?"

"Yes, sir." I squeezed his hand. "For Coach and his wife, Jose and Teri, all the boys Coach has loved and helped, and—most of all—his child. We will find out who did this awful thing."

"Sorrel?"

"Hmm?"

"Thank you."

Chapter 10

Reed and I didn't talk much waiting for our meal. The boisterous music and dance atmosphere would have made talking difficult anyway.

The steaks came exactly as we'd ordered them: his rare and mine well-done. My stomach growled.

"Is this the first you've eaten all day?" Reed asked.

"Of course not! But it was a busy day."

I felt comfortable for the first time that day, sitting across from Reed. Eating with someone who didn't demand anything more from me than just being a companion was a priceless gift after my long day . . . and the past few days as well.

Our waitress reappeared occasionally to refill tea glasses. The last time she stopped by, I asked for a container for leftovers.

"My dad would have said my eyes were bigger than my stomach," I told Reed as I began placing steak bits into the Styrofoam container. "Would you take this to Madonna and those half-grown pups? If I take it home, I'll just forget it's there."

"Sure," he said. "I have a bit myself, so I'll just add to your box."

Reed pulled up to my door after a silent drive, then turned off the truck before turning to me. "I've been a poor dinner companion, Sorrel," he said. "I'm sorry. I meant it to be a sort of celebration for your big day."

"Well, it must be horrible to be investigating a friend's—"

"No, that's not what I mean. Well, that's horrible, of course. But something about this case just isn't right. You know how something is floating out there just out of reach? You can sense it, but you can't quite figure it out? I know Coach is distracted . . . grieving . . . and all of the stuff with the memorial service and stuff. But I guess I expected him to be on me every minute, wanting to know what happened to his son, hounding me about what we know. I'd be doing that if it were my child."

"Maybe he's still in shock. I know I was when Kevin was murdered."

"Really, Sorrel? Your husband had been murdered and you were hurrying to get the services set up and attending a reception—"

"Well, no, of course not. But it was a different circumstance."

Reed didn't answer right away. "True. They were whisking you into protective custody. But . . . something just feels odd."

"We don't want to believe that old adage, 'bad things happen to good people.' Everyone has secrets, you know. We have thoughts we don't share, actions we'd prefer to never reveal, and mistakes that we've made. If we were all perfect, you'd be out of a job, you know."

Reed shrugged. "We hate to think of a kid like him being anything besides a victim. There are some wicked people out there."

"I know. I've encountered more than a few—one of the worst not long ago!"

I shivered at the memory.

Reed reached over and squeezed my hand before opening his door. "Let me walk you to the door—"

"I can—"

But he was already opening my door for me before I could finish my thought. "My mama would haunt me if she thought I had forgotten the manners she drilled into me," he said as I climbed out. Then he held onto my elbow as we walked, and I felt the tense urgency in him.

He continued speaking, almost to himself but aloud. "This kid was a good kid. He never had trouble in school, helped out in the community, teachers wrote about his generous but quiet spirit. How did he end up murdered and dumped out in the country, practically crawling to a church for help? Something's just not right and—"

"And you need some sleep. We both do. Maybe the answer you seek will miraculously appear in a dream!"

"Sure! And I'm sure you have some swamp land to sell me next week!"

He waited for me to unlock my door before leaning over and hugging me.

"I won't come inside," he said. "I hate to admit that you're right, Mother Hen! I promised the team I'd sleep and get back to work early." He gave me a sweet kiss before turning me loose. "Thanks for being my sounding board. Get on in and I'll wait here until I hear the lock."

"Who did you call Mother Hen?" I sang out as I locked the door. He laughed.

An hour later, I finally gave up the pretense of sleep and climbed out of bed amid protests from Van and Flash. "Sorry, felines," I told them. "You two can sleep anywhere, any time. It's a gift. I didn't receive it."

I heated a cup of water in the microwave and dropped a Sleepy Time teabag into it. Since sleep might be far away, I carried my cup to the door adjoining the store and unlocked it. After the sale we'd had today, I had paperwork to tackle. Having a large number of consignees made that paperwork a bit more complicated. And I knew some would be anxious to know how their items had sold. Maybe I could get their checks ready to take out tomorrow when I went for my appointment.

Once I had settled at my desk and begun the task, I felt a whole new rush of energy. The task wouldn't be complicated. Paperwork, I decided, could sometimes be soothing.

When I finally pushed back and viewed the finished ledger and the neatly stacked envelopes with a receipt and cash or check in each one, I felt eyes on me. Creepy, I thought, until I glanced to my right and met huge yellow ones. "Van? What's up?"

Of course, he wouldn't answer. He was a cat, after all. I restored my desk to order and zipped the envelopes into the bank money bag. "Let me put this in the safe and I'll make another attempt at sleep," I told him. "Or maybe not. Now that I'm energized and wide awake, I have some other projects I've been postponing."

I locked the office after I'd finished, set the alarm, and waited for Van to follow through the adjoining door so I could also lock it. We walked back into the bedroom and snuggled in bed, he with Flash and me with a mystery novel I'd not yet started.

A loud hammering startled me. I jerked and my book crashed to the floor. My room was so light. Where were the cats?

The hammering continued. I climbed out of bed and reached for my robe. I felt stiff and clumsy. Maybe I should have exercised a bit before climbing in bed.

Sunlight streamed through my bedroom windows. The knocking continued. When I walked to my front door and peeked through what I called my "spy hole" in the door, I recognized a couple of Teri's relatives who'd constructed the booths for yesterday's sale. I looked down, tied the robe, finger-combed my hair, and opened the door wide enough to peek out.

"I'm sorry to wake you," one of them said when he saw me. "We're here to clear up before we start our other job today."

"Oh, that's fine." I managed a smile around sticky teeth. "Can I make you—"

"We don't need anything. Just wanted to warn you about the noise."

"We're closed for a couple of weeks," I told him. "Don't worry about noise."

I glanced at the clock as I closed the door. I'd agreed to meet with the social worker at three o'clock this afternoon. I had a few hours to work on the investigative reporting assignment for Mr. Byrd before the appointment. But I needed to hustle.

While I changed into a simple shift dress and sandals and applied a minimal amount of make-up, I created a mental list of people I should contact. The library should have copies of the yearbooks, but I would also log onto my computer when I returned home. Teri, of course, might be a good resource for background on Coach and the son. I'd ask where they attended church and other organizations where people knew them well.

"Someone has seen or knows something, but they often have no idea that they do. It's our job to dig it out," my journalism professor had stressed over and over.

What he hadn't told us was that in snooping, we often discover information that is irrelevant but often embarrassing. I started my Jeep and backed out of the driveway. "Sorry, Coach," I whispered. "I'll try to be a gentle snoop, but your baby deserves justice."

As I pulled onto the highway, another thought returned, one I'd pushed back. Why wasn't Coach demanding law enforcement and everyone involved to find who had killed his child?

Chapter 11

"Me and my big mouth!"

Ever since scheduling this appointment with Ms. Janes, she'd had an upset stomach. True, she wasn't bound by confidentiality as a social worker, but she had always practiced discretion. What she'd observed might have been completely innocent, but that didn't guarantee that all parties would welcome its being told to the press. What if the information she planned to reveal backfired and reflected negatively upon people? Influential townspeople had ties to this nursing home, either by donations or as partial owners.

She'd lain awake the past couple of nights, ever since the former groundskeeper had been killed—the papers weren't using the word murdered yet—wrestling with her conscience. He'd been a regular at the senior center for several years. Rarely did a kid volunteer at a retirement home, but this one had also taken time to speak to the residents and even occasionally to play a game of dominoes with them. He'd laughed at their jokes and listened to their stories.

When she'd asked why he volunteered here, he'd just shrugged and said, "I like them. They tell funny stories and everyone else seems too busy to listen. Besides, I don't have any grandparents living to visit, so this sort of makes up for it. Someday I'd like to be a lawyer and represent folks like them."

She'd smiled and thanked him for helping out. That was the first time she'd had a talk with him, but he'd left her a note just two weeks ago.

Reflexively, she reached in her pocket to touch it.

It had been sealed when he gave it to her, but his words as he gave it to her—and his subsequent murder—had nearly changed her mind. "In case something happens to me before you get this mailed, please be sure to deliver it to him personally," he'd said. At the door, he'd turned. "He must be a good guy. It's hard to know who to trust. But this may be a 'life or death' thing. Social workers deal in confidentiality, don't they?"

She'd smiled and assured him that she would mail it.

But she'd been summoned to a meeting, and when she'd returned, she'd been notified of the passing of a favorite resident. Somehow, the letter—and the promise—had been forgotten. She'd only remembered it when she turned on the television news and recognized the young man's face.

She'd immediately thought of the letter and then searched through jacket pockets until she found it. She'd called the sheriff's department, but Christopher Reed had not returned her call. Then she remembered the gossip at the center about how Ms. Janes and Deputy Reed had worked together on a recent case. Maybe she would tell Ms. Janes to pass the message about the letter.

Or maybe she should honor the confidentiality and just try to reach him after this case had died down.

Died. We use that word without even thinking about it, she thought, dabbing at her eyes. Maybe she should think some more before she betrayed the young man's trust.

Chapter 12

I enjoyed a sense of accomplishment as I headed toward Casa de Oro. I'd spent long hours tallying the sales and balancing the books so that I could carry cash to residents who'd sold their craft items. It would have been much easier to write checks, but I'd learned early on that they liked to hold the cash in their hands before depositing it into their accounts. At this stage of these seniors' lives—when they had little control over their bodies or anything else—they desperately needed to recapture some feeling of accomplishment.

At Casa de Oro, I waited for the laundry service and food wholesale suppliers to pull past me, and then parked in the space labeled 'Other' in the small lot in back.

When I opened the Jeep door and stepped out, I noticed a familiar face watching me as he sat at the table under the gazebo.

"Morning, Tim!"

"Morning, Miz Janes."

A brisk breeze whistled by me and I shivered. "Cool out here, isn't it?" I asked. "Smells like rain."

He shrugged. "We need rain. I like the smell of it in the air." He sipped from a disposable cup.

I nodded and smiled, then headed toward the back door. Just as my hand grasped the door handle, I heard a sigh behind me. I must have looked startled, because Tim quickly stepped back. "Sorry. Didn't mean to scare you. I meant to open the door for you."

"You didn't scare me," I told him. "I was just thinking, so I didn't hear you."

"He didn't hear either." At my quizzical look, he elaborated. "The kid who got killed. He always had those things playing music or something in his ears when he was mowing out here." He reached around me and pulled open the door. "Ladies first," he said.

I nodded and walked through and into the small hall. "Did you know him well?" I asked as he stepped in behind me.

"He was a kid. Had lots on his mind. Quiet. But he was nice to us old folks. He didn't talk much, but he was a good listener. Most people don't listen much anymore."

I waited but he didn't say anything more. So I thanked him and walked down the hall toward the front lobby. Tim might be someone I needed to talk with, but I didn't want to be late for my appointment. Maybe I could catch him afterward.

Ms. Hall called for me to come in when I tapped on her closed door. Her office, hardly bigger than a closet, would have made me claustrophobic. She seemed oblivious, however, as she stood and came from around the desk. Somehow, I'd expected someone matronly. Instead, Ms. Hall had a pixie face and dark curls atop a petite frame. She might have celebrated her twenty-first birthday, but she could be mistaken for still being in her teens.

"Thank you for coming on such short notice," she said. I noticed a slight lisp. "I'm Mandy. I've been finishing some paperwork, but it's stuffy in here. Maybe it would be more comfortable if we take a stroll while we talk," she said. "The weather is nice outside, and Tim likes for people to notice his gardens." Then, glancing at my briefcase, she offered, "I'll lock up and you can leave that here while we are gone."

"Oh, that's okay," I told her. "I may need to refer to some notes in it."

Mandy kept up a steady, aimless chatter as we walked back outside onto the patio. I murmured at appropriate intervals as I followed her. So far, nothing she'd said indicated the purpose of our meeting. I wondered if I should broach the subject, then decided I'd wait a bit. Maybe something about me made her nervous.

At the back of the building, several bushes formed a border along each end of the building, giving the patio area a cozy feel. "I love those tiny purple buds," I said.

"They're Cimarron Sage," she said. "Hardy things and ideal for residents who are interested in gardening because they require little maintenance." Her voice held a preoccupied tone. I made a mental note of the name. Low maintenance plants—and pretty—might be a great addition to the grounds around my shop.

As we continued walking through the senior center grounds, we passed a few residents in wheelchairs being pushed by their caregivers. Mandy spoke to each and received a smile or response each time. I could see from those expressions that she enjoyed her job and the residents liked her as well.

Still, when we seemed to be endlessly wandering, I felt I needed to intervene. She'd asked me to come and I felt a little pushy broaching the topic, but I'd told the residents that I'd dispense their money today and I needed to do that before they grew anxious.

"You know how it is," I said, after I'd explained the situation to her. "They focus on something, and I don't want them to stress. They're excited to see how their crafts were received."

"Oh, sorry. I tend to get sidetracked sometimes. I love talking to everyone here, and they are often lonely. Would you like to sit for a moment?"

She gestured toward a couple of small round tables. I chose the more distant one and pulled out a chair, securing my purse and my briefcase in the chair next to me. She sat opposite. Even now, I could sense that she wasn't comfortable—jittery, almost. Finally, she cleared her throat and spoke.

"Are you affiliated with the police department? I notice that your name is often mentioned."

"Not really. I am friends with Chris Reed. When he was a member of the police department, we worked together on a case. Now that he is with the sheriff's department, we don't see as much of each other. But we sometimes go out together."

"I see. Well, I need something delivered to him, and short of sending it special delivery ... "

"I could take it. In fact, I'll be seeing him for dinner tonight."

She hesitated, a myriad of emotions crossing her face. "I'm late getting it sent. First, I set it aside to think about whether I should, and then things were hectic here recently and I just forgot. Only when I read about the young man's murder . . . I'm not sure if I should send it or deliver it personally."

"I don't mind delivering it," I said, "but I could also just tell Deputy Reed that you need him to pick it up tomorrow."

"No!" Then she took a breath. "I'm sorry. I didn't mean to sound sharp. But I had promised to get this to him and then I forgot about it. I hope it wasn't something urgent." She put her hand in her pocket and pulled out an envelope. "I don't know what is in it as it is sealed— only that one of our guests gave it to the young man to deliver to Deputy Reed. And I put it in a desk drawer to keep it safe and just forgot about it." She handed it to me. "Now both he and she have passed and I feel bad about it and all. I should send it to Detective Reed, but since you and he . . . "

"I don't mind delivering it at all," I told her. "And since it sounds like a confidential letter, I should probably sign a receipt that you gave it to me."

She brightened, relief flushing her cheeks. "That sounds like a reasonable solution! This is my first job, and they didn't include this sort of thing in my college classes. Of course, I attended classes online, so it wasn't easy to just ask." She made a face. "My grandma says this isn't my vocation."

"What does she think you should be doing?" I couldn't resist asking.

"Getting married. Having kids." She stopped then, glanced around. "I don't have a pen . . . "

"I do." I pulled a pen and pad from my pocket and tore a sheet from the pad. "You can use this to write your receipt and I'll sign it."

When she'd finished and I'd signed it, she sighed. "I'm glad to pass this! I've had it for a while, but first she died and then he had this horrible—well, I just sort of forgot about it and then I saw it."

"Did you know both of them well?"

"He worked outside. I'd see him mowing and raking and things. He always seemed to take time to speak to the guests." She leaned toward me and lowered her voice. "We've been told to call them guests." Then she continued. "He'd laugh with them and they liked him. But this letter is not from him. I just got side-tracked because he's gone and the lady is gone as well. In fact, she died the night or early morning—I don't remember which exactly as two others departed at almost the same time—but it was the day he'd handed this to me."

"I'm sorry," I murmured. She looked really sad.

"Well, she wasn't warm and fuzzy as they say. In fact, she'd been a high school English teacher, and I think all those years with students must have made her cranky. She corrected your grammar and insisted on having the television in the lobby tuned to that quiz show. When someone hollered their answer out of turn, she scolded them."

"Sounds like she could have been my high school English teacher," I murmured and thought that Reed would really be interested in this!

My comment brought a smile to her worried face. Mandy continued. "She had given the boy strict instructions to deliver this to Deputy Christopher Reed—she frowned if anyone shortened names. So when he gave it to me, I put it in my pocket and then she died that night."

"I'll give it to him today."

"Thank you."

She rose and I did as well and started walking back towards the building.

"Everyone was excited about your sale of their crafts," she told me, relief evident in her whole demeanor. "It's a really good thing for them to do. When most of life is behind instead of ahead, people often get depressed."

I laughed. "Which is why I'd best get to the Business Office to—"

Her giggle interrupted me. I looked ahead. A line of walkers and wheelchairs had formed outside the door to the Business Office and crossed the lobby down the hall. "I'd say you may be receiving some complaints," she whispered.

"Hello, everyone," she called. "Never fear!" she whispered again. Then she whistled for their attention.

"After you conduct your business with Ms. Janes, you will find cookies and punch in the rec room to make up for your wait."

"How much is it gonna cost?" called a cranky voice.

"A smile!" she called back.

"This is your vocation," I murmured before I brushed past her and walked into the Business Office. I bent over to the first one in line and spoke loudly, "You're first!"

Chapter 13

Hopping inside my Jeep awhile later, I turned the ignition switch just as my cell played Reed's tune. Humming, I answered. "You rang?"

"Yep. I need a favor. Are you doing anything?"

"Of course not!" I drawled. "I'm just lying on my chaise lounge sipping iced tea and eating bonbons."

He laughed. "I don't think I've ever tasted a bonbon. You didn't make them yourself, did you?"

I scowled at the phone, but he sobered up just in time and continued in a conciliatory tone. "I bought dog food earlier, but I'm not getting off as early as I'd hoped. Would you be able to come by the office and take it over to my place? It's not a huge bag like I usually get, so you should be able to unload it on my porch."

"Are you at the office right now?"

"Yep. I'm catching up on some paperwork."

"Okay, I'll drop by in a few minutes on my way to a couple of other places. But I'm only doing it for Madonna's sake . . . and those pups!"

Reed laughed. "I owe you one."

"And you'll pay!"

I hung up to the sound of his laughter. Not for the first time, I thought about his laugh . . . and the fact that I could listen to it forever. His teasing? I wasn't admitting even to myself that I sort of liked that too.

After I'd collected the dogfood, which Reed insisted on loading in spite of the bag's small size, I drove by the library to check out the school yearbooks.

I found plenty of photos of our city's latest homicide victim but not where I expected. In the seemingly endless pages of school sports, I only found a couple of shots: he stood in the back of a group lineup of football players and was manager of the track team. He also appeared in group shots of the Student Council and the Honor Society. I studied the photos. Maybe it was my imagination, but he seemed out of place in all but the last group. He was a handsome kid, with more of his mother's looks than his father's.

I glanced through casual shots snapped at parties and conferences for the Honor Society. I noted a couple of guys and a girl with whom he seemed to be comfortable. I jotted down their names in hopes I might find some of them still living locally.

When I returned the books to the counter, the older lady had moved to help someone else, so I caught the attention of a young lady working on a computer at a nearby desk. "Should I just leave these here?" I asked.

She rose and came to look at them. "Oh, I'll take those. We don't want to leave them out. Sometimes people—usually crazy kids—will cut out photos or write dumb remarks on them."

I handed them to her. "I work for the paper," I said, "and I just wanted to look up some information to help me in writing an article."

I could see her face change when she realized whom I had been researching.

"Such a sad thing," she murmured. "He was so nice. It doesn't make sense."

"I've heard that one before," I said. "But you don't always know a person. You see them in one setting and you don't realize that—"

"No!" she interrupted me and leaned across the counter a bit. "I know what the police are implying, that he was running with those guys. But it's not true. He never would have been comfortable there." She glanced over just as the librarian looked her way. She drew back and picked up the books. Then she smiled and said, "Thank you, ma'am."

I nodded. When the librarian returned her attention to her work, I asked softly, "Can we meet?"

Lonna Enox

She unlocked a case and settled the books inside. I barely heard her say, "I go by the Dairy Creamer after I get off at five."

"A date," I murmured and left.

As I walked by the computer desk, I noticed a placard with Sara Cummings, Computer Clerk, printed on it.

Once back in the Jeep, I dialed Teri. She answered right away. "Sorrel? I'm beginning to think we're strangers!"

I heard the teasing in her voice and responded in kind. "Feeling like Old Mother Hubbard? If you can escape, how about we meet up?"

"Where? When? I'm going crazy!"

"Are you free now?"

"Mostly. The boys are at a Cub Scout activity at school. The baby and I are free for an hour or so."

"Meet me at the Dairy Creamer? I have to take dog food out to the dogs, but I'm dying for a sundae."

"Say no more! We'll meet you there!"

Teri was waiting in her car when I arrived. "Is she sleeping?" I asked as she unstrapped the car seat.

"Too nosey!" Teri said. "She's like her Auntie Sorrel!"

I took the carrier from her and peeked under the hood. "Hi, little Sorrel Two," I crooned. "You're the most beautiful girl in the world."

Teri laughed. "She's the most stinking girl in the world just now," she said. "So our first stop inside is the bathroom."

I carried the baby as she followed with the huge bag of stuff. While she expertly changed the diaper and disposed of it, I carried on a nonsensical conversation with my small goddaughter.

Later, after we'd settled into a comfortable corner booth, I handed Teri a bill. "You get our refreshments. I want a lemonade. Medium."

Teri wrinkled her nose. "Yuck!" she said, snatching the bill and heading to the counter. She returned a few minutes later with a whole tray.

"What?" she asked when I grinned and looked at the tray. "This kid eats all the time. I think she's a Sumo wrestler in disguise! So then I have to eat too."

The next half hour flew by as we chatted about babies. Finally, I casually asked, "Who kept her during the funeral?"

"The funeral? We didn't go."

"Why not?"

Teri rolled her eyes. "We weren't invited! Have you ever heard anything like that outside a state funeral or something? Only people with invitations could attend."

"Oh." I felt guilty pretending I didn't know that. "I guess there were just so many—"

"No!" she interrupted. "It was that snooty Mrs. Coach, as she referred to herself when she was sneaking around with him. She hasn't changed." She took a long drink of her milkshake then leaned closer. "Those of us on the Cheer Squad with her could have told Coach some tales. But he was nice, really. She's always been snooty. And for what reason? She grew up down the street from me. Her mama worked at the grocery store checking out groceries, and she had at least two stepdads."

I wisely didn't offer a comment and put a finger out for the baby to grab.

"I don't want to be a gossip, but there are many who wondered if he was really Coach's son," she continued. "But I shouldn't be cruel either. I don't know what I'd do If this happened to either of my boys! I think diapers and getting up in the night brings out the worst in me."

"I haven't had the privilege," I said, "but it doesn't sound like much fun."

We finished our drinks while chatting about our lives.

Sofi began to fuss after a half hour. "Oh, my! Guess I need to stop gossiping! Time flies when we get together, doesn't it, Sorrel? This girl is ready for a snack, and I'm not doing that here."

I helped her carry the diaper bag to the car and waited until she had fastened Sofi in. "Thanks for getting us out for a few minutes," she said as she hugged me.

"Let's do it again," I agreed.

I stood there as they backed out and took off and then walked back into the shop. Someone had cleared the table, so I sat in a different spot where I could watch for Sara.

My phone beeped. When I put my hand in my pocket to take out my phone, I also grabbed Reed's letter. I'd almost forgotten about it!

I checked my message: SORRY. CANNOT MEET. SARA.

I read the message several times. She had given no excuse, nor had she suggested meeting another time. I'd given her my business card, but I didn't have her number. I checked my phone, but her number was blocked. So I couldn't call. Nor did I have her email. What could have happened?

As I pulled out of the parking lot a few moments later, I remembered the librarian eyeing us a time or two during our short conversation earlier. Could she have asked why we were talking? Had someone else spoken to Sara?

I turned back toward town and drove by the library. The guest parking lot was empty. I turned on the side street that passed the employee lot. Only one car remained in the lot. I glanced at the windows along the side of the library, but the blinds were closed.

When I pulled away, I glanced at the window again. Had one moved slightly? Or was I becoming paranoid?

Chapter 14

The letter!

I'd not delivered it to Reed!

The bedside clock's face glowed with the time, 9:00 pm, in big red letters. I reached for my cell phone and texted Reed: Mail 4 U.

While I waited for him to answer, I rationalized my error. First, I'd been distracted by being stood up this afternoon. Then, I'd stopped by the paper to deliver some photos I'd taken at the senior center, using their computer to write small captions for each so the community news editor could run them tomorrow. Finally, I'd ended the evening with small chores like checking mail and feeding my cats.

I'd held out hope that I would receive a text or email explaining why Sara hadn't shown up. She'd obviously been warned about socializing on the job. The librarian wouldn't have known what I was researching, would she? Even if she did, why would she even care? The question buried itself into my brain, but I reached no logical answer. Or the answer might simply be that she was super strict about her workers fraternizing on the job. Or maybe I had frightened Sara in some way? No, that didn't make sense. We had only spoken a moment. No, the most logical explanation was that when she agreed to see me, she'd forgotten she already had something she had to do after work. In fact, she was likely sleeping soundly right now while I was "nattering" about a "trifle" (Kevin's mother's favorite words).

The ding as a text arrived made the cats jump. I reached for my phone and saw Reed's answer: On my way.

I climbed out of bed, threw a robe over my sleepshirt, and turned on a lamp in the living room. Then, I walked into the kitchen, filled the kettle with water, and started heating it on the burner. Chris might want something hot to drink, and I could use some soothing herbal tea.

When I heard his thump-thump on my door, I hurried over, peeked through the spyhole, and unlocked it.

"How'd you get here so fast?" I asked through the half-opened door.

He looked at me from top to bottom. "I was right. You've not been to sleep. Can I come in?"

I stepped back and motioned for him to come in. "I've got water heating."

"I've drunk so much muddy coffee that my veins would bleed it," he said.

"Tea? Hot chocolate?"

"Yeah. Please." He could melt chocolate with those eyes. "Give me the letter, and I'll read it while you choose."

"Have a seat." I pointed to the easy chair. "It's there on the side table."

Reed gently lifted Flash out of the seat, sat down, and put her on his lap. I walked over to the kitchen area and began filling cups with water and tea bags. Reed preferred his tea stronger and sweet, so I added sugar to his cup. I carried both cups into what served as my living room, placed them on the small table, and settled on the sofa on the opposite side of Reed. Watching him while he stared at his name on the envelope, I was concerned by how tired he looked. Had he eaten? He should sleep more. Then I did a mental headshake. Why was I getting these wifely thoughts? Reed wouldn't appreciate being coddled.

He suddenly looked up, caught my eye, and grinned.

"No, I don't need to be coddled," he said. When I made a face at him, he laughed. "But I can use a little comic relief at the end of a very long shift."

He let the letter fall into his lap and took a drink. "This hits the spot."

I picked up my own cup, blew into it, and sipped. "The social worker at the center had meant to get it to you but had forgotten. So I offered to give it to you. I didn't know if it was urgent or not . . . " I let my sentence die off and took another sip of the tea that I didn't really want.

"But you're dying of curiosity."

"I . . . of course, I am a little curious . . . because I wasn't sure whether or not it was urgent or—"

Reed gave a full-throated laugh, then reached for his cup and drained it.

"Want another?"

"No. I need to get home."

"I did get the dogfood over to your place and they have been fed."

"I didn't need to even ask, Sorrel. I knew I could depend on you. As for this letter . . ." He picked up the envelope and carefully tore it open. "Well, I'll be!" He looked up at me and grinned and then began reading the letter aloud.

Dear Christopher,
I'd hoped you'd be more diligent about answering mail than you were about turning in your homework! Yet I haven't heard from my first letter. So I must assume you either are too busy, have considered it too trivial, or

"Or what?"

"I have no clue. It stops there. And the other letter to which she refers? It never came either."

"She?"

"My English teacher during my senior year. Remember? I mentioned her a time or two before. She was a very strict teacher. Loved Shakespeare and all of those English poets. I was always in trouble for not getting work in on time."

I smiled at the thought. "I had a first-year English teacher my senior year," I told him. "And she was the opposite problem. The guys were all crazy about her, hanging around her desk, so—if you were female— you could never get close enough to even ask a homework question!"

Reed grinned at me. "Some guys get all the luck!" Then, he looked down at the letter. "She loved Hamlet . . . made us memorize all sorts of lines. But she was always quoting other plays too. Hadn't thought of Shakespeare or her in a long time, but a line just popped into my head."

"O Romeo, Romeo," I quoted dramatically, giggling.

"No." Chris sobered. "Something about 'how sharper than a serpent's tooth to have an ungrateful child.'"

"Did she have children?"

"No. Never married. She used the quote to describe us—me, especially—when she'd given me a second chance and I ignored it." He looked at the paper in his hands. "I guess I'd lost track of her . . . until I thought of her the other day."

"You must have been happy to get out of her class!"

"Not really." He smiled. "Well, a little. But we knew she cared. She didn't let us get away with anything, but she'd stay there until practice was over so we could come in for help. Even Coach wouldn't cross her. I guess he'd tried. But by the time I had her, he wouldn't argue!"

"Did you pass?"

"Pass? She wouldn't accept less than a B from me. 'Christopher,' she'd say, 'you are smarter than you look!'" He grinned mischievously. "She wouldn't accept failing work. She said Coach needed me on the team."

"Sounds like a real teacher."

"Yes, she was. Was she out there in the senior center? I remember that she lived in this big two-story house. She told us about how she'd grown up there with her grandparents and her mother and then had stayed on after her mother died. It's hard to imagine her at the center." He looked at the letter again. "Who had this letter?"

I explained to him about the young social worker.

"You would have been a favorite," he said. "You also might have helped me out. You'd find her a real classic." He yawned and rose. "But it's time for me to head home."

"Wait! What's happening with the case?"

"You know—"

"You don't have to be specific! Just wondered if . . . "

"A lot of work . . . a lot of unanswered questions."

I followed him over to the door, and he gave me a hug. I couldn't resist the question that had been popping in my mind all day. "Reed? Is it weird to you that the only person who could attend the service was the police chief? And isn't this really quick? I know most people only wait three or four days, so a couple of days isn't outrageous. But when someone is so young . . . and it's unexpected . . . "

He shrugged. "The only explanation I've heard is that they didn't want to wait for the investigation. It was only a memorial service, so I suspect they will have a private burial."

"This service was private enough. What about his friends? And relatives who may need to travel?"

"People are strange, Sorrel. I'm waiting until you go inside and lock the door, by the way."

"You're joking!"

"Not even a little bit. I know you spent many years traipsing around a city of over a million. But you're out here, in rural New Mexico, where you seem to think you can be less diligent. But it isn't safer here than most places. I don't need any more murder cases to work!" He sobered and whispered gently, "I know I'm unreasonable . . . in your eyes. I'm tired from lack of sleep and from losing people I care about. You can unlock the door and take off in the night after I'm gone! I guess this note . . . well, it's something else I need answers about after this case is finished and after I ever sleep a whole night."

I gave him a little push. "Go on home, Deputy. I won't promise to play the wilting violet role longer than three minutes. And I'll wait until tomorrow to—"

"It's not a crime, Sorrel. She was old. I'll check the letter out after this is over."

"Aye, aye, Deputy!"

I turned and stepped inside, locking the door. I heard his laughter all the way to the truck. He needed to think I'd listened to him, so he could sleep.

Chapter 15

He'd spent much of the day in prayer, save the funeral mass at St. Anne's where he'd joined his fellow pastors. He wouldn't have recognized the young man lying in the casket in his football jersey, his hair trimmed and his face peaceful. Instead, his mind recreated the images of agony on his features, death crowding his eyes and desperation in his words: "Father, take this. You'll know what to do."

His heart had not been where it should have been during the mass. Neither could he meet the eyes of one whose black heart had stolen the young life, for he was bound to keep the dark secret. He had transferred the young man's agony to his own.

Even as he bowed his head in prayer, he wept.

Eventually, he rose, brushed his sleeve across his eyes, and moved toward his study. He had paperwork to finish, meetings to conduct, and problems to address.

Yet, as he approached his desk, a vision of the young man's face once more flashed before his eyes, as his ears heard the dying words: "Fair is foul and foul is fair." He'd whispered those words urgently and then begun his confession.

The words were familiar. He sat at his desk, searching his mind. He'd heard them before. Were they the words from a popular song? No, they sounded too old. They didn't sound like any of the scriptures. But that must be where he'd find the phrase.

Hours later, he settled back into his chair in exhaustion. Fair is foul, and foul is fair. Even as the origin of the phrase eluded him, he knew it must have held significance for the young soul. The young man had whispered it urgently several times as he lay dying there in the rain in his priest's arms.

He pulled a notepad forward and wrote the phrase. Perhaps he could stop by the public library to see if he could find the quote. It must be a famous one. In fact, he'd read it once . . . long ago . . . likely in English class. Why hadn't he thought of the library before?

Once the decision was made, he felt driven to follow it up. "I'll be at the city library," he told his secretary.

"Father, your appointment—"

"I haven't forgotten it. I shouldn't be more than twenty minutes or so. Get him a cup of coffee if he arrives before I return."

He found a parking spot near the door of the library and hurried through the front door. When he arrived at the research librarian's desk, however, his good fortune seemed to have deserted him. She was not there.

"May I help you?"

He turned toward the soft, young voice. "I fear I'll have to return," he said. "I need help locating the origin of a quotation. I'll come back another day, as I have a meeting shortly."

"Oh," she said. "Our research librarian is the one who would help you, but she won't be back from a conference until next week. If you want to leave it with me, maybe I can find someone else who can help."

He almost refused, but she seemed so anxious to help. He smiled and handed the note on which he'd written the phrase and said, "Let me put my phone number on it."

She didn't answer. He looked up to see her staring at the note. She looked up and said, "You don't need to write your number. I know this quote. It comes from Macbeth."

"Shakespeare?" He could not imagine the young man reading Shakespeare any more than he'd be quoting it.

"Yes," she said. "We read the play in my Senior English class. Our teacher loved Shakespeare. She even had some of us act out scenes from the play." She smiled awkwardly. "I sort of had a crush on the guy who played Macbeth."

"And this is from Macbeth then?"

"Yes, it is. He even jokingly said it would fit a football chant."

"Football chant? Was he—"

"Yes. He played football. His dad was the coach."

Chapter 16

I could feel my armpits getting sticky and my legs numbing a bit as I ran along the fence line. Only a short distance left. In spite of tiring, I felt terrific. The tension from the past few days had evaporated.

Above, pink and orange fingers threaded through the pale blue sky. A cottontail rabbit and an occasional lizard skittered across my path, making me slow, dodge, then speed back up. A few cows glanced but didn't find me interesting enough to interrupt their grazing.

I loved running through a different world where life meant surviving and death meant . . . well, maybe I didn't like the death part. I passed a couple of buzzards cleaning up the remains of a rabbit. They didn't worry too much about the how's or why's of the death. Maybe they had a better attitude toward the whole process than we humans.

I was so caught up in my surroundings and thoughts that I almost missed the buzzing against my waist. Without breaking my stride, I moved the headset onto my ears and punched the button to answer.

"This is Sorrel."

"Running? Are you far from home?"

"No. Made the turn and on my way back." I skirted around a land turtle who'd drawn his head and legs inside in defense. "Do you want me to call you when I get home, Mr. Byrd?"

"No. I'm parked in front of your place. I'll just wait."

Randall Byrd seldom drove out to my place; and when he did, it was something urgent or important—at least to him. I'd hoped to have a few days to focus on the shop, maybe even take a couple of days off to shoot some new landscapes. His phone call wasn't as welcome as I'd tried to sound when I ended the conversation.

He'd left his car and stood inside the pavilion at the back of the shop. I'd had it erected shortly after moving into the small house. With the shop in the front part and living quarters in back, I'd not really had room for a yard. Instead, I'd hung pots of flowers around the inside of the pavilion so I could admire them, read a good book, and recline on the lounge chair. Reed often referred to it as Sorrel's Shangri-La.

"Did you know you have a horned toad that thinks he lives here?" Mr. Byrd asked by way of greeting.

"Rufus," I said. "He allows me to share the place."

I smiled at the sound of Mr. Byrd's hearty laughter.

"Want to come inside? I can make you something cold to drink or some coffee. I usually drink water before I make coffee after a run."

"I wouldn't say no to a cup of coffee," he said. "I don't drink the nasty stuff they have at the paper, and my wife has turned to that designer stuff." He wrinkled his nose, then followed me through the door. "Hello, kitties," he said to my spoiled felines, who leapt from the sofa into their cat beds.

I took bottled water from the refrigerator and took a long drink. Then I began assembling the ingredients for the coffeemaker and pushed the button for it to brew.

"I'm sorry to catch you on your run," he said. "I saw the place shut up but your vehicle still here, so I thought I'd call and see if you were close by."

"It must be something important." I didn't want to rush him, but a shower beckoned and he actually seemed a bit nervous . . . or anxious? "I could meet you at the paper later if you want."

"I don't want eavesdroppers," he said. "I'll sit here at the kitchen table if you don't mind?"

"Sure." I gathered a couple of coffee mugs and set one in front of him and the other opposite. "Sugar? Cream?"

"Thought you knew I drank it black. That other stuff isn't really coffee by the time you put all those things in it," he grumbled, but I could tell he was just making small talk.

"You sound like my dad," I laughed. I reached inside the cupboard, took out sugar cookies, and arranged them on the plate. By then, the coffeemaker had finished.

Mr. Byrd had already nabbed a couple of cookies when I carried the pot over and filled first his cup and then mine before placing the carafe on a hot pad. "Is it about the funeral?" I asked. "Or was my article—"

"It was fine, like I said. And I've heard nothing really about how the funeral went, except there were some unusual people attending it." He took a sip of coffee. "Strong. Just like I like it."

"You said it was invitation only."

"Yes. And I wasn't mad about being omitted from the guest list in spite of the longtime connection. Funerals, at their best, aren't my idea of a fun activity. But I've never heard of invitations for funerals— outside of celebrities—and this kid wasn't a celebrity—so my newspaper nose tingled. I sent someone sort of undercover—"

I laughed. "How do you manage an undercover person at a funeral?" I asked.

He smirked. "You offer a weekend at your cabin for the guy who was scheduled to work setting up the chairs, etc., with a warning he'll be charged with trespass if he ever breathes a word. Then you pay good money to an investigator from out of town to secure the replacement job."

"Hey! Sneaky! I like it."

"Me too."

We both stuffed cookies in our mouths and washed them down with coffee. I refilled his cup while I waited for him to continue. Finally, he sighed and asked, "Do we ever truly know people?" He reached inside his suit jacket and pulled out a manila envelope. "My guy snapped photos."

As he handed them over to me, he whispered, "Why these people?"

When I opened the envelope, several photos spilled out. Some of the people in them looked vaguely familiar, but most were strangers to me. From their clothing, most were affluent and older. I opened my mouth to ask, but he answered my unasked question. "They're not related. And they're folks I'm not even certain are friends. Coach and his wife obviously are younger than most and in a different social group. Here is our state representative and his wife." So that's why he looked familiar! "This is the president of the board of not only the bank but several other institutions . . . old money." He continued identifying them until he reached the last photo. "This guy isn't from here. I doubt he's even from the state!"

"Maybe an out-of-town relative?"

"Not that we can determine." He picked up his cup and drained it. I motioned toward the carafe but he shook his head. "Something is strange here. Look at their faces. The only two grieving are the parents . . . and Coach appears more worried than sad."

I picked up the photos and looked at them again, this time looking closer at the faces. Mr. Byrd had a point. Not only did they not seem appropriately solemn, but most of them appeared bored.

"You get my point?"

I nodded. "But maybe they were just fulfilling an obligation—"

"By attending the funeral of a high school coach's son who was murdered under questionable circumstances? And why their presence at the funeral? Why not faculty he has known for years, his principal, and his old friends? If I didn't know better, I'd think this was a board meeting, not a funeral." Mr. Byrd leaned toward me, his eyes pinning me into place. "I need someone to find out who they are . . . and why they were there."

"I know you were upset to be omitted," I began carefully, "but—"

"Sorrel, this isn't a fit of pique! I hate most social functions—and a funeral will never be one of those for me, by the way—but I have a nose for news . . . good or bad . . . and this smells bad! If you can't see that . . . or don't want the assignment . . . "

He leaned toward me, his eyes fixed on my face, and let his words hang in the air.

I felt the familiar adrenaline flowing, even as my common sense warned that I was considering stepping off into yet another unwise pothole. "I have to get the shop—" I began.

He sighed. "I guess I could get Will to come."

"Will!" I gasped. "You can't! He's finishing up his degree and . . . "

The gleam in Mr. Byrd's eye, which he didn't conceal quickly enough, made me hush. Will, the university student who had interned at the paper recently, was not experienced enough to take this challenge, I reasoned silently. We'd worked undercover and almost lost our lives—well, my life actually—in the process.

"He can't do this alone," I finally said.

"So you accept the job?" He avoided my eyes. "Will has a week of spring break coming up. That's all the time I'm willing to invest in this. After that, I will accept that maybe I just—"

"When is he arriving?" I finally asked.

"Tomorrow. That should give you today to tie up loose ends here." He rose. "Thanks for the coffee. I'll expect you at the bed and breakfast about nine?" I nodded reluctantly. I had stayed there when I first arrived in Saddle Gap and often stopped by to eat there. "Oh, here." He dropped the photos in front of me as he rose. "I'll let myself out."

I didn't answer. What kind of cover story would divert the attention of Chris Reed? I wondered.

"As little as possible," Randall Byrd answered from the door.

"What?"

He smiled. "I read minds, among other things. Thanks for the coffee and cookies. Oh, and the deputy is easier for you to divert than you think." He probably didn't realize I heard his laughter as he walked down the steps.

"How did I get myself involved in this?" I grumbled under my breath, even as the adrenaline rush rose inside and all sorts of plans began to form in my mind. But first, I needed to call my favorite house sitter, crossing my fingers as I dialed, in hopes she was free.

Chapter 17

"Sometimes solutions just fall in your lap!" I told my feline companions, pocketing my cell phone. Teri's aunt had happily agreed to fill in at my shop for a few days, including feeding my cats. They followed me around the bedroom as I packed spare clothes and limited toiletries into my backpack. "There. I guess I have everything I need." I glanced into the backpack one last time before I zipped it. Instantly, I stopped and looked at Flash. "Sunscreen! You didn't remind me!"

"I have! I've told you at least a dozen times to lock your door! So here's another reminder that leaving your front door unlocked isn't safe when you're isolated. Better yet, to not have it standing open is an even better idea!"

At the first word, I jumped and muted the squeal that rose in my throat. When he finally hushed, I scolded. "Chris Reed! I—"

"Will happily offer you a cup of coffee?" He scooped Flash up into his arms and eased into my overstuffed chair. She snuggled down, purring so loudly her body vibrated.

"The sign outside reads Gifts, not Coffee Shop!" I snapped, moving toward the kitchen counter. He ignored me, snuggling Flash as I filled the coffeemaker with water, the basket with coffee, and pushed the switch. "You—"

"Drink too much coffee. Someone has told me that a hundred times." He grinned. "I guess you don't have anything edible, do you?"

I pulled out the jars of peanut butter and jelly. Luckily, I had bread for three sandwiches. Neither of us spoke while I made them. When I turned around to put the plates on the table, Reed had his head back and his eyes closed.

"I'm not asleep. Just resting my eyes."

I poured him a cup of the fresh coffee and placed it and a couple of sandwiches on the table beside him. He sat up, set Flash on the floor, and grinned. "My favorite meal."

I brought my own sandwich and cup of coffee to the couch and sat down. "I haven't decided yet if that's the truth or that you know it's about all I make that is edible."

"That too," he agreed. He ate the first sandwich in two or three bites and washed it down with a huge gulp of the hot coffee.

"I don't know how you do that! You should be choking or scalding yourself!"

"It's a talent," he mumbled, his mouth already full of another bite of the second sandwich.

"You have an answer for everything," I muttered before biting into my own sandwich.

"Not yet. This one is more complex than one would think. Why the packed backpack?"

"A quick assignment for Mr. Byrd. Will is on break and I'm collaborating with him on a story. It shouldn't be a long one."

"I thought you weren't accepting those for a while." He swallowed the last bite of the second sandwich.

"I wasn't. But I've caught up on the books here and am closed until Monday. Besides, Mr. Byrd—"

"Needed a favor." He grinned. "He can be persuasive when he wants." He picked up his cup and drained the coffee. "I just wanted to drop by and let you know I'll be out of touch for a bit. I've already arranged for someone to feed the dogs, etc."

"Why didn't you ask me? Chris Reed, you know I love those dogs!"

"I know you do. And you spoil them rotten. But you also have a busy life. One would think the store would be enough, but the career you left behind isn't ready to turn you loose."

"Why are you grinning?"

"I wasn't grinning! I don't dare grin when I know I'm right. You don't have the time."

"I won't even dignify that with an answer!" I would have stomped and added 'so there,' but Reed was enjoying this way too much.

"You don't have to." Reed rose, put on his hat, and carried his cup to the sink. Then he leaned his hip against the counter and crossed his arms. "My advice to you—which is cheap since you haven't asked me for it—is to stop apologizing and denying who you are. You're a top-notch reporter. And you're an equally top-notch photographer. And since you've moved here, you are able to pursue both. I understand because I have a similar situation. I love law enforcement and I love ranching. At this point, the first one pays more of the bills. Thrown into the mix is this feisty redhead who I enjoy spending time with when we happen to be free . . . and who I rescue when she gets herself into a mess that I am able to handle. It's the persons we are . . . right now."

"Wow. Do you believe in reincarnation?"

"Why?"

"Because you may just be Will Rogers!"

He laughed. "Well, Will or Roy or whoever, I need to get going." He walked to the door and opened it. "Let me hear. A text . . . whatever. And be careful." Then he walked back to the couch and leaned over to drop a kiss on my forehead. "Do you realize we're sounding like black-and-white television characters?"

"Impossible! We're in color!"

I loved the sound of his laughter. As he walked out the door, I called out, "Get some rest!"

Almost as if on cue, my cell phone rang. It was the newspaper.

"Hello."

"Sorrel?"

"Mr. Byrd, I was about to call you."

"Will is arriving a little earlier than anticipated, so I'd like to make our meeting at the Bed and Breakfast for eight instead of nine tomorrow."

"I'll be there," I said.

"And remember to pack a bag. I don't know if this will last longer than one day, so warn whoever is covering your shop. After we go over things, you two can start right away."

"Reed popped in unexpectedly and saw what I was doing, so I told him I was doing a news assignment with Will."

"That sounds good. Better to tell him that than have him snooping."

After we hung up, I rechecked my backpack to make sure I had all the items I'd need in an emergency overnight job. Even though I shouldn't have to be away overnight, it was smart to be prepared. I could still feel the adrenaline pumping as another thought appeared unexpectedly. Maybe Reed was right. Maybe I hadn't quite cleared this reporter/news thing out of my blood.

Chapter 18

The Bed and Breakfast now sported a new sign advertising breakfast and an afternoon tea. I wasn't surprised when I found only one parking space—and it was across the street. The food was wonderful, something I'd discovered when I'd stayed there while redesigning my little shop. During those months, I'd grown fond of Mrs. Sanchez's cooking. Although I'd moved, I often stopped by for a meal and a quick visit.

"Sorrel!" Mrs. Sanchez exclaimed when I entered. "So good to see you, *chica*!" She gave me a hug and whispered, "The private dining area."

"I'm happy to see you too," I told her. "Business is booming."

"So I've heard," she said. "I'll bring you food."

"Just coffee."

"A meal it will be," she replied firmly. "I'll be with you in a moment," she announced over her shoulder to a tall gentleman.

Then I understood. She was speaking in her own code. She loved cloak-and-dagger drama. I doubted it would qualify as such. I followed her down the short hall into a private dining area. Seated at the only table were Randall Byrd and Will.

"Sorrel." Mr. Byrd rose and pulled out the empty chair facing the door. Will made the mock salute he'd adopted while we had worked together a few months ago.

"Breakfast will be served by Julia," Mrs. Sanchez announced as I sat. "Julia is my niece. She does not speak or understand much English."

I reached across the table to shake hands with Mr. Byrd. "Cloak and dagger," I whispered. He smiled and I thought he would have answered had Julia not chosen that moment to enter with a serving cart.

My stomach welcomed the smells of homemade flour tortillas, sausage, scrambled eggs, green chilies, chopped tomatoes, onions, and shredded cheddar cheese. After serving each of us, she placed a bowl of chopped melons and pineapple beside our plates and filled coffee cups. Then she nodded politely and backed out of the room.

"Make that 'no' English," Will murmured, his mouth already full.

I nodded, already sipping the hot coffee.

Mr. Byrd cleared his throat. "I arranged this meeting to give you information about the assignment. I'd like you to keep it confidential . . . as much as you can."

"But this is for a newspaper article, isn't it, sir?" Will asked.

"Yes, it is. However, some of the information you will uncover will be sensitive. As such, you may encounter resistance. Consider this a sort of an undercover assignment here at the beginning. Depending on what we uncover, we will then decide how to proceed with the information."

We nodded. Will had a full mouth of eggs and sausage by now. I speared a hunk of cantaloupe and bit into it. Mr. Byrd continued. "Will, I've already given you a bit of information about my godson's death. Sorrel has read the recent news articles and can fill in the gaps I may have left. But this assignment is more than just about my godson. In fact, think of it as a treasure hunt. There is a secret connected to this whole thing. Listen and then share what you think."

He lifted a briefcase onto the table, opened it, and pulled out a couple of folders before closing it again.

"I've made you each a copy of the information I have," he began, handing one of the folders to each of us. "Read it as you eat and then we'll share ideas and thoughts."

During the next few moments, I glanced over the notes quickly before adding eggs and sausage to my plate. I'd discovered one should eat when possible as opportunities often did not appear in undercover situations—and certainly not food this delicious. Will managed to consume a huge amount of food in a short time—something I'd learned about him in previous situations—and gulped coffee laced with sugar.

I spooned the last bite into my mouth just as Mr. Byrd cleared his throat. He turned to Julia who had hovered nearby and smiled. In near-perfect Spanish, he asked her to clear the table and bring fresh coffee. Then he turned to Will. "I've included the news clippings of stories that I feel give you background information in this file." He handed over a thick pocket folder. "I've also included a list of concerns, questions, and suggestions of my own. But I want both of you to view those as only starting points. Because of some of the individuals involved, I can promise you will encounter more roadblocks than gates, so to speak. I cannot promise you that you will even be able to find the answers we seek. And maybe the answers you find will be to questions we have not even thought to ask."

I knew he was giving this warm-up for Will, but I was impressed once more with his newspaper skills. In spite of my less-than-excited early approach to this assignment, I could feel the familiar adrenaline pumping inside. Mr. Byrd continued to describe the funeral attendees to Will. I did not see Will's typical bird-dog demeanor yet, but I knew it would follow.

Apparently, Mr. Byrd felt his pitch lacked persuasive punch as well. "Sorrel, do you have something to add?"

I nodded and began reviewing the comments I'd heard from the residents of the nursing home where Brent had worked on the lawns. I included their opinions about him as a person—all very positive. Then I introduced the library incident and my interview with the young lady. I could see both men lean forward a bit and Will jotted notes.

When I reached the point where she had not shown up for the meeting, Will interrupted me. "Have you been able to follow up yet?"

"No," I said. "I intended to do so today. But now that you've joined the team, I wonder if you might be more successful than I in case she's avoiding me."

Mr. Byrd nodded. "I agree."

I continued. "My suggestion would be to make contact at the library. Request her help with something. She is personable but cautious. She was friendly with me, but you have advantages I don't."

Will grinned. "Happy to oblige, ma'am," he drawled in a terrible Western television accent.

Then Mr. Byrd turned to me. "I doubt you'll get much from the priest, but I'd like for you to try. Maybe he'll drop a tidbit without realizing it."

I doubt that, I thought, but I nodded anyway.

"Has Reed given you any statement at all?"

"Not yet. Of course, I haven't seen much of him."

"Check again." He sighed. "You know what to do. Your experience precedes you, Sorrel. I've given you a partial list of the funeral attendees. I'm sure I've not gotten them all, but we tried. This is such a personal thing for me that I guess I find it hard to step back. But I will. I trust you two to pursue any leads that are feasible . . . and contact me should you need my help."

"How long do we have?" Will asked.

"I'd like to have it yesterday," Mr. Byrd grunted, closing his briefcase and rising. "But I do want regular reports. This is an investigative piece, so the deadline isn't the same as a breaking story. But people forget easily and the urgency fades. I'd like to run the story sooner instead of later."

"I have the store covered for this week," I interjected. "So I'm saying this week is probably what I can commit at this time."

Will piped in. "I'm on a tight schedule also. So we have a busy week ahead." He grinned. "This is why I love the newspaper business," he added. "Lots of pressure, snooping, lies, and sleepless nights that equal excitement."

"Stir in blind alleys, close-mouthed witnesses, and irritated law enforcement and you have frustration and long hours," I muttered.

"Sorrel?" Mr. Byrd sounded surprised.

"And I'm in," I said. "This stuff is addictive . . . this news stuff. I wonder if I'll ever be able to totally retire."

"I hope not," Randall Byrd answered. "At least, not until after I do." Then he lifted the pot. "Fresh coffee? I think it's time to chart the course . . . for you two. I'm off to a meeting."

After he left, I looked at Will and shrugged. "Guess we're stepping off into another adventure, partner. You ready?"

"Sure," he grinned. "But first I have to figure out how to handle my parents. They think I'm on a holiday with buddies."

"At least, they're not here," I said. "Christopher Reed is."

Chapter 19

After Mr. Byrd left us, Will and I decided we should choose assignments. Our brainstorming would be more extensive when we had more information, but our first chore would be gathering facts

Will decided he should go to the library first.

"Maybe you can charm her," I teased.

"I can try," he said. "What's your plan?"

I told him I would go to the church first and hopefully get some information from the priest. Then, I'd visit the nursing home. As we discussed whether or not Will should accompany me, he suggested he could go undercover there later.

"We won't have enough time for you to work there," I warned him. "Even a volunteer needs to be vetted."

"Could I be a great nephew?" he asked. "Do they pay close attention to relatives?"

"You could try, but we couldn't be specific about whom you're visiting. It could get complicated. Let me think on that. Maybe if we send you in with flowers or something. Or you might be able to sneak in and out . . . totally unnoticed." I grinned.

"Thanks!" he said. "My ego has missed you!"

Will was booked into the Bed and Breakfast, so we agreed to meet back there at the end of the day—or night, whichever it would be—to compare notes on our progress.

I drove out to the shop and checked my answering machine. I saved a couple of messages from other gift shop owners who wanted some of the notecards and small prints I'd made of various critters in the area. Then I forwarded the phone to my cellphone, fed my greedy cats, changed from my jeans to a slightly dressy pair of slacks, and added a bright scarf to brighten my white shirt. I had grown up with a mother who insisted I should "dress" for church. Of course, I'd be talking to the priest and not attending a service. I looked at the results in my bedroom mirror. Yes, I concluded, the scarf softened the look.

As soon as I met Father Joseph, I realized how antiquated my views had become. He opened the door in worn jeans, even more worn tennis shoes, and a football jersey. Only the cross lying against his throat made me hope I'd found the person I needed to visit. "Father?" I asked.

He grinned and stepped outside. "I'd shake your hand, but I've been painting. May I help you?"

"I hope so. I'm Sorrel Janes, reporter and photographer from the paper. I'd like to visit with you about—"

"The recent murder? I thought the paper had already covered the story. Maybe we can schedule an appointment. I've been working outdoors; and, as you can see, I'm not dressed for photos."

"Well, Mr. Byrd thought we might do a follow-up to help the community deal with the tragedy. I'm only on a fact-finding mission today. No photos."

He shrugged, stepped through the door, and closed it. "Can we go around the side then? I'm painting my office, so it isn't a place for a guest. We can walk around the side here and miss the mess."

"Sure." I followed him down a sidewalk to the back of the church. He unlocked a door and gestured for me to step inside.

"I apologize for my appearance," he said. "But we have a small church, and most of our members are working. We have ladies who come in to clean once a week, but I'm the priest-of-all-trades so to speak. I enjoy painting most, which is a blessing. This church isn't particularly old, but my predecessor had come out of retirement until they could find a fulltime pastor. He wasn't in good health."

I followed him into the room and sat on the worn sofa. He walked over to a counter that ran along one side and washed his hands in the sink. "This is a sort of all-purpose room. We use it for everything from informal gatherings to meals. Some people—especially our teens—feel more comfortable visiting with me here than in the office."

I looked at the yellow walls, simple navy curtains, and colorful pillows on the sofa and overstuffed chair. "This room would put a person at ease," I told him. "It's warm . . . the feel of a den." I gestured to the battered book cases along the opposite wall. "Those don't look like theological books either."

He grinned. "Hardly. You'll find some classics, but mostly we have a trading library here. People bring some and take some." In anticipation of my next question, he leaned forward and stage-whispered, "I tell them I check the titles. But I don't. Please keep that off the record."

I grinned. This was a guy completely different from the minister at the huge church in Houston where I'd attended. I liked his attitude.

"Now, how can I help you?" he asked.

"I'd like for you to tell me about that night," I said. "Do you mind if I record this? I'll just use my phone."

"Not at all. But I really don't have anything more than what has already been reported. I suppose your reporter has talked to the police."

"Yes. But I'd like to hear it again . . . to refresh me . . . and maybe spark a question or two. Did you know him well?"

"Not at all. I can't recall ever seeing him at mass. But as I said, I'm new. In fact, I didn't connect him to his parents until then."

"So you know his parents?"

He looked at his hands then answered carefully. "I'd seen his mother a few times but hadn't yet become acquainted with his father. I've been told he is an outstanding football coach—and this is the season. In fact, scheduling the services took several calls for him to rearrange his schedule."

I paused. Years of experience helped me keep my face and voice neutral, but my heart ached for the young man whose father even thought of the schedule. Still, he'd been eloquent—probably grieving—at the meeting I'd attended.

"Can you tell me about that night?"

"Well . . . "

"I know it is in the police report, and my editor has spoken to them. But I'd like to hear your version. What were you doing? What time of night was it?"

He nodded. "I'd returned from a visit to a sick parishioner . . . an elderly man who likes to help with the gardens. I'd taken him home the day before when he seemed faint. When one of the cleaning ladies carried in a pot of posole, I thought he might enjoy a bowl. Since he lives alone, I stayed longer than I'd expected, visiting with him as he ate. So it was later in the evening by the time I returned home in the middle of the storm. I'd hung my outer garments in the bathroom so they wouldn't make a mess, turned on the television and was just settling into my chair when I heard someone beating at the front door."

"Was that unusual?"

"It is the first time I've had this situation occur since I've been pastor here." He paused, as if searching for words. "I've been called out to the hospital when someone is anxious about a family member, but for the victim to be in his final moments? Definitely my first time. We had spoken of such situations when I attended seminary, but it didn't prepare me for the emotions or reactions I'd experience."

He stared at his shoes for a few minutes, then looked back at me. "Our world is sometimes so filled with evil."

"I spent my early career as a television crime reporter in Houston, Texas," I told him. "No one can truly prepare you for the things you will encounter. After one particularly difficult night—a young girl murdered and discovered lying beneath her grandmother's car—I rode through the city afterward, raging to the cameraman about the injustice of it all. He finally pulled into an all-night diner. 'Here's a Kleenex,' he said to me. 'Then we need to drive back and film your report.'"

"'I can't!' I told him. 'It's too horrible!'"

"'Our job is to report the horror,'" he reminded me, "'in hopes people will try to avoid it. And her family—if she has any—and her friends need to grieve for her without destroying their own lives with needless guilt about what they should or should not have done.'"

"Wise man," Father Joseph commented.

"Smart but not particularly wise. He overdosed at a party a few months later." I looked around the room. "Did you bring Brent, your surprise visitor, in here?"

"No. I heard the banging at the front door of the church. It was pouring rain . . . and dark. The light at the end of the walk had been shattered. I remember a truck idling at the curb. But my attention was on the young man's hands holding his stomach, the anguish on his face, and the blood trickling from his mouth. As he toppled into my arms, I vaguely heard the truck take off, the tires squealing. My attention remained on this young man, obviously struggling to speak, in my arms."

"Did he—"

"He gave his confession, which of course I cannot share." Tears pooled in his eyes and he wiped them with his hands. "Pardon me. My emotions are still raw. But he is with God now. And I am sworn to protect his confession."

I could feel him shutting down, so I switched to another line of questioning. "Did you see the truck at all?"

"The police asked that. I'm not knowledgeable about trucks. It was a dark, late night. . . and with the pouring rain and this poor young man . . . I focused on him. I only glanced as it pulled out. But my concern was the injured. I do think it had an extraordinarily loud idle, or I probably would have ignored it completely."

"Did he tell—"

"Absolutely nothing that I can share."

I rose and handed him my card. "If you remember something else that you can share, please call. I apologize for reminding you of the incident. I can imagine the trauma of such an event."

He rose as well and promised he'd call if he remembered something.

I shook his hand before stepping through the door, and then turned as if I'd only just thought of the question. "Could you tell if the person in the truck was alone? Did she turn toward town?"

He thought a moment. "The truck turned toward town. But I'm not sure whether the driver was a man or woman."

Chapter 20

I drove to Casa de Oro after leaving the church, and sat in the parking lot writing down my thoughts while the interview remained fresh in my mind. Sometimes taking notes during an interview distracts the person, so I'd developed the technique of punching 'record' on my phone before dropping it in my pocket. Listening to the entire interview again helped me develop a broader understanding for the article.

I couldn't—and wouldn't—share exact quotes or sensitive information from the recording unless the person had given permission for me to record; and any direct quotes used in the article would be ones I'd written in my notes down during the interview. In this case, however, Father Joseph had allowed me to record our session.

I'd not asked many questions that I knew he wouldn't answer. It was a technique I'd adopted early in my career with the station in Houston on the advice of a seasoned reporter. He'd said to start with the questions I knew the person would comfortably answer. Then I could slip the tougher questions in without putting the person on the defensive. I'd usually been successful—until today.

Building rapport early on usually helped soften the questions and invited both of us to commiserate together. But it wasn't a sure technique . . . and it hadn't been successful with Father Joseph. He might not be older than I, but he had answered my questions carefully.

Most of the priest's answers had been vague at best. When I'd asked if the young man identified who had hurt him, Father Joseph had said, "He was in much pain, poor man. Speaking would be most difficult." He'd delivered that non-answer earnestly, his eyes pleading with me to agree. When I followed that question with one about the cause of the man's injuries, the priest had given a soliloquy about the "evils that surround all of us" and had hopefully asked if I minded if he prayed for me. Then he'd bowed his head and prayed that I'd be safe in my quest for the events that had happened to the young man and that he hoped those who had performed evil deeds would confess and sin no more.

In retrospect, after I'd left him, I wondered who had actually been in charge of the interview. It wasn't a feeling that sat well with me.

"He's a clever guy," I said aloud.

A man who had parked beside me and was walking toward the sidewalk glanced over, stopped, and asked, "Pardon? Did you say something?"

I grinned ruefully. "It's a bad habit, talking to myself."

He gave a half smile. "As long as you don't start an argument, you're probably safe." Then he raised a hand in a casual wave and continued walking toward the building. I returned my attention to my notes, adding the questions the answers had provoked. Finally, I stepped out and walked up the sidewalk to the building.

"Hello, Miz Sorrel!"

I looked toward the voice. "Hi, Sebastian! What are you up to this morning?"

"Just picking up papers before the groundskeeper mows." He leaned close to shake my hand. Then he whispered, "He's new. Name's Lester I think. Started yesterday and, if that's any indication, he'll need all the help he can get."

"It must be hard to step into the shoes of someone as popular as the last one. He'd been here for years, right? Maybe this new guy will improve once he feels more comfortable."

"I'm not sure he could feel more comfortable!" Sebastian leaned closer and grinned. "Word is that he swiped most of the candy from the dish in the lounge . . . to go along with all the coffee and tea he drank every few minutes. Then that led to the bathroom and flirting with the gals on his way back."

He wiggled his eyebrows with the last few words in a near perfect Groucho Marx imitation.

I grinned. "Guess you other guys need to pay better attention to the ladies before this new guy steals them away!"

Sebastian looked like he'd like to continue, but I told him, "I've got to visit with a couple of people. I'll check in soon to see how the situation develops. I know you'll take care of it."

"Yes, ma'am!"

Then I paused. "Do you know if they have a new volunteer to help this groundskeeper?"

Sebastian's face softened. "They'd not find one as good as the one we lost," he said. "He always worked hard but was never too busy to speak. And he remembered your name. He'd even do small things . . . like mail letters or pick up something at the store."

"Don't they have mail pick-up service here?" I asked.

"Sure but sometimes letters don't get out." He leaned closer to me and whispered, "You know all of us don't still have our brains. Some people take mail."

"Why?"

He shrugged. "Who knows? Nosy? Secret agents?" Then he leaned close again. "I don't think it's always us that does it. Some of these people they hire have sticky fingers, you know. They might be working for someone outside." He punctuated his words with those bushy eyebrows dancing up and down. "Money disappears sometimes, you know. I lost a quarter last week."

I managed to keep a straight face until after I'd entered the building. Sebastian and the other residents often seesawed between reality and fantasy, so one had to listen to them with a discriminating ear. Sometimes, however, they "dropped a pearl of wisdom" as my Aunt Ruth said. But I doubted that Sebastian had left any pearls with me.

I doubted I'd get much information from the personnel office, so I peeked into the break room instead. Empty! But the coffee pot was half full, so I poured a half cup of very strong coffee and added a couple of spoonsful of powdered creamer.

"That stuff is lethal, you know!"

I jumped, splashing some on the counter. "I've had worse." I reached for a paper towel. "I'm Sorrel."

"Volunteer?"

"Sometimes. Mostly, I collect craft items made by residents for my small gift shop."

"Oh, yes. I've heard residents talking about crafts. I'm Elsa. CNA. Otherwise known as Grunge Princess." She indicated the stains on the front of her uniform. "You don't want to know where these originated and I'm trying to forget." She gave an exaggerated shudder. I laughed.

"You are a brave soul, Elsa. I haven't met you before. Are you new?"

"Do I look that young? I can't remember new. Or being idealistic. Maybe I was born old?"

She made another exaggerated face.

"It must be a daily adventure working here."

She grinned. "I like you! Yes, it is an adventure . . . a better word than I sometimes use. I've just spent the past hour trying to find whose dentures fit into whom! Seems like several people decided to trade their teeth to see if food tasted different."

I laughed. "The visions that rise before me—"

"Not to mention the smells!"

We both laughed. She reached into her pocket and pulled out change. "I'm on break and I think I need a soda, in spite of the calories. And to answer your earlier question, yes, I'm fairly new. Staff changes quickly, I've heard. And now I'm understanding a bit more. But it's a job. I've got three kids at home that enjoy eating. You're lucky, having your own business."

She selected a diet drink, then sat on the ancient couch. "Join me?"

I selected a chair near her. "Actually, I'm sort of working. Besides the shop, I do freelance news articles for the paper."

"Hey! Your life is starting to sound much more interesting than mine! Do you have a husband and kids to feed and clean up after too?"

"No. Just two lazy cats who demand to eat more than they should and spread fur on the furniture."

She laughed. "So which job are you on today?"

"The paper. I'm writing a follow-up about the young man who worked here."

"Oh. The one who . . . died."

I sipped the nasty liquid, grimaced, and rose. "This stuff is awful!" I poured it in the sink, tossed the cup, and sat back down. I sensed that our camaraderie had evaporated.

"I probably should—" she began, screwing the lid back on her bottle.

"Please don't let me interrupt your break! I know you get precious few."

She sat back a moment, but I sensed she had elevated her guard.

"Everyone I've spoken with has said the same thing, that he was a quiet kid who must have been a random victim." I took another paper cup and filled it with cold water. "Maybe this will help get that taste out of my mouth."

She relaxed a bit and smiled. "I've never developed a taste for coffee. It all tastes nasty."

The door pushed open and Jen, another volunteer, peeked inside. "Sorrel! I was afraid I'd missed you!"

Lonna Enox

"Almost," I lied. "I'm checking on craft items."

"Oh, then I have bad news for you." She stepped inside, holding the door open behind her. "I forgot to tell you that you won't be getting anything else from Miss Hoskins. She died a couple of weeks ago."

"Really! She's the one I wanted to see. I always loved visiting with her, and her tatted pieces fly out of the shop! I didn't see any notice in the paper. What happened?"

"Just died. No one here is on a lengthy lease, you know. She was nice . . . a crusty sort, though." She waved and let the door close.

I looked toward Elsa. "That must be a hard part of the job . . . saying goodbye."

She nodded. "Some are much easier to let go. But Miss Hoskins . . . she was classy. She never talked down to us. I liked listening to her stories about her years in the classroom."

"She was a teacher? Funny, she never mentioned it."

"She taught here for many years. I didn't have her. I moved here from Tucson after I married." She drained her Coke, rose, and dropped the bottle in the trash. "Time to get back to work."

"Wait! I know you may not be able to tell me, but how did she die?"

"Most everyone here is on the last of their lives," Elsa said. "*Natural causes* is the term." But her eyes stared over my shoulder.

"Is that the official cause?"

She started to the door. "I wouldn't know." She opened it, then looked back. "Look, I need my job. Keeping it means keeping your nose out of things."

"Was she your patient?"

"Yes," she murmured, looking back over her shoulder. She closed the door, leaned against it, and looked at me, her eyes conflicted.

104

"You didn't hear this from me, but she was a precious lady, and I guess I owe her. She seemed different when I took her breakfast in that morning. When I asked if she felt okay, she asked if I'd seen him."

"Him?"

"The young guy that worked on the landscaping."

"Did she say why?"

"No. She seemed agitated, so I changed the subject, thinking she would settle down. But she interrupted with one of her quotes—she liked to quote from poetry."

"Do you remember it?"

"Nah. I was terrible in English. It probably was Shakespeare or one of those guys. Something about something rotten somewhere."

"*Hamlet*," I said.

"What?"

"Shakespeare's play."

She shrugged. "I figured she was out of her head. That proves it. Poor thing. Hey, enjoyed talking to you."

She waved as she left.

"The pleasure is mine," I murmured.

I needed to talk to Reed when he finished with his initial investigation. Further snooping and talking to people here would have to wait until I could focus them better. People had already been guarded enough without my spooking them.

Chapter 21

I turned toward town after leaving the interview. There were no houses close by, but I noted a couple of apartment complexes. Over the next hour, I wandered through them, casually asking people I encountered whether or not it was a quiet area. Only a few alluded to the "accident" near the church. Some, probably thinking I was selling something door-to-door, brushed by without even answering me. Finally, deciding this wasn't productive, I texted Will to meet me at my house after he'd finished his interviews.

Next, I dropped by a couple of gas stations and a shopping mart, picking up a pack of gum and casually remarking that it was "quieter here than last night." The cashiers just grunted and handed me my change. I couldn't decide whether they'd been cautioned not to talk or whether violence had become familiar enough for them to ignore it.

As I drove home, I mentally sorted bits of information I'd received; but none of them added up to anything other than "accidental." Maybe we were trying to find something that just wasn't there. Still, something niggled at the back of my brain. This young man had died a violent death—that much was evident. Even if accidental, why the secretive atmosphere? And if accidental, how?

Once I'd pulled into my driveway and turned off the motor, I dialed Randall Byrd.

"He's out," his secretary told me after I identified myself, "to a meeting. He didn't say when he'd be back, so it may be a lengthy one. Do you want to leave a message?"

"Yes . . . no. Just let him know I called and would like a call back when he can manage."

"May not be until tomorrow. You know how Mr. Byrd is when he gets wrapped up in something."

"Tomorrow will be fine. There's no rush." Acting too anxious would only cause questions that I didn't want to answer.

The parking lot to my shop was empty except for Teri's aunt Celestina's old Ford. I'd peek in to see if she needed anything, grab the mail from the office, and spend some quiet time just thinking about what I'd learned.

Aunt Celestina was busily tidying a display of crochet items at the back of the store. She'd changed the radio station to a Spanish station, and her ample hips swayed as she hummed along with it.

"Hi!" I called.

She jumped. "I didn't hear you!" She glanced at the bell. "That thing doesn't jingle?"

"Sorry. I didn't mean to startle you!" I glanced at the bell hanging on the door. "The cords are tangled. I'll straighten them. How are things going?"

"Fine. We've had some tourists stopping by. They bought two of your pictures!" She motioned toward the wall display near the door where I'd hung photos from the Festival of the Cranes in the fall. "And they bought some of the pottery from that table over there. Then, of course, they just made a mess of this table! But that only means they are interested. People have to touch to fall in love sometimes. Two or three other cars stopped and bought small items."

"Busy morning! Do you want to take your lunch break now? I'll need to leave again this afternoon, but I can work in the office and watch the store for the next hour or so. Would an hour and a half work for you?"

"Yes, I'd like that. Juan likes to eat his beans and tortillas for lunch. I've spoiled him!" She collected her purse as she spoke and started toward the door. "I wrote phone messages on the pad in your office," she called over her shoulder.

A young couple with two young children entered the shop as she left.

"Hello!" I smiled at the children, then added to their parents, "Feel free to ask questions. I have a table with handmade toys and coloring books over there by the window."

They took me at my word. Thirty minutes later, they left with a cloth doll, coloring books, and knitted dish cloths.

A few minutes later, Aunt Celestina called to tell me she wasn't coming back that afternoon. Her refrigerator had suffered a meltdown, and she was busily cooking so the food she'd had in it wouldn't spoil. In the meantime, Juan was off to another relative to get a "new" refrigerator. Later that evening, all of Teri's family would be gathering at Aunt Celestina's to commiserate, celebrate, and feast!

Since we weren't yet in peak tourist season, I decided I could close the shop early. I needed the business, but the timeline for this investigation was already tight. My time would be better spent doing the interviews and making the phone calls I had planned to make this afternoon.

I turned the Open sign hanging on the door to Closed and turned the lock. Then I began my usual closing routine. I checked all the displays, straightening as I went and noting which ones needed restocking. I then counted the cash in the register and placed it in a money bag to take to the bank later.

The phone rang as I was sweeping some dusty footprints at the front entrance. Even though I hurried to catch it, the call ended just as I reached the office. But the red light was blinking. It was Will stating, "Interesting vibes at the library. On my way to follow another lead. Will catch up to you later this afternoon."

"Thanks for sparking my curiosity," I muttered.

My next chore was sorting the mail and writing out checks, if necessary. Aunt Celestina had bundled the mail into a plastic bag and placed it on my desk. I dumped it out and quickly pulled the advertisement fliers out, glancing at some before dumping all of them in the trash. Just as I reached for the letters, my cell rang. It was Reed's number.

"Sorrel? You busy?"

"Always. I've been wondering what happened to you, Reed. Have the pups been taken care of?"

"Yes. I'm on my way from feeding them to your place. Want to bounce something off your stubborn—"

"Brain? How nice to hear from you! I'm in the office."

I hung up to the sound of his chuckles. But they sounded tired.

And he looked more than irritated when he knocked at the locked door of the shop. I hurried to the front to unlock it and let him inside.

"Can you believe it?" he asked when he walked through the door and followed me toward the back.

"What?" I opened the door to my office and motioned for him to follow me inside.

"Haven't you heard?"

"I guess not. Tell me."

Reed plopped into the worn chair at my office desk. "I'm surprised Randall Byrd isn't raising a fit!"

I shoved a stack of folders and perched on the corner. "If I could ever get you to tell me what he isn't 'raising a fit' about, then I'd try to tell you!"

Reed finally focused on my face. "You don't know?"

"Apparently not."

"The boy's death is an 'accident.' The sheriff has officially closed the case. Coach and some other guys spent some time in his office; and when they left, he came out and made the official announcement."

"An accident?" I repeated. "Weird. But that's the same thing I've been getting from anyone I've asked. How can they justify that? I thought he was badly beaten, possibly dumped out of the truck Father Joseph recalled. That doesn't sound like an accident to me."

"Me either."

"How did the sheriff explain it?"

"He didn't explain much except that the bruising, etc., had been the result of his falling out of the back of a pick-up truck. That's the 'accident.' When I questioned how this call had been explained, he told me I was officially off the case as it was going to be closed as soon as he tied up a few loose ends. Then he gave me some time off before I start chasing down some 'malicious mischief calls.'"

"How long?"

"How do I know how long he'll have me chasing internet taggers or looking for some old lady's cat?" He crossed his arms and legs and glared up at the ceiling. "I might as well—"

"Go into my quarters while I finish closing up out here? There are sodas in the fridge."

I gently pushed him toward the adjoining door.

"I'll join you in a minute," I called after him.

He glared at me, then shrugged. "Have I fallen through a rabbit hole or something? Everybody I have spoken to today is—"

"I promise I'll talk to you about it, Reed. Let me make one last phone call and lock up."

He shrugged and walked calmly through the door into my quarters, although he might have closed the door a little harder than necessary.

I dialed Randall Byrd once more. When the call went to voicemail, I said, "Mr. Byrd, this is Sorrel Janes. Strange things are happening. Please call me as soon as you get this message."

Then I locked the door to my office.

When I entered my quarters, I didn't see Reed. Had he left? Then I noticed the door to my framing area slightly ajar. When I pushed it farther open, I saw Reed gazing thoughtfully at a photo I'd shot at sunrise of the cranes lifting up from the water.

"So," he said, "if a coyote attacks one of these fellas and injures his wings badly enough that he crashes during this lift off, do we classify it natural causes because he falls as a result? Do these other birds even care that he dies there, or are they just glad they weren't the one in the coyote's sites?"

I walked closer and put my hand on his shoulder. "These are birds, Reed. Most people argue that they don't have a soul, so they don't feel or think as we do."

"But their young—"

"Are protected as best they can protect them. And they teach them to avoid the dangers. But the young sometimes—"

"Don't listen. I know." He sighed. "But this one listened, Sorrel. People I have interviewed tell the same stories . . . of a quiet young man who had a big heart for helping others."

His voice deepened with emotion. "We either didn't teach him how to detect danger . . . or he had too much heart to avoid it. Either way, he shouldn't have died after having been dumped in front of a church. And his dad should be rampaging through the details of his last days—"

I put my hand on his shoulder, and he turned so quickly that I almost drew back. But I stepped into his hug—almost a painful hug—and held him. "He has you, Reed," I whispered. "And you have me. We'll figure this out. Neither one of us has enough good sense to back away from a soul in need . . . no matter if the odds are stacked against us."

When he finally relaxed and stepped away, he grinned that smart-alecky grin that likely kept him in trouble as a boy, cocked his eye at me, and said, "Guess we coyote hunters had better fuel up before we plan our attack. Do you even have any food in this place? Or is that a dumb question?"

Chapter 22

"So I guess this changes your itinerary!"

Reed shrugged and took another drink of his coffee. "I always have things to do around my place. Now that this investigation is officially ended, I need to concentrate on the thousand and one chores I keep putting off. You?"

"I'm writing another article for the paper. Nothing major." My phone vibrated. "Excuse me."

"Sorrel? You still home?"

"Yes. Reed and I were just—"

"Reed's there? Keep him! I'm on my way."

"What—"

I looked at the screen. "Will just hung up! Weird."

"Trouble?"

"Just weird. He asked if you were here and said—and I quote— 'Keep him! I'm on my way.'"

Reed drained his cup but didn't immediately answer. When he did, he wasn't smiling. "Is everything drama with him?"

"Usually. Before he gets here, let's stop dancing around the subject we need to discuss, namely, how do we proceed with the investigation of a death which we both are sure isn't an accident?"

Reed stared into his cup, then up at me, his eyes deadly serious. "The stakes are high on this one, Sorrel. For sure, they extend to Santa Fe and maybe even to Washington. Both of us could find ourselves in a bad spot. I still owe a bit to the bank for the ranch. I could lose my job. They could call in my note and I'd be homeless."

"You could camp here. This place is clear."

"Except that your business relies on your reputation. 'No customers' would put you out of business just as surely as sheltering an unemployed Sheriff's deputy would. Even with your merchandise being consignment, how would you pay the utilities and taxes? This is a small town, Sorrel, not like Houston. And I don't know yet how deep this thing goes."

"Remember what we said? This boy deserves justice."

"What if it was accidental? Are you absolutely—"

"Never going to accept that it was, Reed. I don't think Randall Byrd believes that either."

"Randall Byrd has to be objective about it. He may be more vulnerable than we are."

"So you're giving up! In spite of what you said!"

"No way! But I'm going against everything I depend upon . . . and I don't want to drag others along. This kid, Will, for example. And Randall. And you."

"You're not dragging me along, Christopher Reed. Get that into your pea brain! I have enough in the bank to maintain this business for a long time. Yes, it would hurt my photography business. But I can't just turn away. Something smells—"

"Rotten in the state of Denmark—or New Mexico?"

Reed and I both jumped. "Will!" I snapped. "This was a private conversation. How long have you been here? How—"

"I saw you hide your spare key to the shop. When I saw Reed's truck, I decided to snoop. I knew you two weren't including me."

He closed the interoffice door and walked over to the couch, tossing the key to me in passing.

"This isn't a video game or some college prank," Reed snapped. "If you've been eavesdropping for a while, you realize that. By the way, before I was worried about you—your degree, your future profession. You can cancel that. By snooping like you just did, I no longer am interested in working with you. And you may have put Sorrel here in harm's way. An irresponsible reporter is worse than the criminal they're investigating!"

I'd never seen Reed so angry. He rose, grabbed his hat, turned away from Will, and addressed me in a barely controlled voice. "Sorrel, I can't discuss or continue a case that has been closed." He strode toward the door.

"Wait!" Will said. "You've had your say. Let me have mine. Then you can continue to despise me or give me a chance to earn your trust. I have important information, and I think both of you may be interested. If not, then I'll leave quietly. But don't think I won't follow this story up—either with you two or on my own! I'm a newspaperman and I have to follow my gut. And my gut tells me that we have stumbled on the tip of something nasty. Of course, I realize that you don't want to endanger your—"

"Will!" I interrupted, standing. "You said in your call that you had something to tell me. Did you learn something important at the library?" I turned to Reed. "There's more coffee if you want it."

He glared at me. I knew him well enough to see his battle between pride and curiosity.

"Maybe Will has something that will help us decide what to do," I continued. I rose and turned to Will. "Get yourself a cup and join us at the table." To Reed, I said, "I wish you'd join us, but I understand if you can't. You have much more at stake than I. But whether you do or not, we're still friends . . . and co-parents to that litter of pups."

Reed sighed. Finally, he walked over, removed his hat, refilled his cup, carried it to the table, and sat down. Will stood a few seconds longer, then poured himself a cup of coffee as well and joined Reed.

"Okay," I said. "Now, we—"

A heavy knock on my door caused me to jump. I looked at Will. "Did—"

"No one there when I came," he said.

Lonna Enox

I walked over and opened it. Randall Byrd stood on the step. "May I come in?" he asked, stepping around me before receiving an answer.

He looked at the group gathered at the table. "Well, well," he said. "I couldn't have planned this any better! Just the people I want to see!"

He looked back at me, standing by the door. "We have a problem," he said.

Chapter 23

"I'll make another pot of coffee." I said as I motioned Randall toward the table where Reed and Will were sitting. He sat down at one end and opened his briefcase.

"Mr. Byrd," Will began, "I have some questions—"

I interrupted. "I suggest we listen to Mr. Byrd and discuss our concerns before we make any rash decisions. We may be more in agreement than we realize."

No one spoke as I filled the empty pot with water, poured it into the coffeemaker, and measured the coffee. But the tension in the air was palpable. I pushed the button and the coffee machine sputtered. Finally, I sat at the end opposite Randall and reached for the pen and tablet I'd left there earlier. "I'll take notes," I told him.

He glanced at Reed and Will for a moment, then nodded to me.

"We've been asked—told—that the investigation into the death of this young man will be closed so that his family may have peace," he began. "At least, I've been asked unofficially to relay this message to 'all concerned parties.'"

"Accidental? This country still operates under freedom of the press!" Will sputtered. "I'd think you—"

"Are smart enough to agree with them verbally." Randall glanced around the table, his eyes and voice steely. "There's more than one way to skin a critter—and we definitely have some powerful critters in this mix."

Will clearly wasn't ready to concede. "Once we agree to back off, we are compromising not only our principles, but those of all journalists!"

"Let's hear him out first," Reed said.

"Reed, I doubt you consider this an accidental death any more than the rest of us," I said.

"Of course not. Without going into specific details, I can promise you that it isn't even close."

Randall and I nodded.

"Then, why—" Will sputtered.

"Because they expect us to object. So they have a solid defense already. Most likely, we'll all be without work shortly and then a carefully planned cover-up will follow." Randall gave a humorless laugh. "It's an old tactic. So we just outsmart them."

"What could they possibly be covering up?" Will asked.

"It could be any of several things, but it most likely comes back to money—and power." Randall Byrd looked around the group. "Do you all agree?"

Will looked like he wanted to pound the table—or someone—with his fist. "It just doesn't make any sense! This is just a high school kid here. He's not even the kid of someone rich or famous! He wouldn't have connections that would make this level of hush-hush necessary."

"But he might have gotten mixed up in something illegal at worst . . . or sensitive at best," Reed told him. "Remember, this kid was likely just an errand boy or something. He may not even have known much about the whole operation; but as the guy on the bottom of a human pyramid, he could cause everyone above to fall with a single word or action. The more powerful they are, the harder everyone above will fight to keep that information secret."

He looked at Randall who was nodding agreement. "So what's your plan?" he asked.

Randall opened a folder and pulled out several sheets. "I didn't make copies. But you may want to take notes—only if you plan to be discreet."

Will opened his mouth but this time closed it without comment.

Reed stood. "I expect I need more coffee first. Anyone else?" Randall shook his head, but Will stood as well.

I rose to place cups, spoons, sugar, and powdered creamer beside the pot. Then I rummaged in the cupboard and added a package of chocolate chip cookies and napkins. Will grabbed several of those, stuffing a couple in his mouth before filling his cup.

Once we'd all settled around the table again, Randall began. "First, I want to reiterate that anything said at this table today must remain with the four of us." His eyes moved around the table, connecting with each of us. "It is sensitive material at the least and must be guarded carefully. At this stage, I really don't know whom we can trust."

Then he pulled out a sheet and continued. "I'd like to first address the report from the medical examiner. Note that it was given priority—unusual in itself—and the body has been sent to a crematorium. At our amazed expressions, he continued. "Again, no one is explaining the rush."

"Cremated? That's—wasn't he Catholic?" I asked.

"Yes," Will cut in, "but times have changed. Catholics may now be cremated, but it's not popular. After all, the church believes that our bodies are the body of Christ, etc."

"Oh. Thanks. I didn't know you were Catholic."

Will shrugged. "I'm not. Well, I was baptized Catholic, but I'm not sure I'm anything just now."

Reed interrupted. "Anyway, the fact that the body is already sent to be cremated so quickly is a notable point. I'm sure an argument may be that the body deteriorates quickly, but that's not usually a consideration. I also had wondered whether his being Catholic would have deterred that."

Randall agreed. "But that's only one of the facts that make me pause. Another is the guests in attendance at the funeral, a funeral that was open only to invited guests."

"What about his classmates?" I asked.

"Only invited guests," he repeated. "Classmates weren't invited. Few of the guests were younger than forty." He paused for a moment, then continued. "His parents were the only family."

"No other family? That's strange. He had no grandparents, aunts, uncles, cousins?" At a quick glance, I saw that all of us agreed on that oddity. "At his age, I also would have expected his classmates to be there. A girlfriend. Buddies."

"I asked," Randall interrupted. "His father said it would be difficult for them, and his son hadn't really had time for dating or friends. His mother mentioned they'd have a family get-together later."

"That's not true!" Will interrupted. "That girl who works in the library was a friend! And she mentioned several from the drama club that intended to go to his funeral when it was held."

"Did anyone attend from the nursing home where he worked?" I asked. "From what I heard, he was really popular with everyone, the residents especially."

Randall shook his head. "The people in attendance were very well dressed—older and affluent. No one from the nursing home. Even his boss, the director, did not attend."

"Curious," I murmured. Reed and Will nodded.

"In fairness, the nursing home management may have wanted to distance themselves, keeping the spotlight off their facility," Randall said. "Scandal is deadly. And a murdered employee, whether a supervisor or a part-timer, can produce negative fallout."

"Will," I asked, "did you have the impression that he'd been romantically involved with this young woman at the library?"

"I'm not sure. I mean, she liked him. I could hear that in her voice. But maybe it was just as friends. They'd been involved in Drama Club in high school, both of them acting. They'd played Shakespearean roles opposite each other. She didn't give the impression that it went any further." Will shrugged. "You know how it is in high school."

I looked over at Reed. "Did they do an autopsy? Would they have had time to do that? This isn't a huge city and the state—could they do an autopsy this quickly?"

Reed looked down at his hands but didn't answer.

Randall answered instead. "Supposedly. But no results will be available for some time. Still, the death is being called an accident at this time."

"An accident is just crazy! We were discussing that before you arrived. Did he have a car crash that is being covered up?" Again, I looked at Reed. "Are you going to be straight with us? What's going on? What sort of crazy cover-up is this?"

Again, Randall answered. "Sorrel, Reed may not—"

Reed held his hand to quiet Randall. He looked into each of our eyes; and, when he spoke, his voice held a seriously cautious note. "It's still an ongoing investigation," he repeated. "I'm not sure how much longer I'll even have access to this case because of my history with Coach. The sheriff has already told me I'm off it and is assigning me insignificant things, Sorrel. Remember?

"I'm--we're all—thinking alike," he continued. "But we need to discuss how we're going to proceed—quickly and quietly and within legal guidelines—until we're hushed. Someone—someone important—wants this investigation to go away. So we have to work as quickly as we can."

"What's the plan?" Will asked.

"That's why we're here, Will. I have some ideas I've jotted down. One of us needs to follow the library angle and the young lady there. Will? Since you've already made contact with her, this would be a good job for you. Another needs to—cautiously—visit with the family. Randall? You already have history with them, so maybe you could take this one. Sorrel and I will approach the priest and revisit the nursing home."

He swept his eyes around the table. "Caution is a priority. Call me if you wander into a situation where you feel uncomfortable." He grunted. "Don't try anything heroic. We don't yet know what is happening here. We do know that a young man was dumped off at his church, very quickly transported to be cremated, and the official word at this point is accidental. Get out your cellphones and let me give you a number to reach me. Put it under the listing Clark."

"As in Kent?" I asked. "Where's the cape?" Laughter does ease tension, I knew; but I didn't feel like laughing. No one else seemed in the mood for it either.

Chapter 24

Before we dispersed, Reed stressed what we did not want to do. "No vigilantes here," he said. "And no blatant snooping. Law enforcement needs to do their job. And you're not law enforcement. You need to keep your eyes and ears open and report to me if something seems out of the ordinary. Do not—I repeat—do not try to interrogate or snoop or talk about this to anyone."

He might have let his eyes linger on Will a bit longer when he said, "I remind all of you that some of the people who seem interested in this case hold more power than any of us in this room. If they have a secret, they have the power to guard it."

I walked everyone to the door, placing my hand on Reed's sleeve and holding on until the others had driven off. "Did you have to be quite so—"

"Forceful? I can only hope Will doesn't go off half—"

"Will is an experienced newsman, Reed. He's graduating soon."

He sighed. "I know. It's just that this is so . . . weird!" `

I removed my hand. "So what's our plan?"

"I have another meeting. I'd suggest you prepare to have your place here covered—just in case. And would you mind seeing that things at mine—"

"Done. But we're talking!"

"Soon." He leaned toward me, ran a finger down my cheek, and smiled. "Don't know how long the meeting I'm heading to will last. Wait for me."

"I'll see about food," I said.

"Don't bother. I'll pick up something and bring it out." He stepped off the porch and called back to me. "Can't afford for us to be sick."

He was still laughing when he drove off.

Once back inside, I reached for my cellphone. Teri answered on the first ring.

"Hello!"

"Hi, Teri! I wondered—"

"If I could watch the store?"

"No. I know you're—"

"Going absolutely nuts! I've got to get out of here soon or I'll forget how to even communicate in words of more than one syllable!" I could hear a cry in the background. "Boys, give that monkey back to your sister. Now!"

"I can call back later."

"Don't you dare! I haven't heard an adult besides Jose in ages, and he hides in the garage or listens to the television with earphones!" I heard a deep breath and a couple of squeals in the background. "Now, where were we?"

"I was about to ask if you knew anyone to—"

"Cover the store? Absolutely not! Anyone I know would be a better fit for looking after these kids. Do you have any idea what it's like to have twin boys and a baby sister who is teething? When the first two aren't fighting, the other one is drooling or howling! I need to escape a little while or I'll—"

"Cover the store for me. Thanks, Teri! I'll need you in the morning. Don't know for long but likely only a couple of days."

"I'll pray for a couple of weeks! I'll call for help on this end. Thanks, Sorrel! You've saved my life . . . or Jose's."

It was late afternoon by the time Reed got back from his meeting and we'd eaten a couple of burritos to tide us over until dinner later that night. I filled him in on the conversation with Teri as we walked to his truck. He chuckled as he held the door open for me. "You don't need to feel sorry for either of them, Sorrel," he said. "They love the misery."

"I know. But it sure makes me rethink any plans of my own."

"Is there something you want to tell me?"

I gave him a mock punch. "I'm just saying that should I get the urge to marry and have kids, I should remember these days."

"You'd be a natural, Sorrel. Look at how you pamper those felines of yours. And my pups are so rotten I can hardly stand them!"

"By the way, where are we going?" I asked as he started the truck and headed toward the highway.

"To the nursing home. I thought it might be a good spot to start. Unless you have another idea."

"Really? I didn't realize I had a vote." Then I relented. "Seriously, why there right now? We've both been out there and talked—"

"To the social worker and the people in charge," he finished for me. "We need to talk to the ones who really knew him."

"Surely they've already been interviewed. Besides, it is dinner time and most of them will likely go to sleep immediately after."

He stopped at a sign and flipped on his blinker before answering. "The people they talked to are the workers, not the residents."

"I tried, but they didn't seem to remember much. And sometimes, even when they do, they get so caught up in the attention that they add facts."

Reed turned onto the highway. "Oh, they remember a lot, depending on the day. And it's the way people talk to them that also matters. Questions make them nervous. So do people in authority. Sadly, they're more accustomed to people ignoring them."

"Surely not!"

"But they do like visitors," he continued as if I hadn't spoken. "And when a visitor casually introduces a topic, they get more comfortable passing on their opinions and memories."

I laughed. "We'll be there all night, Christopher Reed!"

"Let's bet on it."

"On what?"

"On who finds out more? Loser buys dinner afterward."

I laughed. "You know how much I eat! Can you afford it?"

I expected a quick remark but got silence instead. I looked over at him closely. He turned onto the road leading to the center. The silence grew as he parked. "Reed?"

He finally turned toward me and leaned close. In a whisper, he said, "Yes, I can! You hardly eat anything, you know. You're always talking!"

Before I could answer, he planted a quick kiss on my cheek. "We don't want to disappoint the audience," he whispered.

I looked through the windshield at the small group gathered, grinning and applauding. I turned to Reed and whispered through my smile, "Is that the best you can do, Sheriff?"

I cut off his answer with a kiss that brought snickers and a whoop. When I pulled back, he turned and grinned at our audience. He hopped out, hurried around the truck, and opened my door.

"Thanks," he whispered. "That was a terrific diversion!"

He put his hand on my elbow to guide me onto the sidewalk, toward them. "You know how it is, guys," he called to the men in the group. "It's the only way to shut them up long enough to get a word spoken!"

As we neared them, I pulled away from Reed and gave a small curtsey. "Just practicing for a play," I said. "I wasn't sure he knew how to kiss!"

Again the guys laughed. One of the ladies asked, "Does he?"

"Yep!" Chris leaned forward and kissed her cheek. She gasped, smiled, and raised her hand to her face.

"You didn't come here for that," she said. Then she looked around before whispering. "What do you want to know, Mr. Policeman? Is it about our sweet young man who was killed?"

"Where can we talk?" he whispered back to her.

"Everyone besides us is either at dinner or company right now," she said. "The television room is usually empty at this time."

"We'll follow you," Reed told her.

As she started to rise, he stepped forward to hold her walker. "My nephew here is helping me," she told a nursing aide who'd just arrived. The others hastily hid their smiles and drew the attention from Reed and me. "Follow my lead," she whispered.

Chapter 25

The television room was empty, just as our companion had predicted. She led us around several easy chairs to a spot farthest from the television set. "Go and turn the television on, about mid-volume," she told Reed. "That way our voices won't carry."

He nodded and did as she asked. When he returned, she said, "I'm Helen. Helen Williams." She paused until we introduced ourselves, then continued. "Christopher, I have been hoping you would return and talk to me. I may have information you can use. If not, maybe it will make you look in some different directions."

Her voice was soft and she had a lisp, making her almost childlike. But her eyes were serious.

Reed opened his mouth, but she raised a hand to stop him. "From what I've heard and seen, you seem to be looking solely at the young man and his interaction with people here. Is that correct?"

"Not entirely," Reed said. "But as this is an ongoing investigation, I can't—"

"Discuss the particulars." She smiled. "I was married to a policeman for more years than you've been alive. I know the drill." She paused, as if waiting for him to argue. When he remained quiet, she continued. "I have no doubt his interaction with people here may have some bearing on this case, so you are wise to talk to the ones of us who still can remember."

She paused and shrugged. "It happens," she murmured. "I had time"—she grimaced—"to study him a bit, but I didn't want to talk around everyone. You never know who might take offense to what you say. Anyway, something about him caught my attention. Maybe it was his attitude . . . or his expression when he thought no one was watching. Maybe it was a troubled expression that sometimes flitted across his face. He didn't seem happy. It's hard to explain, as we're never always happy. But it was just something . . ."

Reed and I waited silently as she gazed off, searching her memory for the thoughts she wanted to share with us. "I had three boys," she continued. Her eyes misted. When she searched for a tissue, Reed pulled one from a box near him and handed it to her. While she wiped her eyes, Reed pulled a chair up near her. I settled in a chair near but by the window.

Reed carefully asked her, "Do you think this young man was afraid of something?"

"Afraid? Maybe. Concerned. Anxious. Those are the words that come to my mind. I asked him once if things were going well at school, and he brightened up and talked about his friends in the Drama Club. One young lady—I can't remember her name—seemed to have caught his attention. Then I asked if his parents had gone to any of the drama productions, and it was like a curtain fell over his face. He didn't answer, just shook his head. Then he left." She thought a moment. "My son, the middle one, had that look often . . ."

Tears rolled down her cheeks as she stared ahead, searching in her mind for somewhere in the past.

I reached over and patted her hand. "We appreciate your sharing, and I'm sorry that it is difficult. Please don't—"

She looked back at Reed and me. "It's an affliction of old age," she said. "Some things never leave us, but our ability to manage our emotions does vanish on occasion." I could see her square her shoulders and reach inside herself for the resolve she needed. "My son was so different from his brothers, and he somehow decided his father and I were disappointed because of that . . . and, well, he took his life." She sighed and wiped a tear with a tissue wadded in her palm.

"Did this young man have that look?" Reed asked.

"He may have."

We waited for her to continue, but she raised her face, glanced at the door, reached for Reed's hand, and whispered softly. "I'm just an old woman," she said. "Sometimes we don't remember things clearly. Don't pay attention to what I've said. But thank you both for listening to me."

Something made me glance toward the door. A flash of movement caught my eye. Someone stepped away at the same moment. All I could see was a leg encased in an employee caregiver uniform, but it was so quick that I couldn't be sure if the person was male or female. I looked at Chris. He'd seen it also.

"Let me walk you to your room," he said loudly. Instantly, I heard steps hurrying away.

"No need," she replied.

Chris relaxed. "Maybe it would be better for you to walk on your own," he said. "But you be careful, okay? I don't want to scare you, but we'd like to keep our conversation confidential for now." He pulled out his card and handed it to her. "Put this somewhere safe so that when something worries you, you can call me. If I don't answer, someone will get a message to me."

I rose and thanked her as well. She gave me a hug and whispered, "You be careful too, young lady!"

Reed opened the door wider for her; and we followed her out into the empty hall and stood, watching her slow progress. She raised her hand in a half wave over her shoulder when she reached the end and turned the corner into yet another hall.

Once she was out of sight, I turned back to Reed. He was reading a text on his phone. Should I have walked all the way back with her? I looked back in the direction she'd gone, but of course, she was out of sight. Was that shadow across from where she had turned moving after her? I glanced at Reed, thinking he might have seen it too; but he was still reading.

"That was Will," he said as he finished. "He's nosing around the Drama Club rehearsal, interviewing the group about their next production. Of course, he's also picking up any gossip he can. I told him we'd all get together later to compare notes . . . Sorrel? Something wrong?" Reed looked at me curiously. "You have a weird look on your face."

"No." Maybe I was getting just a little paranoid, I thought, seeing shadows everywhere I looked. "No, I was just thinking that maybe we should check in at Reception since someone obviously knows we are here now. Maybe we could talk with some of the staff that weren't here the other day as well as the residents."

A few minutes later, a short, stout man in a brown uniform I'd seen the maintenance men wearing walked up to us.

"Did you want to speak with me?" he asked, his deep voice almost a growl. He waited, one hand holding a cellphone and the other placed on his hip in an impatient pose. "My supervisor said you did, but I get off soon and I don't get paid for overtime. They know that."

Reed stuck out his hand. "I'd sure appreciate your answering a question or two. I'm Chris Reed and this is—"

"I know who you are. And I know why you're here . . . because of that high school kid that used to come around here until he got himself into some kind of trouble and—"

"Is there somewhere we can talk?" Chris interrupted. "I won't take long."

"I have a supply truck due, overdue in fact—"

"Can we sit in the break room and let you have a rest while I ask a question or two?"

He sighed, then turned and waved his hand for us to follow. The break room had always felt cramped, and it felt even more so now, like stepping into a closet. Someone had filled it with the necessary items in spite of the small space. Reed reached into his pocket and pulled out change. "May I buy you—"

"Naw! I don't have time. It won't take long to tell you everything thing I know. And that's nothing."

"Did you know—" I began.

"The kid? Sure. A little. Knew his dad was a big shot coach. Figured he'd expect special privileges and sh—uh—stuff. But he was just a

131

regular kid. Didn't flinch at working on whatever you asked, liked the residents, always polite." His face softened a bit. "'George, he'd say,' . . . George is my name . . . George Wilson . . . 'George, I think these residents are nice people, making the best of what they have to be right now. They can't help it because they're sick and old.'"

"Did he seem worried or upset the last time you saw him?" Reed asked.

"Naw! What did he have to worry about? He was a high school kid . . . with an old man who could buy him anything he wanted. So what if he didn't want to play football? He was a good kid." He edged toward the door. "Look, I've got work to do. I don't get involved in things besides work. And I don't know nothing anyways." He held a hand up and slid around the door before either of us could answer.

I looked at Reed. "Well, that could have gone better. But not a total waste."

He grunted. "Really?"

"Really. He knew this 'high school kid.' And I think he liked him. They talked or he wouldn't have known as much as he does. But I didn't get the feeling he knew much about what happened."

Reed grunted but didn't disagree. We interviewed six other people the administrators had lined up for us: cafeteria workers, a couple of caregivers, social workers. Everyone gave the same answers . . . almost by rote: "No, a good kid"; "no, never seemed unhappy"; "no, always got along with everyone."

Watching the last one leave, Reed turned to me. "This is a waste of time. They couldn't have prepared these people better. It's like they've all been programmed. And I'm getting claustrophobic in this place!"

I couldn't argue with him. "They made the list of who we'd see. What if we sneak out and try to find someone who hasn't been programmed? Maybe if we split up?"

We met back up in the break room an hour later. I could tell at a glance that Reed hadn't had any more success than I.

"Maybe we need to brainstorm and find another approach," I told Reed. "Everyone keeps describing the perfect young man . . . at least the ones who will speak to us do. I was beginning to feel like I have the plague or something!"

Reed stretched and motioned for me to walk through the door first and grinned. "It would be contagious then because I got the same treatment."

As we passed the ladies' room, I paused by the door. "I'll meet you at the truck," I said.

Inside were only two stalls. One was filled, so I stepped into the second one. The person in the next stall flushed and opened the door to leave. Then I heard a hiss. "You the girl with the cop? That crazy photography lady?"

"Yes," I answered cautiously. "Well, the crazy—"

"Asking about that kid? You didn't hear it from me—I'm not telling my name. And don't open that door till I leave!—that kid ran errands for some of the people. It's what got him into trouble." The voice sounded weird. The owner obviously was disguising it.

"What errands?"   "

"Mail."

"Isn't mail sent out here?"

The voice turned to a whisper. "People go through it."

"Why?"

I heard her—was it a female?—step away. So I pushed on my stall door to open it, but it was stuck. I pushed again but it wouldn't budge. Then I bent down and squinted so I could see along the edge of the door. It had a padlock on it!

"Help!" I yelled.

133

The outer door opened and I heard footsteps.

"Hey, I need help!" I called. No answer. "Anybody in here?" Still no answer. Then the outer door shut again.

"Well, that was rude!" I muttered. Why had I been locked in? Could it be a prank on the crazy photography lady? How long would it be before someone came inside? Not long, surely.

I glanced down to the bottom of the bathroom stall, estimating the measurement. Maybe eighteen to twenty inches? I then looked down at my body. Of course, I'd worn my new silky blouse! This would be the only time I'd wear it for sure. The floor tiles looked clean, but the idea of crawling on them made me shiver. Still, the idea of staying in there until Reed got impatient enough to rescue me—that was unthinkable! He'd never let me hear the end of that, sharing the story with the whole town!

My purse—a small shoulder bag—wasn't too big. I gripped it in my hand, knelt down, and peeked under the door. Maybe . . . if I flattened myself and held my breath I could squeeze under the door. I pushed the germs on that floor to the back of my mind and gingerly lay my chin on the tiles. No, I'd have to turn my face sideways. That meant putting my cheek on that nasty floor.

"This is mind over matter, Sorrel," I muttered. "Maybe this floor is not too nasty. It didn't look bad at first. Think positive, Sorrel," I whispered, "and pretend this is just another slumber party adventure!" I took a breath and put a foot on each side of the toilet so I could push against the wall.

The first push moved me a few inches, scratching my cheek and snagging a strand of my hair in the door hinge. "Lucky I have plenty of hair," I muttered, pulling it loose and leaving a few strands stuck in the hinge. I bit my lip. My cheek felt like it was bleeding. I'd be lucky if my hair was all I left behind!

I counted to ten and thought about the person who'd locked me in here. For a few seconds, I imagined dunking her head into the toilet bowl. The thought appealed to me, but I needed to get out of here first. I took a deep breath and again inched forward, pulling my purse behind me and pushing against the toilet with my feet. A piece of tile grout scratched my cheek again and I yelped. I lay there another moment and reviewed the situation. Maybe I was approaching this totally wrong. Maybe I should go out feet first. At least the only thing that might get scratched would be covered up. Or maybe I could stand on that wretched toilet and climb over.

I scooted back and stood up. My cheek burned like fire. I reached in my purse, pulled out a tissue, and wiped the blood. It stung and, if I hadn't been so angry, I might have given up right them and just waited until someone finally missed me! But I remembered thinking earlier that no one visited the residents here, especially at this time of day. Since this was a guest bathroom, I could be here indefinitely! I had to rethink my options.

I doubted I could climb over the top of the stall. Even if I stood on the toilet seat . . . and it was split so I would be in danger of sliding in. The walls of the stall were slippery. I didn't have enough strength in my upper arms to pull myself up without getting traction from my feet. "Toss another great option," I muttered.

I lay back down and held my breath, imagining anything but what was likely only been a few short inches from my face. Reaching over my head, I grasped the bottom of the door with both hands and pulled as hard as I could, counting to distract myself from the stinging scrapes on my back as my blouse rode up. I turned my face sideways, wincing as the rough edge of the tile scraped my other cheek. My hair caught in the grout groove and I bit my lip to keep from crying out. I moved my feet until they touched the bottom of the toilet bowl. I took a deep breath, gritted my teeth, and pushed as hard as I could. I felt the new blouse rip as I dug my elbow into the tile and gave a hard shove. "I didn't like this blouse anyway!" I growled.

"I do."

I hadn't heard the door open. But I certainly recognized the voice. "This is the ladies' room!" I snapped. "What are you doing here? Get out!"

Reed took a couple of steps into the room and looked down at me and then the stall door. "Why is there a padlock on this door? I'll go get something to cut it off. Stay still. I'll be right back."

"Don't you dare leave me here like this, Chris Reed!"

"First it's 'get out!' and then 'don't leave me!' I don't really want to wait around until you make up your mind. It would be difficult to explain why I'm standing in the ladies' room!"

I heard the outer door close again. I wiggled faster, focusing on all the things I'd like to see happen to one smarty detective! I finally staggered to my feet, my new blouse in tatters and leaned over the sink.

The door to the bathroom opened and a familiar voice drawled, "Should I give you more privacy?"

"Shut up!" I snarled. "I'm just catching my breath!" I stood there in silent tears, wishing he'd leave and afraid he would!

Reed managed to keep a sober face as he walked toward me and pulled me up into his arms. "My brave partner," he whispered, as I leaned into his shoulder and sniffled. "I wouldn't have had the nerve to put my face or anything else on that floor!"

He held me a few seconds longer as I tried to compose myself. "I asked why they had this hasp on the toilet," he drawled. "Seems some of the residents like to slip out and parade around. But they only use a zip tie sort of thing. Not a padlock. Maybe a handsome prince locked you in here to keep you for himself!"

I bit back a giggle. "Hush! I'm having a meltdown! At least let me do something right today!"

His laughter didn't irritate me like it usually did. It comforted me, instead. And a few minutes later, I joined in with him.

Behind us, the door rattled and opened.

"Oh, my!" a prim voice said. "Uh, what . . . uh . . . oh, my! I'll call maintenance!" Then she focused on my face. "And get you to the nurse."

The nurse cleaned my scrapes in spite of my protests. When she finished, she lent me a uniform top to wear home.

"Do you want this?" she asked, holding up my shredded blouse.

"No." Glancing at the remains of one of my favorite blouses, I felt indignation refueling itself inside.

"I'm sorry for this incident," she murmured kindly, opened the door, and stepped out. Reed passed her on his way in.

"There was a padlock on the bathroom door?"

"Yeah. I asked the maintenance man who came to get it off and clean things up, but he didn't have a clue . . . or wasn't saying. You okay?" he asked.

"Sure. I have some ugly scrapes and abrasions, my favorite blouse is in shreds, and this whole place is either gawking or snickering when I approach. I'm just dandy!"

"Not to mention grumpy. I suspect we're finished here for the moment. Let's get out of this joint before something else happens. We can come back another time."

Chapter 26

"Are you hungry?" Reed asked as we walked toward the main entrance.

"Not really."

"Then you're sick! How about we pick up about a dozen burgers and fries and whatever comes to mind and head to your place. After you eat most of that, you can replace this designer outfit before we meet up with the other members of the team?"

I knew he was trying to lift my spirits with his outrageous teasing. He probably thought I was hurting . . . or embarrassed. I was neither. I was mad and determined to find the person who had tried to make a fool of me. No, they hadn't tried, they had—and they'd scared me too!

"Hyperbole!" I grumbled as we walked out toward the door. I could feel curious eyes, some grins, and even a few sympathetic smiles.

Reed nodded and spoke to several, telling them we'd be back another time. Once in the truck, he turned on a country music station and didn't speak.

I leaned back and thought about that crazy experience in the bathroom. The first sticking point was motivation. Well . . . maybe not. Whoever locked me in the stall had wanted to get away before I saw them. But for what purpose? Locking me in the bathroom must have been an attempt to intimidate me! And it had worked. I'd never admit it to Reed, but I still felt shaky inside.

So I focused inwardly on the culprit. Who could he/she have been? What details could I remember? Shoes? Had they been black? Maybe. No, white. Lace-ups maybe? Where had I seen those earlier? Well, duh! Almost every person working there wore them! The legs. Had they been pink? Peach? Lavender?

Reed finally spoke up. "Let your mind rest, Sorrel. You know as well as I that the details will appear when you least expect them. Relax."

"Says the guy who wasn't wallowing around on that filthy floor! And I saw those hidden grins when I emerged!"

Reed stopped at the light on Main. Then he looked over at me and grinned. "I didn't notice the grins. I saw those guys looking at your cute—"

"Reed! Get serious here! We—"

"Need to get you fed and let you relax a bit. Then we need to brainstorm." He slowed, signaled, and turned into the Bed and Breakfast parking lot.

"I thought we were going for burgers!"

"I scrapped that idea. Mrs. Sanchez has that private room where we can have a decent meal and think about what just happened." He parked the truck and shrugged. "Besides, you weren't in the mood to be told that we're meeting up with Randall Byrd."

"I'm still not in the mood!"

He turned off the ignition. I stared out my window. "Sorrel, you need to eat something. Then we need to regroup. Obviously, we've gotten someone's attention . . . someone who may or may not want to silence us."

"Make me look like a fool!"

"Maybe. Anyway, Randall has information he gathered this morning. When we share—over Mrs. Sanchez's delicious enchiladas— we can focus better."

As if on cue, my stomach growled. I caught Reed's eye. He was struggling. A giggle escaped and he laughed. "Well," I said, when I could talk again. "I've never been told that I was boring . . . and nothing has ever affected my appetite."

We climbed out and walked across the parking lot. Reed guided me down the hall toward the private dining room. I'd begun to ache a bit and regretted not taking the painkiller I'd been offered. I hadn't been seriously hurt—just my pride—and focused on the earlier event to ignore the pain in my cheek and back. *How did I get myself in that crazy situation?* I asked myself. *Who would do something like that? And, for sure, what had been the motivation?*

"No sense dwelling on it. It will come to you sometime when you're doing something else . . . like sleeping."

I jumped as Reed's voice interrupted my thoughts. "Have you always been a mind reader, Reed?"

"Don't have to be. You have an expressive face. And I've been thinking along the same lines."

"Come up with an answer?"

"Not really. It could be someone who wanted to make you look—"

"Ridiculous?"

"Well, it was a diversion, at best. It gave them the opportunity to get out of there without our seeing them or noticing them."

"But what if we didn't know who we were looking for?"

He thought a minute. "Did it scare you?"

"Heavens, no! Made me mad though."

"It also interrupted your focus. In fact, it drew everyone's attention away from our victim." He reached for the door. "I don't know about you, but I'd like to put the incident to rest and enjoy a good meal."

"I don't think I can eat."

"That would be a first!"

I walked in ahead of Reed. My back was on fire, my other muscles had already stiffened, and I was struggling to focus on not letting it show.

"Fashionably late? At least, you could speak!" The question startled me. Will and Mr. Byrd had already settled at a table in the far corner of the private dining room and, from the look of things, had been drinking a cocktail or two.

"I'll speak later. I'm ready for enchiladas!" I told Will. "You haven't eaten them all, have you?"

"Not—hey, what happened to you?" Will asked. "You—"

"Just an undercover exercise," I told him. "You should see the others!"

He whistled. "What exercise? Is that a nurse's uniform?"

"I needed it for my role."

Mr. Byrd hadn't commented. I looked at him and said, "I hope you gentlemen are hungry. I've had an interesting day."

"Wait till you hear—" Will interrupted.

Randall Byrd cleared his throat. "Later," he muttered and motioned for me to sit. The door opened and Mrs. Sanchez entered. She took my appearance in at a glance but didn't react at all.

"The special for today, as I suspect you already know, is enchiladas. Ice water or iced tea? Salad? Josefina will be serving you." She smiled and slipped out as quietly as she had entered.

No one spoke until after Josefina had served drinks and food. Randall Byrd watched until she had closed the door before he cleared his voice and spoke. "I suspect we have all had an interesting day so far. Let us eat first and then discuss it." He pointed to his ears as he glanced toward the young waitress who had just entered.

Will reached for his glass. "To an interesting day," he muttered, taking a healthy gulp.

Chapter 27

Neither Mr. Byrd nor Will asked why I didn't remove my jacket, although I saw them glance at it a time or two. Reed hid a grin, but I glared at him until he looked away.

Everyone commented on the weather or ball teams and plowed into their food. As usual, the enchiladas were hot, spicy, and delicious. Each of us had been given a small bowl of pinto beans and a dish of guacamole salad. I gulped my iced tea in a useless attempt to cool my tongue several times, but it didn't slow down my appetite.

The waitress cleared our plates before returning with sopapillas, honey, and small plates for each of us. Then she filled our glasses one last time and quietly left.

Mr. Byrd rose, placed the Do Not Disturb sign on the door, returned to his seat, and cleared his throat. "I understand you encountered an interesting situation at the senior center. How about you tell us what happened, Sorrel?"

"I'll start," Reed interrupted. "Sorrel's misadventure came at the end of our visit."

Mr. Byrd raised his eyebrows at "misadventure," but he simply nodded.

Reed checked his notes and then named the people we had interviewed, taking time to detail the information we'd gleaned. Listening to him reinforced the feeling that we weren't being given all —or even half—of the picture. It was something my mama had often said: Tell enough truth to make the listener trust you but not enough to give away your secrets. These people might fear losing their jobs or other repercussions.

I looked up and caught Mr. Byrd staring at me. He gave a small nod. "Do you have anything to add at this point, Sorrel?"

"*Guarded* is the word I'd use. But it's also only natural. The people working there likely not only need their jobs but also have been trained in keeping their mouths shut. I'll bet they share more around the dinner table than they did with Reed and me. But, for sure, someone is discouraging any information being shared.

"As for the residents, I'd say they've been cautioned not to talk. They've seen small things, which may or may not be useful. But they are vulnerable at this age. Their families—if they have any left—either can't or don't want to care for them. And, truthfully, I'm not sure what they've actually seen or what they've invented in their minds. Still, they seem more anxious than I'd expect."

No one spoke for a moment. Then Randall Byrd asked, "Do you want to share your misadventure with us now?"

I briefly described the bathroom incident, omitting my terror and embarrassment. Reed's lip quivered only once, and Will covered his mouth during a fake cough. However, when I reached the part about the voice and the warning, Reed sat up.

"Hey! You didn't tell me that!"

"I guess I didn't . . . you know . . . well, Reed, it sounds really cheesy. And I'm not sure if the speaker was male or female."

"Weren't you in the ladies' bathroom?"

"Yes. But if someone had put a sign indicating the bathroom was being cleaned—and I did smell cleaner—then either a male or a female could have been there. The voice was a sort of harsh whisper. It could have been either."

"And you planned to tell me when?" Reed growled.

"Actually, I'd forgotten it until just now."

Reed looked at me searchingly but didn't pursue the subject. Instead, he asked, "Is there anything else you remember about the voice?"

"It was obviously being disguised . . . as I said . . . sort of rough and mean . . . all at once. I certainly felt threatened. But he also made me mad."

"He. You said earlier you didn't know if the person was male or female."

"You're right." I thought for a minute, even closing my eyes to recapture the sound. "I can't be sure, but I'd vote for male."

"Did you notice a sign on the outside when you entered?" Reed asked. "Something like Workmen Inside?"

"I didn't notice."

All three men had questions about anything else I'd noticed, but we couldn't pull anything else up in my memory. Finally, Randall Byrd cleared his throat and sighed. "I think we wandered into something we shouldn't," he said. "I've not been sure—and I still am not— whether we should just leave this alone. After this incident, I fear the choice has been made for us." He looked over at Will. "How about you tell us about your experiences with the . . . Drama Club?"

Will perked up. "Ah, yes. Well, you remember that girl at the library? It seems there was a bit more feeling there than she'd shared. Whether it was all on her part or on both, I don't know. But I think she's shared as much as she is going to share . . . at least with me. I got the impression that his parents weren't happy with his Drama Club participation—not parents, his father."

Reed nodded. "Someone mentioned that to us as well . . . about Coach not liking his interest in those areas. Has Coach ever said anything to you, Randall?"

"He didn't have to say anything. When his wife mentioned it, his facial reaction was enough to let you know. But you have to give him some slack. After all, he's a football coach. People expect his son to not only play football but to be a star. And in this part of the world, being in Drama Club may not be regarded in the same light."

"Very diplomatically spoken," Reed murmured.

Will shrugged. "My dad wasn't too sold on my choice of journalism either. I guess it's more common than people think."

"What's wrong with journalism?" Randall asked. "There's nothing soft or cowardly about it!"

"There is when the first thing your co-workers ask is which position your kid plays in football."

"I'm sorry," I told Will.

"Don't be." Will grinned. "My dad hates football. His dream is for me to become a stockbroker so I can help him with investments."

A chuckle lightened the room that had gradually grown darker.

"What's this about the death being declared natural causes?" I asked.

Mr. Byrd sobered. "The actual cause of death has been listed as an asthma attack."

"What about the obvious beating he suffered?" Chris asked.

Mr. Byrd answered carefully. "The official answer to that question has already been given. He suffered an asthma attack and lost control of the vehicle."

"Our findings do not have him driving the vehicle," Chris argued. "In fact, he didn't have a driver's license."

"Have you seen the latest official finding?" Mr. Byrd drained his water glass. He set the glass on the table and stared into Reed's eyes. "There not only is no mention of his driving without a drivers' license. Neither is there mention of the beating he suffered before he 'accidentally' died."

Chapter 28

"Can you find my glasses?" The voice quivered, almost in a panic. *"I need my glasses to see."*

"There's nothin' to see!"

The harsh voice made her draw back into her pillow. She could vaguely see an outline of a large shape bending over her roommate's body.

She wanted to cover her head. Instead, she whispered, *"Who are you? We don't have men working on this floor. Did you get the wrong room? I don't think we've met."*

"We haven't met, lady. I'm just here handling some issues with the building. Don't worry! We'll be finished soon."

"Sylvia? Why isn't Sylvia answering me? Is she okay? I should ring for the nurse. Silvia, are you okay?" A sob escaped. *"Who are you? You don't sound like the therapist who comes. Where are my glasses? Why is it so dark in here? I need to ring for the nurse!"*

"Just calm down, dear. You're getting too excited and it ain't good for you. Just let me put this over your nose and mouth and you breathe deep. It will feel good soon. You'll be fast asleep."

"What are you doing, Jo—uh—Smith?" a third voice burst out *"We were only told to—"*

"Shut up! Grab her arms and keep her from fighting!"

Smith dripped the liquid onto the gauze patch he held over the old lady's mouth. Almost immediately, her flailing hands slowed. *"Check the door."*

His partner tiptoed to the door and glanced out. *"Nobody's here."*

"Good. And the other one?"

"Out like a light."

Both men stared at the figure lying in the bed until her breathing slowed. The one called Smith lifted her wrist, checked her pulse, and nodded to himself. "Okay, now," he murmured to his partner. "Cover her with the sheet and check the hall. See if they are still eating. Hurry!"

His partner eased out into the hall. Smith counted silently. They didn't have much time before the nurse's aide would be making rounds, checking to see that the patients were sleeping. He looked over at the roommate, Sylvia. She snorted, sleeping deeply with her mouth open. Then he lifted the wrist again and checked for a pulse. None.

Quickly, he drew back the sheet and tucked her up as if she'd just dozed off to sleep. He glanced around the room. Everything looked in order. He patted the signed will in his pocket.

"Ready?" his partner whispered.

"Yes. You go first."

They walked down the dimly lit hall, carrying their plumbing cases.

Just as they reached the door at the end of the hall, a young nurse's aide came out of a room, her arms piled high with folded sheets. Smith touched the brim of his hat and she nodded absently, fighting to keep the stack from sliding sideways. When she had the stack secured, she looked back. But she only heard the swish of the door leading outdoors. For a moment, she wondered why they'd been called in at night. Then she remembered that the head nurse had already warned her about working too slowly. She hurried off down the hall, the two workmen fading from her thoughts.

Chapter 29

"This case we're working on is impossible!" I told Reed as he sped down the highway. "I call it an Alice-in-Wonderful experience. Everything we encounter doesn't seem to connect and, although it feels like we have fallen into something, no one acknowledges it."

When he didn't speak, I continued.

"Our purpose in returning to the nursing home was what? Yes, this kid volunteered there and, I think, may have even worked there and . . . how does it connect to what happened to him? Everyone has nice things to say about him. So since the official statement is death by accident, we should be finished, right?"

He grunted.

"So what are we doing here? Is there even a case at all?"

"I might have agreed with you, Sorrel, until the incident in the bathroom. *Incident* doesn't even sound like the right word . . . but it's all I can think of to call it just now. Motivation is troubling me. Either way, there was the attempt to embarrass or scare you, wasn't there?"

"Or make me mad!" I could feel my face flushing.

"My point is, if you are embarrassed—or mad . . . or scared . . . or distracted—you aren't looking for the basic motivation. So I have these questions: Why? Who? What's the motive? What's the end game?"

"We just spent hours trying to figure that out," I snapped. "Why are we going over it again?"

He turned off the key to the truck and I looked around in surprise. We had parked in front of his house.

"I thought you were taking me home."

"I'm making a point here. While you were concentrating on our conversation and the bathroom incident, you were distracted. You didn't notice that we'd taken a different route. Come inside, you can take a nap, and I feed you again, we can talk or you can sleep."

His dogs—Madonna and the one pup Reed hadn't wanted to give away—escorted us to the front door, wiggling with excitement and barks. Reed waited patiently while I took a quick moment to pat each of them. Then he unlocked the door and held it open for me. "You've ruined my dogs," he muttered.

He touched my back to guide me inside. When I gasped, he yanked his hand away. "Oh, Sorrel, I'm so sorry! I forgot! You go on in to the bathroom. I'll rustle up something for you to wear when you want to get out."

The warm shower didn't hurt as I feared it would. I dunked my head under and scrubbed my hair with the shampoo Reed had given me. It—and the conditioner—had a floral scent that I doubted Chris used. He must have bought it for me to use—or a guest. I stood under the warm water longer than I should have. Finally, I turned it off. Almost immediately, a knock on the door was followed by, "Be careful with drying your back and face. I have something to put on both that should help when you come out. Wait to put on your nightclothes. I've hung a robe up for you."

It was a soft, oversized terrycloth robe. I wrapped up in it after I'd patted my body dry.

"Ready?"

"Yes."

The knob turned and Reed looked in. He had a towel in one hand which he wrapped around my hair. Then he lifted me up in his arms.

"Reed! I'm not an invalid! I can walk!" I protested.

He carried me into his bedroom and set me gently on the bed. "Shucks!" he whispered. "Then I guess you'll insist on putting this stuff on your back yourself?"

I made a face at him, privately loving his laughter. "Here's a brush," he said, "for that wild mane of yours. And before you ask, these 'lady' things—they were my mom's. But I've also gotten Teri to come here and . . . "

149

"Sorrel? Where are you, girl?"

Teri entered like a small whirlwind, gently pushed Reed out the door, and pretended not to be horrified at the damage. "These are surface. But I've also brought my *abuelita*'s remedy. I'll be gentle."

The salve soothed the burning, and Teri insisted on dressing me in a voluminous but very soft and worn nightgown. Then she brushed out my hair and blew it dry before braiding it. Finally, she stepped back and grinned.

"Now I know how you must have looked as a little girl," she said.

I looked into an antique oval mirror. "I look like I've stepped back in time," I agreed.

She gathered up the things she'd brought, strangely quiet.

"Are you upset with me?" I asked.

"No. But I am worried. Please let Reed protect you, Sorrel. Whoever did this is not someone to ignore. Until they are found, please be safe."

"I'm not . . . I've been looking after myself. "

"So, looking at the mess you're in, maybe it's time you let someone do that." She glanced at her watch. "It's late and I need to get home before your goddaughter wakes up for her next feeding. If you need anything—"

"I'll take care of her," Reed said, as he started into the bedroom. "Thank you, Teri."

"Do you have any tea, Reed? I think she needs a cup to help her relax before she sleeps."

"Already thought of that. Kettle's on and should be ready any minute now."

I cleared my throat. "Uh, is this a private conversation? Or can anyone participate?"

Teri laughed. "Let's get you into the kitchen." She wrapped the robe and tied it to make it fit better . . . but not well. Then Reed scooped me up and started toward the kitchen.

Before I could remind Reed that he could put me down, Teri leaned over and whispered, "Goodbye."

As she left out the door, Will entered and took in the sight of me in Reed's arms. "Did I miss the wedding?

"If—and I underline that word *if*—I ever marry again, it won't be in a bathrobe!"

I could feel Reed's chest shaking, but he kept a straight face as he settled me into a chair at the table.

"Well said!"

"Mr. Byrd! I didn't know . . . "

"I'm not staying. Just wanted to set eyes on you to see if you're really okay. Looks like our sheriff's deputy has done a decent job caring for you. I'll see you guys in the morning. Will?"

"He's staying the night at the shop," Reed said.

I felt like a puppet, looking from one to the other. I watched Mr. Byrd and Will leave. Then I turned to Reed.

"I'll get your tea," he said and turned toward the stove. A few seconds later he set a steaming cup of Sleepy Time tea in front of me.

"When did you start drinking this?" I asked.

"I don't. I thought I should have some on hand for those times when I have to calm you down a bit, Red." His eyes reflected the grin he was trying hard to stifle.

He then settled into the chair next to mine. But instead of popping back at him, I simply breathed in the delicious aroma of the hot brew. As I took my first sip, I looked around appreciatively. "This place is looking nice too. I haven't been here since you painted. Are you liking the color now?"

When he'd first discussed the renovation of this older home with me, Reed had argued against anything but white. I'd argued for something light instead because white would be too stark. He'd reluctantly settled on the one I'd privately loved most—a delicate shade of pale yellow that the paint store had labeled Almost Cream. But he didn't accept everything I'd suggested. When he'd stripped the cabinets, he'd painted them Delft Blue even though I'd suggested a dusty rose.

I looked at the walls and cabinets. "I'm not sure about—"

"I like them! Besides, food tastes the same no matter what color the walls, cabinets, etc., are. Women must spend hours dreaming up things to keep a guy too busy for what's really important."

"And that is?"

"Eating with someone you care about—even if she talks constantly—and enjoying yourself." He took a drink of the coffee he'd poured himself.

I had to admit that he was almost right about food shared with someone you cared about. But, I didn't I talk too much, did I?

Neither of us spoke for a while. When we'd both finished our cups, he took them to the sink, rinsed them, and placed them in the drainer.

"You look like you are sleeping," he said when he'd finished. "Let's get you settled in bed."

I'm not an invalid, Chris!" I snapped as he started to pick me up again. "Really, Reed. I know Will is feeding my cats, but I'd feel better if I stayed there and let Will come back over here. My spoiled critters miss me."

"Stubborn woman," he muttered.

I felt the weight of the day settle as we drove toward my store. Reed must have felt it too. He reached over and turned on the truck stereo. "George okay?"

"Always."

I liked that wicked chuckle. The painkiller had worn off and the tea hadn't relaxed me enough to ignore it, so I welcomed the distractions of twinkling stars, music, the soothing rhythm of the wheels on the highway pavement—

"Distraction!"

"Sorrel? You say something?"

"Distraction! That's the motivation for the bathroom thing."

"How do you figure that?"

"Think about it, Reed. We must have been rattling some cages, as Dad liked to say. We must have been making someone nervous, so they staged this incident in the bathroom. Why didn't I see it? I should have—"

"Don't be too hard on yourself. They counted on the surprise factor. You were thinking about our case. And, face it, who would have suspected anything that crazy in the ladies' room at a retirement home?"

Suddenly, Reed burst out laughing.

"What's so funny about it?"

"Think about it, Sorrel. You're not the only one who was surprised. I would have never imagined your reaction. Crawling under the door? I've never seen—or heard—of anyone doing that? If you could have seen yourself!"

He was laughing so hard that I couldn't control the curve of my lip. "It isn't that funny," I muttered. Then I realized what he'd said. "Reed, you said they. Do you think there were two people in that bathroom? I never—"

Lonna Enox

"Not two inside the bathroom, but someone may have been helping. Was there a sign outside when you walked into the bathroom?"

"No. I wouldn't have gone inside if there were."

"Was the person inside when you walked in?"

"Yes."

"So someone was probably making sure no one interrupted."

"You're right! I never thought of that. If someone had walked in before the one there locked me in, it wouldn't have worked out."

"So there must have been a sign up after you walked in . . . and the other person was already there. Did you notice anyone hanging out?"

I shook my head. "It was prearranged all right. And thought out." The enormity of that statement left me nearly speechless. With all of the teasing, I hadn't considered the danger of the situation.

Reed reached over and covered my hand with his. "I doubt he/she planned anything more than to scare you." Returning his hand to the steering wheel, Reed turned into the parking lot of my shop and parked outside the door to my apartment.

"Then he/she accomplished it . . . now. I was too mad to think of it then."

Reed burst out laughing again as he turned off the key and hopped out to open the door for me. Before I could put a foot out, he pulled me out of the truck and into his arms for a gentle hug, careful to keep his hands from my shoulder area. "Life is never boring when you're around, is it?"

I allowed myself to snuggle close for a minute. Then I pulled back and looked up into his eyes. "I have a question."

"Shoot."

"Uh . . . not shoot. But I wonder why a boring life is something people tend to think is bad."

"I'm beginning to think boring is something neither of us are ever going to know."

"Reed, let's not ignore the elephant in the room . . . although here, I guess, it would be a buffalo." I looked straight into his eyes. "That young man did not die of natural causes, and someone powerful is covering it up. Since we're making noises, this person . . . or persons . . . needs to shut us up."

"You're right."

"What are we going to do next?"

"Get you inside and into bed and Will can return to his place or come over to mine."

"What are you two doing here?" Will asked as we came into the kitchen. He was seated at the table, his notes spread around him. The cats were nowhere in sight.

"Sorrel is determined to stay here with her kitties. So you can pack up your sleeping bag and either go back to the bed and breakfast or stay the night at my place."

"I'll just head back to the bed and breakfast and crash, but I really want to go over my interview notes with you two. Maybe when we all are better rested. In the morning?"

A few minutes later, we watched Will get in his car and drive off the parking lot. Then Reed turned to me, gently holding my shoulders. "Now, it's time for you to get some sleep, too."

"And you?"

"As soon as I know you are safely tucked in, I'm headed to my place to catch a few hours of sleep while I can."

I nodded, the exhaustion of the last few hours finally catching up with me. "Come over for breakfast and we can figure out what comes next."

"I'll bring breakfast! It doesn't look like there's much left in your pantry after Will's short cat-sitting adventure." He grinned. "And that way I know we'll have real food to get us through the morning!"

"Chris Reed—"

"I know, I know. Just let me take care of you a bit, okay? Now, get to bed." He hugged me gently so as not to aggravate the scrapes on my back and shoulders, then turned me toward the bedroom.

As I headed there, Van and Flash fell in behind me.

"Guard her well, you felines! See you all in the morning."

I giggled but continued to the bed, laying down gingerly and pulling a coverlet over me. I didn't even have the energy to change clothes.

As I drifted off, I heard the sound of Reed's truck starting up and pulling out, followed by the soft purring of my fur babies.

Chapter 30

A little before nine, Reed was at my door, a small grocery bag in hand.

"Coffee's already on," I said as I opened the door wide for him to come in.

"Don't look now, but we've got company for breakfast," he said as he sat the bag on the counter and began taking out breakfast burritos, bananas, and orange juice.

I peeked out the door to see Will getting out of his car. As I watched him approach, I called to Reed. "Do we have enough to share?"

"Yes. But he's staying at the bed and breakfast, so doesn't he get breakfast? He must be the only person who has more of an appetite than you do?" He chuckled but Will was at the door before I could respond.

"Is the coffee ready yet?" Will asked, skipping all preliminaries, as usual.

I pointed to the pot and cups already set out on the counter. "Help yourself, Will."

With both Will and Reed at the counter, space was limited so I sat at the table and watched Reed putting the burritos on a plate and pouring glasses of orange juice. Will filled his coffee cup and looked longingly at the food.

"What brings you here so early?" Reed asked, placing the burritos on the table.

I started to get up to finish setting the table, only to be waved back into my seat by Reed, who was obviously going to take charge of this breakfast meeting. But before Will could answer, Reed's phone rang. He looked at the number and started toward the door. "I've got to take this," he said.

Will brought his cup to the table, eying the burritos. "Mind if I—"

"Help yourself, Will. Just leave some for Reed and me. We haven't eaten yet and if the past few days are any indication, we're going to need nourishment." I then got out the cat food to fill Van's and Flash's dishes, as Will sheepishly returned one of the three wrapped burritos he'd grabbed to the platter. "There are some plain sugar cookies in that cabinet if you'd like."

He got up, opened the door, and got the bag of cookies out. Eyeing the bag, he asked, "Do you ever have homemade cookies?"

"Not since Sofie was born." I grinned. "Teri's too busy. Since when did you get so finicky?"

With the first sound of the kibble hitting the bottom of their dishes, the two cats dashed from the bedroom.

"So they are still here! I didn't see them at all yesterday evening. I was beginning to think I'd inadvertently let them get out of the house!"

I grinned as I set their dishes down and they began to eat. "They're just particular about who they hang out with," I said.

"Sorrel? Are you having a party and didn't invite me?" Teri asked as she zipped up the steps and through the door. "Reporting for duty? Oh, those smell great! Mind if I—"

"Help yourself, Teri. Orange juice or coffee?"

"Oh, coffee, please! It's the fuel I live on these days. Thanks again for rescuing me. I've missed working at the store and getting to interact with adults! Mmm! Delicious!" she mumbled over the mouthful of burrito. "I'll just take this with me and get the store ready to open."

"I'll get the door for you," I said and went with her into the store to get the cash out of the safe and make sure she had everything she needed for the day.

Although I hadn't been gone long, when I came back into the kitchen, I sensed a tension I'd not expected. Will was reading something on his phone, his shoulders tense. Reed was still outside, talking in soft hushed tones to whoever had called.

"What's up?" I asked Will.

He shrugged without looking up. Something about his whole demeanor alerted me. He was clearly not happy. In fact, his clinched jaw signaled anger.

I poured a cup of coffee for myself, then I asked him if he wanted a refill before I sat down at the table. He shook his head without looking up, although he shut off his phone and put it in his shirt pocket. Then he burst out, "Why do you women always send mixed signals?"

"We do? What did I—"

"Not you."

"Girlfriend?"

"Not yet, but I thought . . . when I did the interview, Sara and I were getting along so well I asked if she'd seen that new movie. She hadn't and gave me her cell number. And now I've been blocked from her phone completely! There's a message saying that her phone service has been stopped. That's a little drastic! All she had to do was send me a message saying she was no longer interested."

"Did—"

"Sara seemed really interested. I know I wasn't the only one."

He didn't seem to need an answer, so I decided to just let him vent. But he had already run down and stopped talking. We sat there a few minutes longer before Reed walked inside.

"What's going on?" I asked him.

"I have to go to work," he said. "We have either a homicide or suicide."

"Who? Where?" Will and I chorused.

Lonna Enox

"You know I can't say yet. And, truthfully, I don't know the particulars. I've been called in to work. Can't tell you anything yet." He leaned over and kissed me on the cheek. "You don't need to get involved in this one, Sorrel."

Something was off. "Reed—"

Will's cellphone rang. He grabbed it and stood. "Mr. Byrd? Yes, sir. I'm here at the store with Sorrel and—"

His face paled. "Yes, sir. I'll tell her. Right away."

He opened his mouth, but before he could speak, Reed interrupted. "He wants you to cover it?"

"Yes. And Sorrel."

"I figured as much." He grabbed his hat and turned to the door, then added, "I was ordered to keep it quiet. Since Randall knows, it's in your court. But I still can't discuss it." His shoulders slumped, and he didn't look at us. "This is not good." Then he stepped out of the door.

I turned to Will. "What is going on?"

"We can talk on the way, Sorrel. Grab your camera and hurry! Mr. Byrd wants us there like fifteen minutes ago!"

I held my temper until I'd thrown on slacks and a top, loaded my gear into my Jeep, and began backing out. "Where are we going and what is going on?"

"All I know is there's a dead body," he said.

"Where?"

"The high school gym."

"Why would Mr. Byrd want me there? I doubt they'll need photos. The school will likely only allow a shot from a distance. For sure, law enforcement will object."

Wil shrugged, his attention on his phone.

160

We drove in silence until a few blocks from the school. Up ahead, I could see emergency vehicles, as I'd expected. But the vehicles lining the streets and the crowd in the parking lot, including vehicles from the television station from a city more than an hour away, set off my inner alarms. Something about this murder wasn't ordinary. In fact, as we drew closer and I noticed the news van from Albuquerque, chills ran up my spine.

"What are you not telling me, Will?"

"Mr. Byrd didn't tell me any more than what I've already shared with you." He gave a small whistle. "Obviously, he left us both out of the loop! Look at this crowd!"

I crept along until I saw a clear spot at the end of the faculty parking lot. I turned into the lot and was instantly flagged down by a police officer. He didn't look familiar, which was unusual. In a town this size and with my work for the newspaper, I knew most of the force either by name or sight or both. Then I looked more closely at the uniform. He was a member of the state police force.

"Ma'am, only official vehicles are allowed in this area. Do you have ID?"

I showed him the permit Randall Byrd had given me for such occasions and pulled my driver's license from my jacket pocket. He looked at both, then stepped a few feet away and spoke into a handheld device.

"This is big," I told Will. "Are you sure you don't know anything?" Silence. "Have they had a school shooting?" Silence. "Either you fill me in or we're leaving and going back to my place!"

"Okay! But if Mr. Byrd asks, you'd better tell him you threatened me!"

I sighed. "Cut the drama, Will! If Mr. Byrd gives you trouble, I'll tell him I threatened you."

He sighed. "Okay," he finally said. "Coach has been murdered. His wife is dead too. Mr. Byrd said it appears to be a suicide. He didn't elaborate, but you know he has lived here forever and has good sources. He said he's not sure what else is happening." He swallowed. "He sounded different, Sorrel."

"Ma'am?"

I heard the officer's voice, although it sounded as if it were coming from a well. I focused on his badge and nodded.

"Here's your ID. You have been cleared. Park over there, where you were headed. Someone will come for you and take you inside."

We crept toward the spot the officer had indicated, waiting for people to move out of the way. Neither of us spoke until I'd parked and turned off the motor. Then I turned to Will. "Do you have any experience with these kinds of crowds?" I asked.

"Not really."

"Then follow my lead. Keep your eyes ahead, focused on my back. Do not let anyone engage you in conversation or dialog at all. Yank your arm loose if they grab you. Got it?"

"The whole town must be here," he muttered.

"Will, did you hear me? Can you do this?"

"Yeah. I've got your back."

"I'm counting on that!

Chapter 31

I'd actually had more experience interviewing people at scenes like this one, so it felt a bit strange to be the one with the camera and not the microphone. Will and I had to push our way through the crowd at first, but an officer managing the crowd parted the way ahead of us. Finally, we stepped into the small clearing at the gym doors and signed the clipboard held by a young officer at the door. He looked at our signatures and then spoke into his cellphone. He listened, then hung up.

"Follow me," he said as he grabbed the door handle. "Straight through the foyer. Someone will instruct you."

His eyes never rested on us as he spoke. I knew he worried about someone charging in when the door opened.

"Yes, sir," I said.

He opened the door and we slid inside, Will almost glued to my back. I moved my camera bag from under my arm to my hand as I hurried across the foyer after the officer. When Will stepped on the back of my heel, I stopped, shoved him in front of me, and gave him a small push. Clearly, this was the biggest story he had investigated—for this part of the state, at least. I knew he had the ability he needed, so his panic surprised me a little. But then the huge crowd outside had been unnerving, even for someone with my years of experience with crime scenes.

Randall Byrd stood near the door. We again signed a clipboard and presented our IDs, then walked over to him. He was impeccably dressed as always, but the strain and sorrow etched in his face lent him a vulnerable air I'd expected but had never seen before. As we approached, he seemed to stiffen his spine.

"Thanks for coming so quickly," he murmured as he led us into the gym, through the door, and directed us to step right so that we weren't blocking the entrance.

"Did it happen here?" Will asked.

Lonna Enox

No answer. I swept my eyes over the gym, resting briefly on Reed standing near Jose, his hand on Jose's shoulder. I knew that Jose and Coach had been close, and I could certainly see the grief on Jose's face, even with his head bowed. I felt a hand on my elbow.

"Sorrel, I trust you to be discreet. Any shots shouldn't include Coach or his wife—unless they are covered," Mr. Byrd instructed me.

"Yes, sir. I thought I might photograph some of the awards on the walls."

"Yes, that would be good. It gives a positive look at the legacy he leaves behind." His voice wobbled a bit on the last word, and I instinctively touched his arm. He straightened and continued. "You'll want photos of the outside, even with the crowds, and—what am I doing? You know what to do."

I gave his arm a squeeze. "I do, but it's never easy. I'm so sorry, Mr. Byrd."

He turned to Will. "The information officer has material for you." He pointed him out. "I don't need to tell you that the paper has someone who routinely writes obituaries. This is, of course, not routine. I'm looking to you to write the story with dignity, capturing the person he . . . was." He swallowed and took a breath.

"Do they know who . . . was he shot?" Will asked. When Randall nodded, Will continued. "Do they have suspects?"

"Not that they're sharing yet. You'll need to—"

"Oh, I know how to do that, sir. And his wife?"

Mr. Byrd nodded.

"They've mentioned suicide, Mr. Byrd," I interrupted.

"We won't use that term until we know, of course." Then he turned to Will again. "This is a huge story, son. Even after the article about this horrible incident, we'll be publishing articles about his life. He's a legend in this town. Most of these cops played ball for him. Handle your questions, your expressions, and your whole demeanor

164

with courtesy and respect. They won't let you—either of you—but, of course, Sorrel knows that—near the crime scenes. Don't anger them. It alienates. Keep your ears open and keep good notes."

I'd heard Randall's instructions to Will, his eyes scanning the gym as he spoke. The crime scene, which appeared to be in the dressing room area, was closely cordoned off. I could see a trail of markers coming out of the visitors' dressing room and alongside the bleachers, which were folded back against the wall as they would have been during cleaning. Those were probably markers for blood drops, but we wouldn't be allowed close to them. In fact, I was surprised we'd been allowed this close.

Then I took a breath and focused on my job. It was a difficult balance of respect for the victims and probing the evidence for details of their horrible deaths. The question hovered in the back of my mind—as it always did: What right did we have to know? No one had ever been able to answer that question. I doubt they ever would.

Chapter 32

We had only been inside the gym for a few minutes when the doors were closed. I was surprised that we'd been allowed inside at all. Randall Byrd had more clout than I'd known. Even so, the large—and steadily growing—numbers of law enforcement formed a wall of sorts between us and the crime technicians.

I'd snapped a few shots, making sure they were discreet. Will's attempts to speak to anyone had largely been unsuccessful. Both of us lingered on the fringe, feeling as useful as barbers at a baldness convention. I spotted people from the regional television station hovering against one wall, occasionally sticking a microphone out to people who shook their heads and kept walking.

Suddenly, a stir of activity at the door leading into the locker room caught our attention. Will stepped in that direction, ducking around a guy with a television station logo on his shirt. The guy leaned over and said something to Will, but Will elbowed past him toward the locker room door. I hurried after him, but before we reached it, the doors flew open. Two state policemen, their hats in hand, held the doors open.

As if on cue, a hush swept through the gym. The first body, large and covered, was hand carried by four policemen, their hats tucked under their arms. In the silence, all eyes followed their procession to the back door where an ambulance waited. I glanced at the faces in the crowd, many with tears streaming. I quickly focused my camera and snapped a couple of shots as adults and teens placed their hands in a final salute to their much-loved Coach. They continued to stand there in the gym, hardly seeming to breathe. When the ambulance started and we heard the crunching of the tires, silently, hands dropped. Then, one by one, the gym emptied, no one speaking, some wiping faces and eyes.

"Why didn't you take more photos?" Will whispered. "You're some journalist."

I looked at him. "I did snap a photo of some people saluting. As for the others, I think some moments should remain private. I didn't have that option as a television journalist. But now, for the newspaper, I do. And, as for you, you're the one who must create the photo with your words. We saw grief today. The public can see it through your words and still give privacy to those who need it."

His facial expression clearly disagreed with what I'd said. "No wonder you're no longer a news journalist—if you ever were!"

I ignored the challenge. It could wait. "They're bringing someone else out," I said, instead.

I aimed my camera toward the doors, shooting the back of the officer as he backed out. Will hurried closer. He didn't notice when I stopped taking photos and walked toward the door we'd entered. From the signal one of the officers had given, this was the last victim.

"Sorrel?"

I jumped. "Mr. Byrd, you startled me."

He put his hand on my elbow and walked with me through the crowds around the gym entrance. "Where's your vehicle?" he asked. I told him and he steered me that direction, nodding but not speaking to the voices calling out questions. I kept my eyes trained on the path that parted for us.

When we reached my Jeep, he took my key, clicked opened my door, and helped me inside. "Thanks for keeping an eye on Will," he said before he shut my door. "They will likely do autopsies in Santa Fe, so you may want a shot of the plane at the airport—you know the drill. You can head out there when you finish at the paper. They're not flying out until the evening. The morning flight has already gone. At least, that's what I overheard."

He paused and stared back at the gym where the bodies were being transferred to ambulances. "I would normally have Jose on this story, as this is routine, but because of his longtime close relationship with Coach, I thought you'd be a better choice. I plan to have Jose interview some of the athletes—cover more of the sports part. We'll do a special sports edition for the Sunday paper covering his career. Oh, and please email your photos to me instead of Jose or Will."

"I will, sir." I started my car, then turned toward him a last time. "Do you—"

"Yes! I want you to investigate this story! You have years of experience with that, and you are more neutral. Even though you have met Coach, you've not been as closely connected to him as the rest of us—Chris included. Chris, of course, will do his best even though I know it will be heartbreaking for him. He's a professional in law enforcement. As for Will, because he is young, he tends to act without thinking. He'll be great one day, but not today. I'll keep him busy with other parts of the story so I can keep an eye on him. I'll be in touch." He reached inside and patted my arm. "I trust you, Sorrel. Thanks."

I watched as he walked across the lot toward the gym, his shoulders back and his head up. How difficult this job was! My respect for him doubled at that moment.

Easing the Jeep out of the parking lot was a challenge. Clusters of people stood in the middle of the exit, only moving when I tapped my horn. Some gave angry shouts while others stood with heads bowed in grief or anger or shock.

As I waited for one large group to move, I had that feeling of being watched. I glanced along the side until I caught a slight movement toward the end. It was too far to see a face, but I recognized the slump of the shoulders and the hair. "Sara?" I asked, then sighed. Of course, she couldn't hear me!

A horn beeped behind me. I glanced in the mirror and saw a police car. The officer stuck his hand out and gestured for me to move on. I nodded and started forward. The cars ahead had started up as well. By the time I reached the spot where Sara had been, I could see no trace.

I pulled over to the edge of the lot, got out, and focused my camera toward the path I'd just come. The gym stood tall and proud against the sky. But in the lot before it, clusters of grieving students, parents, and friends stood staring at the doors. They almost resembled statues, neither talking nor moving.

What was it Will had said? Had I forgotten my trade? I turned off the motor, gathered my recorder and camera, and walked toward them. In the gym, I'd been protecting the privacy of the victims. Out here, I had a different duty. I needed to provide a voice for the people left behind to grieve. I didn't have long, but I could spare fifteen minutes.

As I neared a small cluster of people, I clicked on my recorder. "Excuse me," I said to a young man who looked to be in his twenties. "Did you ever play football?"

"I'll say he did!" answered an older man to his left. "God gave him the talent, but Coach made him a winner!"

As if on cue, others joined in, animatedly telling their own stories, their faces mirroring their sorrow, their pride, and their memories. One by one, they talked until I could see what I'd witnessed so many times before: the beginning of closure and acceptance. It wouldn't be fast or easy. But it had begun. There would be tears, stories, disbelief, anger, and countless other emotions. It was difficult to witness, but that was what I'd done so long.

When I felt I'd spent as much time as I could spare, I once again settled into my Jeep. Moving through the crowd, I'd looked about, but I never saw Sara again. Why had she fled? What did she fear?'

"Sorrel," I told myself. "You've got to talk to that girl."

I glanced at my watch. Where had the time flown? Even if I found the girl, I wouldn't be interviewing her today, unless some miracle occurred. And I'd never found miracles on my doorstep.

Instead, I needed to look to the next stop: the paper and the morning's story. I also had photos to prepare and captions to write.

My stomach growled as I sped along. I'd never had a chance to eat that burrito! Maybe the paper had something in the snack machine.

Chapter 33

I hit the key to send my article about the townspeople grieving at the gym just before Will walked into the paper office.

"I was calling you next," I said, "in case you hadn't found a ride back here. How did it go?"

Will had that animated, restless look he always has when chasing a story. "I'm in a hurry to get this thing submitted by deadline," he said. "But I have news for you when I'm finished. Sorry I can't talk now."

He took a gulp of a canned soda and headed over to the cubbyhole area he claimed as his office.

Always drama with Will, I thought. But I needed to focus just now, so I was glad he had his own agenda.

My next task was to continue following—and snapping photos of—the unfolding story. I rang Randall Byrd on my cell as I began gathering my equipment. He answered on the third ring.

"Sorrel, where are you?"

"Walking out of the door here at the paper and heading for the airport. My photos are filed and ready to accompany Will's story. I included captions, which he can use if he chooses."

"Good. I'm—" The rest was difficult to hear over the talking behind him. "I'm sorry. Noisy," he said. "Anyway, I'm texting some information to you. I know I don't have to tell you to be discreet. This is a small community and Coach is . . . was . . . revered."

I lowered my voice as I passed the circulation desk. "Sir, I'm operating in the dark here." I opened the outer door to the parking lot and continued. "I appreciate discretion, but I need to know the barebones—"

"Give me a minute."

I opened the door to the Jeep and slung my camera into the passenger seat. I could hear the noise behind Mr. Byrd fading.

"Okay," he said. "I think I'm in a better place. I know I don't need to remind you that you need to be discreet." He paused, cleared his throat, and continued. "They haven't declared officially why Coach and his wife are dead." He paused again.

"Murdered?" I finally asked, sliding into the driver's seat and closing my door.

"Nothing official on that. There's no official statement for cause of death. That can be added before press time if needed."

"So at the moment . . . "

"At the moment, it's either suicide or murder." He cleared his voice. "Both he and his wife."

"So do you want me to continue with the article?""

"There's nothing official at this moment, so we'll wait for the official word and then I'll write the article."

"Then you need to let them know right away! I've just written an article to go with photos."

"Okay. You go ahead. You need to be at the airport for me, Sorrel. I overheard some names being mentioned. And even though this is a tragic event, I'm surprised that they are coming here. A popular coach . . . much loved . . . " His voice softened and he took a breath, "is a news event. But it hardly warrants the immediate attention of some of the names I overheard. I'll text them for you. Anyway, you'll know what to do. Listen. Keep your eyes open. Snap photos that you may or may not use and report back to me." His voice had dropped so low I could only catch an occasional word after that. "I'll see about the article you have turned in at the paper. I'll call on my way there."

"Yes, sir," I said, interrupting him. "Check in soon."

I'd covered this sort of situation as a television journalist in Houston. The glaring difference was that I was essentially solo here, whereas before I'd had a crew filtering and gathering information for me. For a moment, I allowed myself to review what Mr. Byrd had—

and hadn't—said. Apparently both Coach and his wife were dead. If they weren't suicides, then someone might have attempted to make them appear to be suicides. Mr. Byrd had not mentioned a weapon, but I suspected gunshot.

Motive could be complicated as well. With their only son murdered, maybe grief had pushed the couple toward murder–suicide. But before the thought could even settle into my mind, I rejected it. Coach had hardly seemed the type. He loved his son, but wouldn't he be more determined to find his son's killer than to kill his wife and himself? And his wife certainly—well, I could see her taking pills but not pulling the trigger on a gun.

Mr. Byrd hadn't specifically said gunshot, but something in his tone implied as much. "We don't want to take photos here," he'd said. "They have crime scene photographers here." He was uncharacteristically protective.

Saddle Gap has a small airport. Most of the airport traffic is private planes, but a regional jet arrives at noon from Albuquerque with a continuing flight to Dallas. Another arrives in the afternoon from Dallas bound for Albuquerque. They are usually half full—often even less—but the news had spread quickly. When I turned into the parking lot, I didn't see an empty spot. I drove past television vans from Albuquerque and Tucson. Finally, I parked on a grassy spot under a tree across the road. Did they tow vehicles parked beside the road in Saddle Gap?

"I hope not," I grumbled to myself, loading up my camera equipment.

The airport, usually tomblike, had transformed into the chaos of a mall at Christmas. A few fortunate travelers had wedged themselves into seats, guarding their carry-on luggage from the constant stream of people walking by. A few listened curiously to the bits of conversation, sometimes adding their own opinions and asking questions. Descriptions of the scene at the gym and events were passed along the rows, growing more gruesome and incorrect with each account.

I grabbed a bottle of cold water from the machine just inside the door, checked arrival schedules, and spotted a seat near the glass windows facing the runway. I smiled, engagingly I hoped, at the older lady whose shopping bags filled it and asked, "May I move these? Thank you!" As I began stuffing them under her seat, I lowered my voice and explained, "I'm the local news."

"Oh, yes!" she responded, helping to move her bits and pieces, her eyes alive with curiosity. "Are you—?"

"Covering the tragedy? Yes." Then I leaned closer and added, "I'm not at liberty to share—yet."

She nodded, her eyes alive with curiosity.

I had no clue how long I'd be here. Even without the unfolding drama at the gym, these things could extend for a long time. I turned on my cell and opened my email.

Sorrel Chatter is for personal email, and I don't share the address often. The other, assigned to me by the paper, is simply Byrd's Blurbs. It is publicized in the paper with a note that I am available for news and photos for the paper. Besides the senior center, almost no one uses it. But they keep me—and the newspaper—busy enough. The seniors love for me to photograph their activities and put their names and faces in the paper. In turn, they buy extra copies of the paper, sending clippings to their families. They also pass along notes about upcoming activities and tidbits of news I may want to pass on in the column Randall Byrd created a year ago, "Sorrel's Snippets." Sometimes, I find interesting news. More often, I find gossip or ramblings that only would interest the writer. Still, Mr. Byrd is pleased that the circulation for the paper has increased.

For the first time, I wished my photos and short news pieces were today's only enterprise instead of this current tragedy. When I looked at the number of emails in my box, even I hadn't expected so many.

Of course, I had more emails today than normal. People were talking about Coach, sharing memories and stories. He'd been a celebrity for this small city over the years, a colorful character who not only put Saddle Gap's name on the map with the winning football team, but also presented a strikingly handsome man whose charismatic personality had been the subject of legends.

I'd seen it time and again while reporting the news for television. People are attracted to tragedy. How many times had I seen people collecting souvenirs, selling refreshments at the scene, snapping photos, or just edging in as closely as possible while staring at the covered bodies and grieving families?

I glanced around the familiar, noisy scene. My own husband had lain, dying in our home while I'd been jockeying for a spot next to the latest drug lord, recording his answers to my shouted questions. I hadn't known it until I'd come home, of course. But that image had returned in the late night for a long time—and now again.

I pushed those mental images away and focused again on the scene around me. The speaker announced an incoming flight, so I stood and slung my photo bag on my right shoulder while keeping my camera in my left hand. "Show time!" had always been the signal when I worked with the Houston station, and I found myself whispering it as I threaded through the ever-growing crowd at the arrival gate. My mind had already formed questions, shots, and information I needed to record.

Chapter 34

As I waited for the passengers to deplane, I clicked the icon for Byrd's Blurbs on my phone and scanned the names or titles. The note at the top indicated eighteen entries, but it was the eighteenth message that made me take a second look. The entry had no title and simply read:

> Once upon a time, a prince and a lady's maid fell in love. When the King and Queen discovered the romance, they threatened the lady's maid. But she ignored their threats and continued to love the prince until someone murdered him. Now, she is scared of the danger she, a mere lady's maid, may face. She has gone into hiding until she can devise a plan of action—which she may have done. She drowns her sorrow secretly . . . and considers the plan . . . which she may share . . . with a sundae . . . at four.

I found no signature, but I knew who had written it: my "no-show" friend from the library. My first reaction was to ignore it. After all, I had little time for this hide-and-seek drama. Then I reread it. The word *threatened* gave me pause. Obviously, the King and Queen—his parents—would be powerful adversaries. Could someone else have threatened her? Does she know the murderer? How much does she know about the whole family's demise?

People began moving around me, gathering bags and lining up to move through the security gate. I glanced at the flight schedule on the monitor. The last incoming flight was scheduled to arrive at 3:05 from Phoenix. Another, from Dallas, was arriving within the next few moments. I'd promised to meet those planes and interview—or get statements—from the people on the list Mr. Byrd had given me. No other flights were listed until early evening, but I hadn't planned to spend the evening here anyway. So, I should be able to slip over, grab a milkshake at four, and visit with my elusive storyteller. She would likely be a better lead than anyone I'd meet here. Still, I'd been a journalist long enough to know that leads come from places and people we often overlook. I'd have time to do Mr. Byrd's interviews.

"Stacy?"

It took me a moment to realize the person was calling me! I'd abandoned that name when I'd moved from Houston to Saddle Gap. I'd never liked it anyway, but the station felt "Sorrel" was too "country" for television news.

I would have recognized that voice anywhere! My first instinct was to pretend I hadn't heard her. She called out a second time, and I remembered that—like mosquitoes and other distasteful creatures—the voice's owner would follow me like a bloodhound. Her voice had attracted attention.

Pasting a gracious smile on my face, I turned toward the gate streaming with new arrivals and waved to the anorexic, bleached blonde who had yelled across the small waiting room. I waited until she neared before answering, keeping my voice polite. "Hi, Renee. Fancy meeting you here."

"I could say the same!" She swept her eyes around the room. "This whole terminal is smaller than one waiting area in Houston. You poor thing!"

"That's because few residents want to leave the breathtaking sunsets and friendly people, not to mention the delicious food." I smiled. "I can give you some delicious places to eat."

She moved closer, as if to whisper, but kept her voice pitched for the room. "You poor thing. Are you working for the city council now? I'm sorry you lost your job with the television station, dear. But you remember how it is. Eating is the least important activity for news professionals."

I focused on her last statement, pitching my voice to match hers. "Moving to a better position isn't losing, Renee. Look at you! No more maid work?"

Watching her face flush a deep red, I knew I'd probably gone too far. Part of me hated that I'd fallen to her level. She had actually been in charge of designing and rearranging the sets for the station in Houston. But at times, that had included janitorial work for short periods until the staff she'd insulted could be replaced. I hurried on. "Are you travelling on your own?"

"Unfortunately—no."

The deep voice so near my shoulder startled me. I'd not noticed Dan. "You're here too?" I whooped. "How—"

"Did you get our things?" Renee interrupted, turning a shoulder toward me and smiling sickeningly up at Dan.

"It will take a few minutes," I answered for him. "This airport isn't usually so busy. Follow me. We can wait near the carousel."

When we reached the baggage claim area, I noticed camera crews from Albuquerque and Denver already grouping in the area. Renee must have noticed them at the same time, because she tamped down her irritable demeanor, ran her fingers through her bleached curls, and pasted a smile on her face.

"Dan, I'm so glad to have someone strong to help with my luggage!" she cooed.

Dan, who'd been surveying the area himself, said, "You shouldn't have packed so much!" He turned to me. "Sorrel, great to see you! But—"

"Dan," Renee interrupted, "I really need to get to the hotel so I can rest up!" She gave a sigh. "You remember, Sorrel . . . Stacy? You've changed your name?"

"I—"

"Dan, we need to see about our car. As little as this place is, we don't have time to chat. Sorry . . . er . . . Stacy . . . we'll be lucky if we get anything besides some big truck with horns on the front."

She grabbed Dan's elbow after she handed him her carry-on and started away. He looked back over his shoulder and called, "I need your number."

I raced forward and stuck a card in his pocket. "It was interesting to meet you guys . . . I think," I murmured.

Renee drug him along, announcing loudly, "Move over for television news!"

I smothered a giggle. I'd always suspected a monster lurked inside Renee. Looks like this had opened the door for it!

"Good Luck!" I called to them.

Renee didn't answer me, as she hurried past people and pushed her way toward the luggage area. Dan gave a shrug and hurried after her.

Another reason why I'm here instead of still working with her, I thought as I turned back to the lounge area. I had others to catch and I needed to focus on that, else I'd never make the 4:00 pm appointment Mr. Byrd for me, interviews of people who had known Coach and were arriving on the flight.

In fact, the interviews went smoother than I'd thought they might. One, a former athlete who'd revered Coach, spoke briefly about his shock and sorrow. "He was my idol," he said at the end of the interview. "I can only hope I can do as wonderful a job as he did instilling pride, hope, and joy in my students."

Another, now a state legislator, told me, "I can't answer anything about the legal issues. I'm here to honor a man I admire above most." I hadn't known there were legal issues. Wisely, I didn't share that with him, but I made a note for Mr. Byrd.

It wasn't easy seeing the shock and pain, but I'd slipped right into my former "shoes," distancing myself from their emotions and concentrating on the list Mr. Byrd had given me.

On my way out to the parking area, I stopped by each of the other television crews and collected cards.

178

"I'm with the local newspaper," I told each of them. "Could I snap a photo?"

I seriously doubted the paper would print one, but should we have a spot for a photo and a caption, I'd have something handy.

When I finally walked out to the Jeep, I had only just enough time to drive to meet my mysterious emailer. My lips twitched when I saw Dan trying to stuff numerous pieces of luggage into a small white economy car while Renee, her mouth moving and her arms crossed, watched. It reminded me of some of the things—or people— connected to my former job that I didn't miss.

Chapter 35

Will answered on the first ring. "Yes?"

"I'm meeting our young library aide, but I'm a few minutes late. Traffic. I hope she'll wait a moment or two over the time. Anyway, would you let Mr. Byrd or Reed know, if they ask, that I'm turning my phone ringer off so they should just leave a message?"

"Good luck! Since you say she's been so skittish, she may not show," Will answered. "But I'll tell Mr. Byrd that you will try to meet us afterward, say . . . in an hour?"

"I'll do my best. We may talk a bit longer than that. I need to go. I've not been inside yet, but if I don't see her, I'll wait a few minutes, just in case she has cold feet. I should still be able to make the meeting in an hour anyway. Is the meeting at the paper?"

"That's the plan. I'm already here, writing up a couple of interviews."

Before I could respond, someone came in and Will said a quick goodbye.

There were no cars in the parking lot, and I didn't see anyone sitting in any of the booths as I walked up to the door of the ice cream shop; but a few booths located on the other side were not yet visible. She would likely choose one there for their privacy.

"May I help you, ma'am?"

I jumped and only barely managed to avoid ramming my elbow into a cardboard stand-up cutout of a strawberry ice cream dish.

"Sorry. Didn't mean to startle you." The lady's voice had a breathy quality, almost as if she'd been running. One might expect that she'd be tiny and younger. Instead, she had a generous build, and I could see white strands in the dark hair she'd pulled into a ponytail.

"No . . . to both. I'm here to meet a friend so thought I'd wait to order until after she arrives."

"Oh. Then . . . "

"Maybe you know her. Sara? She works at the library and when she suggested we meet here, she sounded like she's a regular."

"Actually, I'm only part time. I usually work the early morning shift, and it's so busy I wouldn't remember anyone!"

"I understand that one. I'll just glance around first; and if I don't see her, I'll get something and sit by the window."

She smiled and might have said something else, but someone called for her and she turned toward the voice. "You might consider this strawberry concoction," she said and hurried toward the kitchen.

"I'll take one of those, too!"

I managed to swallow the yelp coming in my throat and whirled around. "Sara! You startled me!"

She smiled, her eyes glancing around us. When she'd checked out the other customers, she stepped closer and lowered her voice. "There's a spot back toward the restrooms," she said.

"I'll pick up two of these and join you," I answered.

"Oh . . . I—"

"Just two friends enjoying a gossip," I murmured.

"Oh . . . right."

I turned and casually studied the menu before stepping up to the counter. "What can I make for you?" a young man asked.

"Two of those sinful strawberry concoctions."

He smiled and turned toward the ice cream machine. When he'd made them both, he placed them on a tray, still smiling. "Sinful treats coming up!"

I paid him, picked up the tray, and winked. "On our way to Weight Watchers!"

His delighted laughter followed me.

Sara had selected a table between two high school groups here since school had canceled. She had sat so her head was facing the back wall. Smart. The teens would make enough noise to draw the attention their direction, providing an effective shield for us.

"Thanks," she said, scooting the dish in front of her and smiling.

I settled across from her. "We'll enjoy eating these with no talk of calories. I refuse to even think of the f-a-t word! Dig in!"

Sara grinned and obediently filled her mouth. "Mmm! I'm in love!"

I didn't immediately broach the topic on my mind. Instead, I simply asked about school and her activities. She relaxed gradually. She was a bright, witty young lady. I could think of no reason for Coach to object to her dating his son. Of course, I wasn't a parent.

When I'd eaten more of the delicious treat than I'd planned, I placed my spoon in the dish and shivered.

"I love this . . . but it's much bigger than I expected!" I told her.

Sara finished chewing a strawberry, nodded, and then dropped her spoon beside the bowl.

"Want something else?" I asked.

"No, thank you." She glanced around. The table behind her had emptied, but she leaned closer and lowered her voice anyway. "I heard about Coach and his wife," she said.

"Tragic!"

"They didn't like me much, but I wouldn't want this to happen."

"Why didn't they like you?"

She shrugged, picked up her spoon, and made circles in the ice cream before she finally spoke. "They didn't think I was good enough for Brent. They wanted him to pick someone more like his mother had been—popular, outgoing, a cheerleader, maybe."

"Did they tell you that?"

"Not in so many words." She cut a strawberry in half, lifted it to her mouth, stared at it, and abruptly dropped it into the dish. "When they came to take Brent home from the library, they were almost too nice . . . talking, you know, in that high, fake voice people use when they're pretending. His mom did, anyway. His dad seldom spoke to me at all. Then one day Brent didn't show. Later that day, I got his email."

"Was he angry?"

"No. He was very proper and polite . . . like someone was dictating the letter to him. And I'm sure that's how it went. He regretted that he couldn't see me as he needed to concentrate on his grades . . . and sports, of course. He wished me a happy life."

Her voice wobbled on the final sentence. She took a deep breath before she continued.

"I'm sorry." Tears filled her eyes.

I reached for my purse and handed her a small tissue package. She pulled one out and returned the package to me.

I picked up my spoon and toyed with a strawberry before biting into it. I could sense her pulling herself together, and she breathed deeply a couple of times before she resumed talking.

"Brent didn't write it, you know. He hated sports. And he had never concentrated on his grades because he never needed to. He was so smart. In fact, I don't think he ever needed to study. He was one of those who could read something once and almost repeat it back to you." She leaned closer and lowered her voice. "He'd discovered something . . . a secret, I think. He didn't tell me what it was, but it troubled him."

"Did he ever mention it again?""

"No. He was often careful . . . almost like he was scared to say anything. Then he'd change the mood and clown around."

"Did you two see much of each other?"

She grimaced. "He'd stop by the library mostly. Then my boss complained about my socializing. So we'd schedule times to meet up elsewhere . . . sort of like Romeo and Juliet. My parents liked him the one time they met." She paused and when she spoke again, her voice wobbled. "Brent was a nice guy, but he was caught up in something."

"Did he tell you what it was?"

"No. He only told me to not tell anyone we'd been friends. And he said that maybe . . . when we went to college . . . we could date." She dipped her spoon into the melting ice cream, stirred it around a bit, and laid it down again. She glanced over her shoulder, then leaned over the table. "He said once that he thought he'd stumbled upon something illegal . . . some bad stuff. Then he made this face and told me that no one would ever believe it could be true."

"What kind of stuff?" I asked.

"He wouldn't say, but I wondered if it had something to do with that senior center."

"Why?"

"Brent was devoted to his job there. He told me he could think of nothing worse than waking up one morning old, sick, and with no one who cared."

I waited for her to continue. When she didn't, I asked, "Did he explain himself?"

"Well, he had worked quite a while at that senior center, you know, and he said he saw some horrible incidents of how their relatives mistreated them."

"He must have been a caring person," I said. "I talked to some of them recently, and they had nothing but positive things to say about him. I find it admirable that he'd connect with senior citizens while he was still a teen."

"Oh, he didn't begin with the Casa de Oro. He told me that he'd begun doing yard work for some older people in his neighborhood when he was thirteen. He bought his first bicycle with the money he earned mostly from mowing lawns. But he also ran errands for them, picked up small items for them from the stores in the neighborhood, and even took small dogs walking."

"You loved him," I said softly.

Sara looked down. Tears dropped onto her hand. "Yes," she whispered. "But it never would have worked. His parents had big plans for him." She wiped her hand, then her cheeks, glancing self-consciously around at the other booths.

When she'd calmed herself, she continued. "He said he wondered if he'd been adopted or something. That he just didn't fit in his own family."

"Well, I think we all wonder about that at one time or another," I said. "I did. I made up this whole story about my family drowning in a flood. Right before they went down into the water, they tied me onto a small raft. I floated away until I washed up on the shore near my house. Only problem was my house wasn't on a shore."

"You have a wild imagination," she said, relaxing a bit. "I wondered if I was adopted because I didn't look much like my mom or dad."

"Were you?"

"No."

"How could you be sure?"

"I discovered some family secrets, and they proved that I had definitely been born to my mom and dad. I also have my granny's beaky nose," she said. "So there goes my adoption story."

I reached over and squeezed her hand. "I have to go. But before I go, I have one last question. Did his parents share his love for the theatre?"

Sara shook her head. "His father was Coach, you know." She pushed back her chair, as did I, and stood. "With Coach for a father, how could he admit that he hated football?" She toyed with her spoon. "Maybe," she said, "we are all trying to fit into roles our parents expect."

Chapter 36

I couldn't think of an answer for her, so I handed her my card. "Thanks for meeting up with me," I told her. "If you remember anything, let me know?"

"I'm still not sure if I should have met up with you or said anything," she whispered. "What if someone saw us here and . . ."

I reached in my purse for the disposable phone I'd bought several months earlier for just such an occasion. "The number is taped on the back," I said as I handed it to Sara. "If you need to talk, use it. Memorize the number and throw it away."

"You sound like a television cop!" She grinned for the first time.

"I'm not," I said. "Maybe in a second life I'll try that career. Take care. I'll leave first."

I drove down the street, pulled into a florist shop, and pretended to look at the window displays. I realized as I waited for Sara to drive by that she'd never really talked much about her own parents and what they thought of the relationship. But from our conversation today, I knew one thing for certain: Sara, at least, had loved Brent. And I would wager that their relationship had been more than she was willing to tell me.

After I saw her drive past and out of sight, I went back to my Jeep and waited another few minutes to make sure no one had followed her. Next, I drove straight to the newspaper office, but didn't immediately go inside. Instead, I took a few moments to jot down notes about my recent conversation while the things we'd discussed were still fresh in my mind. I included questions that she had either not answered or that appeared now as I reviewed our talk.

My psychology classes—a bit vague now after these several years—suggested that she was more an introvert than I'd first thought. But her love—and I was sure it was love—had pushed her to meet up with me and say as much as she had. I noted her nervousness about our meeting, her lack of self-esteem, especially when she referred to parents, both hers and his. Their romance, if one could truly call it that, bore a juvenile romantic quality when she described it. Her voice held a secretive tone even now after he'd been killed and his parents had died as well. She hadn't asked anything about his parents besides the brief reference at the start of our conversation. I noted that and added a question mark to remind me to investigate it.

I wrote down the questions I'd asked and her answers as closely as I could remember them. She had seemed really nervous, so I'd left my recorder in my purse. With noise in the shop, I knew it wouldn't pick up her soft voice unless it was sitting on the table next to her. The one time I'd written something on a napkin, she'd withdrawn until I'd put my pen in my purse and wadded up the napkin to toss.

Years as a news television reporter had taught me alternate methods of interviewing and of noticing nonverbal signs during interviews. The misery I'd seen in her eyes wasn't new.

It was too late now to ask Coach why they didn't like the romance. I doubted it held any real significance. Brent had been an excellent student and a good athlete. Maybe they feared he'd make choices that would keep him here, away from college, and send him on a path they hadn't wanted. It was a natural thing for parents to wish.

Something, however, had posted a target on him. Was it connected—or even the result—of something his parents had done? I couldn't ignore the fact that they were both dead so closely after his own murder. He hadn't appeared to be involved in drugs, but that wouldn't be impossible. Unfortunately, many kids—both good and bad students—fell into the temptation of the money drugs offered.

A glance at my watch warned me that I needed to move on. Maybe Will and Mr. Byrd had some ideas to add to my own speculations.

I hopped out of the Jeep and then reached back inside to grab my purse and notebook. I almost skipped to the door of the paper office.

"Whoa! Are you late to something important? A fire? Another litter of pups to spoil and add to the herd I suddenly am feeding?" A muscular arm encircled my waist and pulled me against the irritating cowboy detective.

Wriggling to loosen his grip, I said, "Reed, turn loose. People will get the wrong idea!"

Reed removed his arm, reached for the door, held onto it, and whispered as I tried to brush past. "They already have the right idea, you know." Then he sobered. "Sorry. I know this isn't the time to be silly. Just tired of all the craziness here."

I glanced up into his face. "I'm sorry, Reed. This must be a nightmare for you." I reached for his hand and squeezed it. "I've been so insensitive."

"Another time, another place. For now, let's do this!" he whispered. Then he opened the door and gestured for me to enter first.

Mr. Byrd's secretary looked up at the door's chime. "Hello. We're meeting with Will and Mr. Byrd," I told her, glancing over my shoulder to include Reed.

"Go right on in. He's waiting on both of you," she answered, her voice and manner softer than I'd ever seen. Then she lifted the telephone and spoke our names into it.

As we entered the office, Will glanced up from a square table by the window. Mr. Byrd rose from his desk and motioned for us to sit with Will.

"Thank you for getting here as quickly as you could," Mr. Byrd said, his voice strangely polite. "Would you like something to drink before we start? Coffee?"

"Yes!" Reed said. "Black."

"No," I replied.

He dialed his secretary. "One coffee, black, please."

I sat in a chair next to Will and pulled out my notebook. Reed settled between me and the last seat where Mr. Byrd settled.

"Before we share, I'll let you look at the front page," Mr. Byrd said, handing each of us a mock-up of the paper's front page stacked in the center of the table. The bold headline in large print grabbed my attention: *Legendary Coach and Wife Dead in Possible Double Murder*. Beneath, in a slightly smaller font another headline followed: *Officers Continue in Probe of Son's Death*. Scattered over the front page, I glanced at related articles, as well as at a couple of photos I'd emailed to him from the airport this afternoon. Spanning across the bottom was a photo I'd emailed of the crowd clustered outside the gym, many with heads hung in grief.

No one spoke until Reed and I looked up.

"Nice tribute," Reed told him. "Coach would have been honored."

"He'd be more honored if we manage to clear up this mess!" Mr. Byrd glanced at his phone, reading a text before continuing. "What do you have? Can you tell us anything, Reed?"

"I wish I could, but the department is sitting tight on this one. Because it happened there at the gym, our department isn't the lead on Coach and his wife." Reed sighed. "I don't know a lot."

"Off the record? These are our longtime friends, Reed. You know you can trust me!" He looked hard at Will and me. "Us! We've shared a lot of secrets! No one at this table," again looking hard at each of us, "will share anything from here without the agreement of all of us! Agreed?"

Each of us nodded and said, "Agreed."

A tap at the door interrupted him. "Enter." His secretary entered with Reed's coffee. "Thanks," Mr. Byrd told her, then looked at Will and me. "Cold bottled water in that mini fridge by my desk. Get it when or if you want it."

When the door shut again, he continued. "Frankly, I think the police are looking at this as a murder–suicide. In fact, that's how they referred to it in the information sent to our paper. Does anyone have anything that would confirm or dispute that theory?"

"It fits," Will said. "Their only child had been murdered. They had seemed distraught—almost inconsolable."

"Coach wouldn't kill himself," Reed interrupted. "He is—was—a fighter. He'd be looking for those who killed his son and kill them—whatever it took! And he wouldn't kill his wife—ever!"

"I have to agree," Mr. Byrd finally said, softly, almost as if talking to himself.

"Then why this headline? This article?" Will asked. "If you don't believe it is true, why—"

"Bait!" Reed said. He stared into Mr. Byrd's eyes. "Who are you expecting to trap?"

"I'm hoping you . . . and Sorrel . . . and Will . . . can find the answer to that question for us. We need to put our heads, our notes, our information, and our ideas together. This is not a simple murder or a double suicide. We can't let it pass as that. Someone smart . . . and evil . . . and angry is behind this. We owe it to our friends to discover the truth and make the guilty parties pay!" Randall Byrd handed around lined tablets. "First, let's share what we know! Who wants to go first?"

I spoke up. "I will. I just spent time with the young woman, Sara, I'd met earlier at the library. She sent me a cryptic email, and we met for ice cream at the place where she'd stood me up before. She confirmed that she and Brent had a romantic relationship. The romance began in drama class, but it hadn't developed further than a couple of dates, if I can believe her . . . and I'm not sure I do. But while we were talking, a couple of things came up that were interesting. First, his parents didn't approve of their relationship, and they didn't like his interest in drama. She said the only reason she'd been told for him not seeing her anymore was that Coach didn't want his son distracted from football. So their relationship had taken on a sort of Romeo-and-Juliet tone. Brent was interested in drama and, in her opinion, talented in it. The parents felt drama . . . and she . . . distracted him from football. But she found it strange that they encouraged his work at the senior nursing home and said that took much more time."

Mr. Byrd nodded. "Anyone have anything to add to that?"

Reed spoke first. "Coach would expect his boy to be like him. But this kid didn't seem to be tough enough. I watched him playing a few times a couple of years ago. He just didn't have the drive . . . the instinct . . . he needed. He played a fair game, but my opinion is that his heart wasn't in it. When he wasn't on the bench the past year, I suspected he'd dropped out. Coach would have taken that very badly."

"I agree," Will said. "That seemed to be the consensus from people who knew him."

"And this girl," I said, "isn't decorative enough."

"I'm afraid you're all probably right." Mr. Byrd paused and, when no one spoke, continued. "My observations have been focused on the airport. More specifically, the guests arriving for the services. Sorrel, how did that go?"

"The place is buzzing with news people—many television news crews," I said. "I'm not sure anyone I spoke with could tell me why they were here. One recognized me from my old station in Houston. She mentioned a fax from the local chamber of commerce office. I struck up a conversation with a young guy at the car rental counter. Didn't last long as he was busy. But he did have time to tell me that several politicians and 'big wigs' had reserved vehicles."

Randall Byrd didn't comment but added his own news. "Coach, interestingly, had plans for the services in his will. They are to be held as quickly as possible, followed by cremation. Since the bodies will first be moved to Santa Fe for autopsies, cremation will not be immediate. So the services as such will be memorials . . . likely at the school gym."

"So why are they all here?" Will asked.

"Who are 'they'?" Reed asked.

"They are some big names in our state," Mr. Byrd answered. "Reed, that's why I'd like for you and Sorrel to find out as much as you can about this unusually sophisticated list of people, especially since their appearances are unusual . . . given that he was a high school coach. I've given Sorrel a list of people that I—and others—recognize,

192

as well as the hotels where most are staying. These are political types mostly." He passed copies to the three of us. "I'd also like someone— Will?—to revisit the priest to hear his reaction to these plans of cremation and haste. Sorrel, I'd like you to mingle with those who have arrived recently. There's a cocktail party this evening at the mayor's house. Here's the address and any names given me. Reed, I'd like for you to accompany Sorrel, of course, but I realize you're likely busy."

"I'll see what I can do."

"Good. I've added to the list of people I recognized from the television cameras any bits of information and thoughts. Sorrel, I know our job is not to solve the murders, so I advise you to turn over any questionable information you find to Chris first. If he thinks it might endanger the investigation, he'll let you know. And, Will, Sorrel has lead on this."

All of us could easily recognize Will's disappointment. "You're an apprentice here, Will," Mr. Byrd reminded him gently. "Neither of us— nor the university—needs the problems some of these people can cause us." He stood. "Now, I must go. Check with my 'right arm' outside before you leave."

He nodded and turned to leave. For a moment, I saw his shoulders hunched—likely from grief for his friends—before he straightened, checked that his tie was straight, and reached for his suit jacket. I thought he sounded much as Coach would have sounded before a game. "Let's do our best to help the authorities but not to cause problems for them." He directed a sad smile at Will. "This is the best—the only thing—we can do for them now." He stepped out quietly, his shoulders squared, and pulled the door closed.

Chris reached over and squeezed my hand. Then he looked at both Will and me.

"Well, troops, do we need to decide on a secret code word now?" he asked.

He didn't get a smile and didn't seem to expect one.

193

Lonna Enox

"Lead on," I said, instead. "Will and I are at your command. And Madonna sounds like a nice code word!"

Chapter 37

When the well-dressed stranger dumped his trash in the garbage bin and slipped out the door of the ice cream shop, no one glanced up. Instead, they continued to complain about the focus of their mundane lives.

The young girlfriend and her companion, the news gal, had not seemed to reach any real conclusions before they left. Instead, they had wasted their time with useless speculation from what he'd snooped through the new listening device. Wasn't it Shakespeare who had coined the phrase "much ado about nothing"? From what he'd overheard, this current situation was contained.

He backed the rental car out of the slot and turned onto the street. He'd make a call when he found a pay phone. They weren't as common any more, especially in these small, isolated towns; but he didn't want to use the burner phone he'd bought unless he could find no other alternative. People who paid this much money for his services expected precaution.

His mind wandered to the old lady he'd helped along to her rewards. She had whispered a phrase from Shakespeare as she struggled for air those last moments of her life. He had looked the words up afterward. "Cowards die many times before their death," she'd gasped. He'd wondered if it could be a code or something. Who knew? Her mind might have just been wandering, as old as she looked.

She hadn't looked afraid as she'd struggled to continue her miserable existence. Why had she struggled? This stranger had been giving her a gift, as he had done to the other souls, by removing her from her useless life.

"Whatever makes a person a hero instead of a coward?" the stranger mused. "Money? Success? Good Looks? Perhaps brains? If so, I'd qualify. But the real question is why Coach would think he qualified also?"

The stranger chuckled at his wit, cruising slowly through the gym parking lot. He stopped a couple of times to avoid hitting mourners who darted out without looking. No one seemed to be in their homes.

Instead, cars filled the gym parking lot, their owners standing outside in groups talking, crying, looking up at the sky or down at the pavement. How many stories could a person tell? How many condolences could a person offer? How many people knew the truth about the famed Coach?

The stranger chuckled, imagining the reactions if these mourners knew the truth about their hero. How would they react to their hero crying for mercy, pleading for his life? Would they expect Coach to plead for his wife's life? Would they be surprised to hear him bargaining for his life but not for his wife's? Who would have imagined her courage!

"Please," she'd whispered. "Take me. I no longer have a reason to live."

Then the stranger's whisper into her ear had changed her face from sorrow to horror and then to desolation. Finally, she looked up with resignation and reached for the gun.

"I love you," she had whispered to her husband, even as she squeezed the trigger. Then she had closed her eyes as she turned the gun on herself. The stranger had been impressed as he watched her stroke the gun's barrel, then whisper an inaudible statement before squeezing the trigger again

The stranger rolled away from the gym parking lot, nodding to mourners and forcing down the joy the memory filled inside him. What a sight they had made!

Once back onto the road, the stranger sped up and turned toward town. A busy day made a body weary. Time to rest . . . perhaps to dream . . . the images of the famous coach's terror still filling his thoughts.

Chapter 38

"Wow! You clean up nice!"

"Reed! You almost made me spill this awful punch!" I whispered through my teeth, avoiding looking straight at interested guests. Carefully, I inched away until I could meet his eyes.

Attempting a more appropriate expression—sad yet welcoming—I leaned toward his ear as if to console him. "This is a sad occasion, so check your hormones and grieve!" I then raised the tissue to my nose.

He put a hand on my waist and leaned close enough I could feel his breath on my cheek. "We have been instructed to act as a couple by your boss. I'm just trying to follow his instructions."

Reed didn't move away, and his intimate smile promised all sorts of activities for the nosy onlookers. I leaned close to his ear and continued through gritted teeth. "Behave or I'll have to employ some of my karate moves."

His mouth opened but—thankfully—he was interrupted before he could continue. Randall Byrd held out a hand to shake with Reed, forcing him to remove his arm from my waist. "Hello, Deputy," he said. "Sad occasion here. Coffee or punch is at the table over there."

Even Reed knew an implied order. Mr. Byrd and I watched his progress toward the coffee table for a moment. Then he turned toward me. "Sad occasion here, Ms. Janes. I doubt you knew Coach or his family, but this town not only knew but also loved them."

His voice, pitched just slightly louder, caught the attention of several around us. He continued, including Reed as he approached with his coffee. "I'm sure there are many here who would like to tell you stories about this family. They are our family as well."

"Hear, hear." The speaker, a distinguished older gentleman, moved closer and held his hand out to me. "I'm Carl Ponte, retired high school principal. I could tell you many stories about Coach, but this young man here can tell you even more."

Reed stepped forward, moved his coffee cup to his left hand, and shook hands. "He was a legend," he said.

"It is inconceivable for us to be here grieving the death of him and his whole family," Mr. Ponte continued. He patted Reed on the shoulder. "I feel better that you are investigating this tragedy."

He moved on then and Reed followed, greeting people and hugging some of the ladies. I inched back close to Mr. Byrd, listening to comments people gave as he greeted them and then offering some of my own as he passed them toward me.

Finally, I broke away to return my punch cup to the table, only to have a young waiter take it from me instead. While Mr. Byrd and Reed were occupied, I wandered to a quiet spot beside a fake tree and watched the group, paying attention to occasional tidbits of conversation. Most fell into the traditional exclamations of horror, surprise, outrage, and fear. Traditionally, people in situations like this one seem compelled to ask each other 'why' and express their horror, even while gathering details both horrifying and gory. Others sit or stand nearby, listening to the reactions and words of others.

"Will they have an open casket?" an older lady asked her friend.

"I doubt it," her friend answered. "Maybe they'll have cremation. Guns cause all sorts of damage."

"Sad," the first lady sighed. "It doesn't seem like a proper funeral when you can't see them one last time."

They moved away, only to be replaced by an older gentleman and his wife. She sniffed and he reached over to remove the tea cup from her fingers and hand it to a passing waiter. Then he reached for her hand. "They were good neighbors," he said.

I casually moved closer. "Hello," I said. "I'm looking for people who knew this family well . . . possibly neighbors or church members?"

Both brightened a bit. She opened her mouth, then shut it at her husband's clearing his throat. "And you are?" he asked.

"Sorrel Janes," I answered, reaching forward to shake his hand. "I work with Mr. Byrd part time."

His wife brightened. "You're the photographer! You have that adorable little shop. I've only been once, but I love the photos of the cranes!"

"Thank you. After years of television news reporting . . . and situations like this current one . . . I love nature photography more and more. Death and violence are part of their world as well, but it doesn't feel . . . "

"Senseless?" The man stepped forward. "I'm Daniel Burns and this is my wife, Sheila. We were their neighbors all these years, since they moved in as newlyweds and then raised their son."

I asked, "Do you mind if I record this?" I pulled a small cassette recorder form my pocket. "I'd like to hear about them as you knew them." I looked into her eyes apologetically. "Unfortunately, when something this horrific happens, people tend to focus on the event and forget the people."

Both visibly relaxed.

I glanced over my shoulder and spotted a small table. "May we sit?"

Before they left me, Sheila spotted someone and waved her over. "You will want to speak to Brent's second grade teacher! She taught his mama also."

By the time Reed rescued me—almost two hours later—I'd filled a couple of cassettes and my tiny notepad.

"Sorry," he said, smiling his best charming smile at another couple who'd known Coach and his family for many years. "I must steal this lady on orders from her editor, Randall Byrd."

He shook hands with each, and I gave the lady a hug. "Thank you for sharing with me," I told them both.

Mr. Byrd stood by the door, his demeanor calm and serious. We threaded our way toward him, apologizing to numerous people for not being able to stop or for bumping into elbows. Finally, we arrived, where he expertly whisked us out the door and to the parking lot.

"Exhausting," he said over his shoulder as he strode to his car. "I hate these things. Why—"

"Because we all are wondering why," Reed answered.

He sighed. "I know. But no one ever finds a real answer. It's impossible. I don't think there is a real answer. Mankind is really just a collection of animals." He clicked the key button to unlock the doors, opened the driver's side, and slid inside. Once there, he opened his window.

I'd never seen him like this: tired, dejected. "People are a bossy bunch of critters," I said. "We think we are in charge, so we try to explain everything that happens as if we can either stop or manage things. We know better, but we feel this need to convince ourselves and everyone that we are in charge."

"Well said." Mr. Byrd sighed. "I'm off to my house to collect Mrs. Byrd for yet another of these things. And I suspect you two have some long hours ahead of you as well." He started his car and waved to us as he drove away.

Reed turned to me. "Our evening is just beginning," he said. "How about we drive over to Teri and Jose's place? I've been instructed—by Teri, of course—to bring you so she can feed you. And don't say a word . . . if that's possible!"

He dodged my swing, laughing, as he said, "You need nourishment if you expect to land one of those puny punches!" He pretended to duck. "Only telling the truth!" I sensed that he was trying to lighten the situation for both of us. He walked me to my Jeep and waited until I had started it and pulled out before turning to walk to his truck.

I thought, as I'd thought many times in recent months, that life without Chris Reed would be unthinkably calm . . . and empty.

Chapter 39

Wonderful, spicy odors greeted us even before Jose, his arms filled with a sleeping Sofie, opened the door.

"Ssh. I was just going to put her down. Teri's in the kitchen."

I kissed my goddaughter lightly on her forehead, not wanting to awaken her, and headed toward the kitchen.

Just then, the twins peeked around the corner of the hallway, then raced over for a hug.

"What are you two still doing up?" I asked.

"Boys, back to bed. You can visit with Sorrel some other time," Teri scolded mildly. "And don't wake your sister!"

As they released me to run back to bed, I followed Teri into the kitchen.

"Here," she said, after giving me a big hug. "Even though you and the kitchen are almost strangers, you're a great taster. What do you think?" She then blew on a spoon and held it up to my mouth.

I swallowed and leaned over the sink to rinse the spoon. "I think I'm going to gain five pounds with this meal!"

"You always say that and you just get skinnier! I wish you'd share your secret! This is ready if you like it."

"I'll set the table--."

"No need," Teri interrupted. "It's posole. I just fill bowls here and everyone takes theirs to the table."

"Then I'll carry in the bowls," I said. "You don't want spills. And the guys are too preoccupied to be careful."

Teri sighed. "I won't argue with that."

In spite of the greeting and smiles, I could feel the underlying sadness as we ate. Even the delicious posole couldn't distract anyone.

None of us adults ate as much as we usually would have done, our minds full of unsaid questions: the *who*'s, the *why*'s, and the *how*'s.

After the meal, Reed and I insisted on clearing up while Teri and Jose checked on the twins and Sofie.

When we'd finished, we gathered in their den. Reed looked around at us all. "Now I understand that phrase about the elephant in the kitchen," he said. "We need to talk."

No one spoke—or even reacted at all. We sat quietly for what seemed like an eternity. Finally, Jose rose abruptly and left the room.

I looked over at Reed and arched my brows. He shrugged. "Maybe we need to slip out," I whispered. He shrugged then reached for his hat, which he'd placed on the arm of the chair.

"Found it!"

Both of us jerked around to see Jose, a huge grin on his face, holding up a bottle of sparkling cider in one hand and a framed football photo in the other.

"Remember this game, Reed?"

Reed reached for it. "There you are—were you really that chunky?"

Jose pulled it back. "Chunky? That was a well-toned, athletic body, man! Look at you—that scrawny excuse for a—"

Reed and Jose spent a minute grappling over the photo, grinning like the young men they had been.

"Boys! If you wake the children, Sorrel and I are taking off and letting you get them settled again!" Then Teri turned to Jose. "Where are the glasses? We're not going to drink out of the bottle like you guys did back then!"

He walked over to the china cabinet and pulled out four crystal flutes. "Well said, Babe. This calls for something fancier than water glasses." He looked at Reed. "Remember?"

"Yeah, I do."

Reed rose, took the bottle, twisted until it was uncorked, and began filling the flutes. Jose passed them around.

When everyone held a filled one, Jose continued. "Softly, Reed."

We all held our flute high and the men softly sang their school fight song, both of their eyes misty. When the last note—a whispered note—died, Reed said, "To playing hard, to trusting hard, to winning. But, most of all, to our team—one body, one mind, one heart—to the end."

As we raised the glasses, everyone whispered, "To Coach." Then Reed added, "To Mrs. Coach." And Jose finished, "To Coach Junior." I somehow managed to swallow over the lump in my throat.

Teri reached for the flutes and I carried the empty bottle to the kitchen. We could hear the guys talking softly. "I'm so glad!" Teri whispered. "I'd hoped they'd start grieving. Talking is always better than angry silence."

I agreed. "I hope the authorities find out what happened—soon"

"Me, too! The town is crawling with big shots, television crews, and reporters. I wish they'd get out of here!" Then she gasped. "I'm sorry, Sorrel. I know you were—"

"Yes, I was. But I'm not anymore, and I can now appreciate how people felt. The whole town is filled with strangers. You should have seen the airport!"

"I can only imagine!" Teri carried the clean flutes to the cabinet and I followed her into the den.

"Speaking of strangers," Reed said, cutting his eyes toward me. "I met a friend of yours from the Houston television station."

"*Friend* is a misnomer," I corrected him. "She was a co-worker."

"Good looking gal!"

I agreed, trying to ignore Teri's gasp and Jose's snicker.

"Reed! Behave!" Teri scolded. "You said earlier that the station had dropped in quality if she had replaced Sorrel!"

"Really!" I shrugged. "She was just an extra when I was there, but I've been gone awhile now. If they have her covering this story, she is likely good. When I was out there at the airport, I could only think about how glad I was to be here . . . and not just arriving here to work."

I noticed Teri trying to discreetly hide a yawn. It was late and we were all running on adrenalin. "I hate to break this up, but I think we all need to get some rest."

"Yes, neither of us has been keeping regular hours during the investigation," Reed said.

"Us either!" Teri put a hand on Jose's shoulder. "We will be awake early, and it's your morning feeding, remember?" Jose moaned and stood as well.

"And thanks for the posole," Reed said as we walked toward the door. "Those little snacks at the reception weren't very filling."

Teri looked at me. "I forgot to tell you that the store is covered tomorrow if you need it to be."

"I appreciate that! I need to check mail and messages, but I have other things also."

"No problem. I'll just call her before she leaves tomorrow to let her know she doesn't have to be there right at nine." Then she hugged me and then Reed.

"I'll be in touch," Jose murmured to Reed.

As Reed walked me to my Jeep, he drew close, leaned down, and whispered, "Any chance of you making a pot of coffee so we can throw around our ideas from the party while they're still fresh?"

"You really need to get some sleep, Reed. You've been working nonstop—"

"I'd really like to talk. I didn't want to say anything in front of Teri and Jose, of course, but I'd like to hear what you have to say. Besides, I miss those two mangy cats."

"Sure you do! Are you ever serious, Reed?"

Then he said, softly, almost as if to himself, "Sometimes being serious isn't what it's made out to be. I'm serious all the time . . . just don't always share it." He looked over at me and half-smiled. "That line came from some comedian I saw once. I thought he was dumb. Now, I understand what he meant."

"I know you tease sometimes to reduce tension in situations. It's just that this case is so—"

"Heartbreaking? Personal? Frustrating?"

"Yes."

"They all are, if you think about it.

As he opened the door for me to get in, he said. "I'll meet you at your place." Then he closed the door and waited to get in his truck until I started the Jeep and began to drive away.

Reed pulled in behind me at the store. Before I could get out of the Jeep, he parked next to me, stepped out of his truck, and walked around the Jeep to escort me to my door. He opened the door, and I stepped out, but he didn't move.

"The hardest part of this job," Reed continued as if we had been driving together all this time, "is the weight of the trust people have in me to find out who destroyed their lives . . . as if I could restore their lives to what they were before this happened."

"I'm beginning to understand that, Reed. I'm frustrated, too . . . and a bit short, like I always get when a case is this twisted. I mean, we don't know much more than we did the moment we learned about the body out at the rectory!"

He moved closer and caught my hand. "Sorrel, we know more than we think. In fact, as far as the cases we've been involved with together, we must be nearing the finish line."

I laughed incredulously. "You're joking!"

"You need a new line, Sorrel. You say that every time."

"Really!"

He started toward the house. "Let's see what we've got and then sleep on it. We don't need a whole pot of coffee, but a cup might keep me awake long enough to drive home. And we need a few moments of down time. Share what we know—or think we know. Like any puzzle, the pieces all fit. We're probably missing a few, but we need to share the ones we have."

We walked to the door and he took my key to open it. "I'm checking inside."

"That—"

"Your place is isolated out here. Besides, the cats like me!"

It is hard to not grin when Chris Reed is being his normal self. When I told him so, he gave me a quick hug. "I don't want these cats hurt," he drawled, chuckling.

I might have laughed with him, except that suddenly something didn't feel quite right. I couldn't explain it—or why—but I pulled his hand away from the knob. "Don't!"

He looked at me as if I were crazy. "Why not?"

I turned on my pocket flashlight and turned it toward the knob. Almost hidden beneath it was a tiny bit of wire. Reed squinted over my shoulder.

"Is that what I think?" I breathed.

"I'm afraid it is. Hands away""

He pulled me with him back off the steps, already dialing his phone. "I need our bomb expert out here immediately." He gave the address. Then he pulled me back away from the building.

"You said bomb expert!"

"Yes. It looks like some sort of explosive device, and these guys are trained in handling them."

"My cats are in there, Chris Reed!"

"I'll warn the experts that they are facing the greater danger on the inside!"

"Not funny!" I mumbled, my head buried in his chest.

"I'll try to protect them, Sorrel," he whispered. "I promise. But you're my priority."

We could hear sirens in the distance. They, Reed's arms holding me, and the tension in his grip reminded me that sometimes the "single" route isn't as glamorous as it may seem.

Chapter 40

Reed had forbidden me to go inside to rescue my "roommates"; so while he was occupied briefing the various law enforcement officers about what we suspected, I sneaked in the shop door and into my quarters to gather up the kitties. They weren't happy about being stuffed into the same carrier, but I assured them that they'd be even less happy should a bomb explode in their home.

The carrier was both awkward and heavy. I perched it on the counter long enough to remove cans of their favorite food from the cabinet and stuffed them into my jacket pocket. Both filled the air with feline yowls as I started the awkward process back toward the door connecting my living quarters and the shop.

I bumped into a chair back and they slid toward one end of the carrier, their yowls turning into howls. "Hush, you sissies," I muttered. "If you get Reed's attention," I whispered, "we'll all be in hot water."

I opened the door and slid into the shop, taking a moment to adjust to the lighting. I planned to rely on the ambient light streaming through the windows of the shop to not draw attention. However, I'd been absent from the shop a few days and hoped someone hadn't moved a display a bit.

Turning the carrier in front of me, I continued a soft, nonsensical conversation with the cats. Flash, whether because she was female or just spoiled, ignored me. I moved cautiously down the aisle toward the front door, managing to avoid knocking anything over besides a stack of embroidered tea towels.

We'd almost reached the door when I slowed. The windows on either side of the door were long and narrow, with security wire crisscrossing them. Still, I could see a shadow in the window to the left, tall enough to be a human form.

"Trouble," I whispered. I eased the carrier to the floor, but the cats protested loudly.

"Hush!" I whispered.

The shadow moved slowly toward the door knob. I reached down to lift the carrier, but both cats slid to one end and I lost my balance. The cats yowled louder than before, their bodies moving in a panicked attempt to right themselves. I fell against a table, whacking my elbow. "Ow!" I yelped before I could stop myself.

The shadow jiggled the knob. "Sorrel?"

"Oh-oh!" I told the increasingly panicked cats. "Get ready for that hot water!"

I eased the carrier to the floor and reached until I could unlock the front door. Reed yanked it open, shined a flashlight into my face, and growled, "Don't you ever listen to anyone?"

I doubted he expected an answer, so I didn't give him one. Instead, I said, "Hurry up and help me get this heavy thing and these irritated cats out before we all blow up!"

"No danger in that now," a gruff voice answered.

Reed turned and asked, "Secure?"

"Yep! At least, they're working on it. Jose sent me to see if you two needed any help."

"Got it!" Reed answered, lifting the carrier and stepping onto the porch. "Sorrel, you take these noisy critters over to my house."

I followed him cautiously until we had cleared the building. Reed helped me settle them into the back of my Jeep. Then he led me to the driver's door and opened it.

"Reed, I can let the cats sit here for a bit. There are things—"

"Sorrel, if this thing blows up, there is nothing in there as precious as human life. The bomb squad will be here what's left of tonight and maybe a bit of tomorrow. Take these critters on and get them settled."

"But—"

He opened the driver's door, put his hands at my waist, and urged me inside. "You could help me most if you'd feed those mutts when you get to the house," he grumbled. "They're so spoiled now they think food only comes in a bag or can!" He reached over and fastened my seat belt.

I grabbed his hand. "Be careful, Reed."

"Always." He reached in his pocket and pulled out a key ring. "Here's the key to the house and this one is to the barn for the mutts. If you'll put the food in their kennel, they'll follow you in."

"Reed?" a deep voice called. "Can you come here?"

"Gotta go," he said.

"Stay safe!" I called, but I doubted he heard me. Still, I felt better for having said it.

"He will."

I squealed and jumped. The voice had come from the passenger side. I hadn't even noticed that the door had opened. "Will! Don't you know—"

He stepped in through the open door and settled into the passenger seat. "Reed said the team will meet at his place sometime later, so he wanted me to go along with you."

"Really! So now I'm some—"

"Someone who needs to catch a little sleep so she can light into me when I get there!"

I looked over my shoulder at yet another familiar voice. I squinted at the tall figure. "What—"

"We need to meet and discuss this latest development as well as our next options," Randell Byrd said. "You two try to catch a nap. I'll be there in the morning with doughnuts.

Will followed me as I took the shortcut to Reed's ranch. When we arrived, he offered to feed the dogs while I settled the cats in the guest room.

"Are you hungry?" I asked him when he came into the living room from the barn, carrying a sleeping bag and a bottle of water.

"No," he said. "I'm just tired. Reed said I could use this and sleep on the couch." He dropped it on the floor beside the couch and looked around. I pointed toward the bathroom. "Thanks. I hope you don't mind if I crash."

"Long day," I agreed. I glanced at the wall clock and gasped. "When did it become three o'clock?"

"While we were having fun," Will muttered.

Neither of us wasted time getting settled into our sleeping arrangements.

"I'll just lie here a bit," I told the cats. They complained until I'd finally let them out of their carrier, fed them a bite, and scrounged a cardboard box from the porch and filled it with sand for a temporary bathroom for them. "When Reed gets in, I'll check to see if we can go back home. So this is only a short stay. Think of it as a kitty hotel."

From their whining meows, they weren't happy about it. I could appreciate their upset, I thought as I changed into one of Reed's shirts that I'd found in his drawer. It only fell about halfway down my thighs, but it would do. I climbed into the narrow bed and wished I'd brought a book to read. The kitties snuggled against me, one on either side, and I warned them, "We're just here for a minute."

I continued telling them what we had found. Somewhere in the middle of the bomb discovery, they fell asleep. "I'll just rest my eyes," I whispered.

Chapter 41

Freshly brewed coffee awakens me faster than anything, especially when it is sitting on the small side table by my bed. I forced my eyelids open—my eyes feeling grainy and dry—and reached for the cup. It wasn't close enough. I sat up, pushed my hair out of my eyes, and squinted at the handsome sheriff's deputy watching from a rocking chair nearby.

"Chris Reed, you—"

"Enjoy watching you—anyone—getting some sleep! And sharing my coffee is a bonus!"

"How long—"

"Long enough to listen to your snoring . . . louder than these cats—almost!"

I wiped my eyes and focused on the two purring traitors perched on his lap. "Some watch-cats you two are!" I leaned over and picked up the steaming cup, blew on it first, then took a sip.

"Microwaved, so it's really hot," Chris warned.

"Did you sleep at all?" He still looked good, but his eyes looked tired.

"I caught an hour or two. Oh, by the way, a friend of yours from Houston said hello."

I raised my eyebrows. "I didn't see—"

"She replaced you at the station."

"Oh. What was she doing?"

"Besides trying to scoop everyone else? I'm not sure I approve of your friends, Sorrel."

"She's not—"

"No, she's definitely not! She's—"

A knock at the door interrupted what he'd planned to add. I glanced down and pulled the covers up, then Reed called, "Come!"

Will peeked around the corner. "Uh, Mr. Byrd has arrived."

"He's early!" I said. I looked at the wall clock. "It's—"

"Let's give Sorrel some privacy to get dressed," Reed interrupted. He rose and headed to the door. "I'll start breakfast."

"Don't bother," Will said, backing out. "Mr. Byrd brought it."

By the time I'd refilled the cats' bowls, climbed into my clothes, and combed most of the tangles out of my hair and bunched it into a semi-tidy ponytail, I could smell delicious odors drifting under the door. I grabbed my empty coffee cup and followed my nose.

Mr. Byrd, Reed, and Will were just finishing up. "Morning, Sorrel!" Mr. Byrd called. "I'm refilling my coffee cup. Do you want me to pour another for you?"

"Yes, sir, that would be great."

When I sat in front of the empty place setting, Reed grabbed my plate. "Scrambled eggs? Bacon? Tortilla?"

"Yes to all."

Reed filled the plate and placed it and the coffee before me. "Anyone else need any more."

The other two shook their heads.

"Then, Mr. Byrd, if you'd like to begin while Sorrel eats?"

Mr. Byrd set up an easel and placed an oversized tablet on it. "I thought if we brainstormed, we might see something that we're missing," he began. "The first thing that drew us into this tragedy was Brent's death, which drew heavy attention because he was Coach's son." He paused. "That sounded cold and I'm sorry. The death of any healthy youngster is a tragedy, but this one received more public reaction because of his father." He printed his comment on the tablet with a marker. "Anything one of you would like to add under Brent?"

"He was dumped out of a vehicle on the church lawn during a rainstorm," Will said. "Why there, specifically? Why not the football field or somewhere like that?"

Mr. Byrd listed the question and looked at me.

"Motivation?" I asked. "His most noteworthy asset was being Coach's son. He was a good student, apparently, and he liked Drama Club. He also volunteered at the senior nursing home and earned pocket money mowing yards. I'd call him wholesome, nice, but hardly the sort that would draw such media attention around the state."

Both Reed and Randall Byrd nodded in agreement.

I pushed away my cooling breakfast and took a swallow of coffee before finishing my thoughts. "His girlfriend—for wont of a better term—described a son who wanted to please his parents but was finding it a difficult job."

"It would be a challenge to be Coach's son," Mr. Byrd agreed. "Average seemed to describe him in every area in which his parents expected him to be excellent, while he excelled in the areas they didn't support. That's not a new scenario. In fact, it has been repeated countless times through the ages, and it doesn't often lead to murder."

"Tell that to Shakespeare," Will muttered.

Mr. Byrd shrugged. "You got me on that one," he said, adding the point he'd made. Then he flipped over the page and wrote Coach and his wife at the top. "What about these?"

Reed began. "Both murdered . . . either at the gym or dumped at the gym."

Will looked at him in surprise. "I thought the murders were conducted there."

"Maybe, Will. But they could have been moved there and the killer wanted us to think they were committed there." Reed spoke straight to Mr. Byrd. "The last scenario would be easier for the killer, of course. Coach would have had access to the gymnasium. It's located away from neighborhoods . . . almost out of town . . . and no one would have been there if you chose the right time. Of course, someone could have shown up unexpectedly . . . but maybe that increased the enjoyment for the killer."

"Coach habitually spent time in his office at the gym. Weird hours," Randall Byrd murmured. "It was quiet, he said, and he didn't have to deal with interruptions from the family or unexpected company." He glanced almost apologetically at us. "He didn't mean it to sound quite like it does, I'm sure. He was a single guy for many years longer than the rest of us, so this was a pattern he'd established long ago. Unfortunately, that widens the suspects as almost everyone would know that—especially anyone whom he'd coached."

"We also have two other points to consider," I spoke up. "I just met with the girl from the library . . . possibly Brent's sweetheart. She seemed intimidated by someone. I thought it might have been Coach, but he was already dead when I spoke to her last and she was still scared."

Mr. Byrd entered my point on the tablet. "I don't want to speak ill of a friend," he said, "but I'd like to enter the point about Brent's funeral."

"The fact that it seemed more like a political convention or something instead of an ordinary high school kid's funeral?" Will asked. "I hoped I wasn't alone on that one. I've never heard of an invitation only funeral except for national heroes or big politicians. A high school kid?" He shrugged incredulously.

Chris Reed spoke up. "The senior living home."

"Yes!" I said.

"What about it?" Mr. Byrd asked. "That hardly seems to—oh, Brent worked there."

"More than that," Reed said. "He spent a lot of time there and was popular with the staff, apparently. So why are they so jumpy?"

"The activities director seemed scared," I murmured. "But the residents all spoke well of Brent. The picture they painted of him was a polite young man who took the time to treat them with respect . . . almost friendship."

"You were assaulted in the bathroom," Reed reminded me, "although it seemed more a scare tactic than an assault."

"Speak for yourself," I mumbled. "Scare tactic or not, it was an assault! I was scared!"

Mr. Byrd added the last points Reed and I had made, then stepped back. "We have a full sheet here. Does anyone want to add anything else?"

"What about the media attention?" Will asked. "This place is buzzing."

Mr. Byrd didn't write it down. "It's news, Will. Here we have the son of a, well, almost legendary coach murdered. But that wouldn't have been enough to keep the media here . . . and I wonder if that may be part of the motivation of our killer—or killers—to commit the murders of the parents."

I decided not to share my next thought, but something just out of reach niggled at my mind. Then I heard a deep voice to my right speak my thoughts. "What if these killings weren't related? What if, instead, most of these are simply to confuse and distract us?"

"What do you mean?" Will asked.

"The first person murdered was the only son of a legendary—at least, in this area—football coach. That seemed to be the only reason for his murder. But what if it weren't?" I paused. "What if it was a distraction . . . or a warning?"

Mr. Byrd stared at Reed. "It would be big," he said. "Complex. Involving more than one killer . . . likely in high places."

"Why high places?" Will asked. "Maybe someone had a beef with the Coach and killed his kid. Or maybe some guys in town had a score of some sort to settle with the kid? Or it could always be a random act."

"High places because of the people here—the media attention," I told him. "Why is the media attention continuing? Even a well-known coach's kid's murder would be a short-term story. You wouldn't have stations as far away as Houston and Dallas—even a couple of people from Los Angeles—here. Even the "big" news shows are sniffing around." I made quotes with my fingers. "I noticed familiar faces."

"Not random," Reed shot back. "Say Coach was being blackmailed about something."

"And he didn't meet the blackmail demands," I whispered.

"There goes the 'confuse and distract' theory with that explanation." Randall Byrd stared at the ceiling for a bit, then turned to Reed. "But I don't buy random either. However, I do think it is connected with Coach himself—and I think I'd vote for the personal aspect. Maybe the person didn't mean to kill Coach at first. Or maybe he owed money . . . or crossed someone important . "

"Man!" Will whistled. "This sounds . . . huge!"

"And we still have no real idea about motivation," Reed murmured.

Chapter 42

Since everyone had different ideas concerning where to start next, we agreed to collaborate and chose our focus. Except for Reed, of course. After breakfast, he'd taken a quick shower, changed clothes, and returned to the crime scene—or wherever. He'd been understandably evasive.

So that left Randall Byrd, Will, and me. We'd gathered around the table. Mr. Byrd had jotted some notes for himself that he consulted before speaking to us.

"Media attention around Coach will only continue to be big," Mr. Byrd told Will. "You would be a good one for that aspect."

"I'd put Sorrel there," Will argued. "She worked much longer in that career . . . and most of the media are television, her area."

"What do you think, Sorrel?"

"I think Will continues to surprise me! Let me handle the media."

Mr. Byrd nodded. "I'd planned to send you to the Casa de Oro again, but that lead seems to have dried up."

"Maybe not," Will said. "I'm willing to check it out. Maybe I can get some of those old guys to drop some information they don't know they have."

"Go to the bathroom here before you leave," I warned.

Will grinned. "I won't comment on that one."

"Wise decision." Mr. Byrd consulted his notes again. "Something is strange there. I wouldn't have given them a second look until the aggression against Sorrel. It's still a weak lead in my mind, so don't plan to spend a long time. A casual comment might garner details we've not been given, but your focus—as far as they are concerned— is a human-interest story about a young man who had a big heart. Who knows what sorts of stories some of the residents—or employees—may share?"

"I wouldn't discount it, Mr. Byrd," I said. "Something *is* strange there. Whether or not it connects to this set of family murders or not isn't clear. But we shouldn't ignore the fact that one of our victims spent a great many hours volunteering there. What if he angered some family member?"

"I'd vote for something less aggressive," Will argued. "They're hungry for attention in these places. A neighbor of mine went to one. I needed a project for Scouts, so I went with a couple of other guys for two Saturdays and just listened to their stories."

Mr. Byrd nodded. "That wouldn't be a bad way to approach it now, Will. I'm afraid many of us, myself included, tend to view them as weaker minded and just wanting attention, as you said. When you look at them today, look at the intelligent, educated people they were . . . and may still be. They have more time to observe, and many may be sharp judges of character. Sorrel is popular with them as many contribute items for her store, and they may have forgotten her background as a crime reporter. But please remember to treat them with respect, Will."

Will nodded. "I—"

"Know you do. But I also know how desperate we are just now to get to the bottom of this horrific crime, which may make us more anxious." He looked into Will's eyes. "I trust you, Will. These people are family to me, so I can't be as unbiased as I know you can be."

I could see Will's shoulders square. At that moment, I could have hugged Mr. Byrd for his gentle intuitiveness.

"Sorrel?"

I could tell he had spoken my name at least twice. "The library?" I asked.

"Yes, I'd like for you to check there. The young lady seems to trust you. Even if she has nothing to add about this series of deaths, maybe she can give you more details about Brent that might help us. See if you can get her talking about his interaction with other students, athletes, even his parents. Was he bullied? Maybe he confided

220

something to her. But, as I said earlier, I'd also like you to mingle with the other news people, especially the television crews. See what you can pick up."

"Without giving anything." I smiled. "It has been a bit, but I haven't forgotten the drill."

Mr. Byrd gave a quick nod. "I'll handle the funeral visits and mingle with the various dignitaries who have flown in. They know I'm newspaper, and you'd think they wouldn't want me around. But as in everything, there are those who will use this tragedy to their own advantage if they can, promoting their private causes and rubbing shoulders with the politicians." He grinned. "I can rub shoulders with the best of them."

Almost as an afterthought, he said, "We're not in the business of solving this crime. We're in the business of sharing the crime with the public. It's a totally different thing. When people this well-known in a small community are murdered, the community wants to know why. But they also want to grieve in the way they know best, shared meals and shared stories. It's how we are best able to go on with our lives when the process is finished."

"Gruesome," Will mumbled.

"Not any more than those video games you guys are so immersed in," I told him.

"How about some of that music?" Mr. Byrd added.

Will rolled his eyes. "That's a whole different topic! And I'm taking off before you two remind me any further of my parents!" He turned away, then back. "Where and when do we meet up?"

"The paper, of course," Mr. Byrd said. "Whenever you get there. I'll have someone there to let you in."

Will nodded and hurried out to his car. Mr. Byrd stared after him. "I'm afraid to become attached to yet another young man."

"It's already too late, I think," I told him.

Chapter 43

Where to begin? Maybe with the mundane but necessary chores. I could take care of them quickly and then concentrate on Mr. Byrd's requests.

Everyone had left, but I doubted Reed had thought to feed the dogs. He did have an automatic feeder, but I decided a bit of canned food would make a more appealing start to the morning.

It proved a popular decision I decided a few minutes later while fending off dirty paws and dripping kisses. A person could do worse than begin the day that way: being greeted with love and joy.

After making sure their watering fountain wasn't clogged, I climbed into the Jeep and turned onto the shortcut to the store. My own critters would appreciate getting back to their home and I'd like to see if the latest shipment of framing materials had arrived and been stored appropriately.

I had my place in sight when my phone began playing the "William Tell Overture."

"Hello, Detective!"

"Do you still have me connected to that ridiculous tune?" he growled.

My giggle answered his question. "I've taken care of the dogs, and I'm pulling into my own place to check on things here. What's up?"

"Paperwork, politics, jockeying for positions, and everywhere reminders that I've lost a friend and don't know why!" He sighed. "What's on your radar?"

I pulled into the small circle drive in front of my living quarters and parked. "I've agreed to work for Mr. Byrd part of today, taking some photos to accompany Will's stories. You heard him tell me to look into the library's connection, but there's no real story there. I suppose I could do a feature, maybe review Brent's activities with the Drama Club. The other news sources here, Reed—I didn't say anything to him, but I have no influence on them. They'll broadcast whatever they want. But I didn't want to upset him just then."

"I know. We're all exhausted, grieving, angry, and any number of other things. I didn't want him sending you all off to . . . I don't know how to say it any other way . . . to interfere with us. This is a complicated crime already."

"What we can do," I answered, "is to keep our eyes and ears open. That's what I told Will, and I told him to call me or you if he encounters anything suspicious."

"I told him the same thing before I left. Processing a crime scene of this caliber, where we have three victims who are related but were killed—or died—in different places at different times—or at least it appears so—and complicated by political connections—it's a nightmare!"

I didn't answer. He didn't need one really, just someone to listen. When he'd come to the end of his rant, I told him as much.

"Are you saying I need a wife?" he asked.

"You don't have time for one of those," I laughed. "Besides, you have the dogs."

I could hear his chuckle and felt the tension lifting just a tiny bit as I stepped out of the Jeep. "I need to get my kitties out of the Jeep and out of the carrier," I told him. "Maybe lunch? Or a taco on the run?"

"I'll see but don't count on it. If it is possible, I'll call. And, Sorrel? Thanks."

I'd scarcely opened the door of the carrier when Flash bolted out, dashing to the bedroom. Van followed, although a bit slower. When I peeked in, both were settling on the bed, one up against my pillow at the top of the bed, the other on the coverlet at the bottom. Obviously, they'd had enough togetherness for a while, yet were wary of being alone. "I love you both, you know. Last night was for your own good, even if I do think Reed may have overreacted."

I dropped my bag, walked over to the bed, and stroked each of them, their purrs signaling their delight with being back home. "Welcome home to us!" I said, giving each another scratch behind their ears.

I made a cup of hot tea. Then I put fresh water in the cats' bowls. First Flash and then Van padded into the kitchen, drank, and looked up at me expectantly. I gave the cats a treat and a couple of extra pats, before assuring them that I was checking messages in the office and wouldn't be long.

Several customers were wandering through the store when I stepped through the door later. I smiled and spoke to Teri's cousin, Emma, before unlocking and entering the office. I could hear the front door tinkle with each opening, and I was thankful for Teri's assistance in staffing the store until she and I could focus on it.

Closely following the next tinkle came a thought I'd entertained recently. Hadn't I left the fast-paced world of television crime news to follow this dream? Records showed that my business had gotten an extraordinarily good start, but small businesses—even ones with good starts—were closing every day.

I settled down to work through the necessary paperwork for the shop. The first thing I noticed was the stack of mail on my desk. Then I saw a couple of phone messages, neither signaling that they needed to be returned immediately. Maybe I should handle mail first.

Glancing through the stack, I found most of it was advertising circulars and requests from local charities. I sorted the charity requests to consider later and tossed the circulars. Next, I pulled out the utility bills, wrote checks, sealed the envelopes, and dropped them in the mail bin to go out tomorrow.

"Oops! I didn't put stamps on them!" I scooped them back out of the bin and rummaged in the desk drawer until I found the stamps and put them on the bills. "Here you guys go again," I murmured. Then something weird caught my eye.

At the bottom of the bin was a handwritten letter. "That's strange," I murmured. "Where did this come from? And who writes letters anymore?" I looked for the return address, but there was no name or return address. I turned the envelope over, then back to the front. The stamp from the postal authorities noted that it had been mailed in Saddle Gap last year. The date had been stamped as well, but it was smudged. I squinted at the faded mark. The only thing I could clearly make out was the date and Saddle Gap.

"This can't be right," I murmured as I squinted at the faded mark.

"Oh, you found that!"

Teri's cousin Emma giggled when I jumped. "Sorry. I guess I'm quieter than usual. I just came in to get some change." She held up a large bill. I exchanged it for her and watched as she made change for a well-dressed man who held two of my Bosque photos. He spoke to her and she pointed to the office. Then he waved, pointed to the photos, and smiled!

I rose and stepped out. "Thank you for your business. I had such an exciting weekend shooting those photos!"

I didn't tell him that the whole weekend had been not only exciting but deadly and terrifying.

"My wife loves birds and these are gorgeous! It's our twentieth anniversary, so I wanted something unique and special. And I've found it!" He waved and hurried out.

"That makes my day brighter," I told Emma. "By the way, I found a strange letter in the incoming mail box." I held it up. "What do you make of this date?"

She squinted at it as I had done. "Oh, this is that letter I found in the box a couple of days ago. But I didn't notice this! It is dated over a year ago!" she said. "That can't be right! And look! It's so thin! Are you going to open it? Oh, there's the bell. I need to get back!" She darted out the door.

I sat and looked at the thin letter. The envelope was creased, as if it had been carried around for a long time. I picked it up to open it, but it had been slit across the bottom. Nothing remained inside. "Curious,"

I murmured. I turned it over and gasped. I had been so busy perusing the postmark that I'd ignored the address. Actually, it was lacking an address. It merely said, "Mr. Christopher Reed, Sheriff's Office, Saddle Gap, New Mexico."

Sometimes writing is clearly feminine or masculine, but I couldn't decide which this might be. But the strangest thing of all wasn't the address; it was the alteration. Someone had used a pen to slash through the address and printed instead "c/o Sorrel Janes, Saddle Gap, New Mexico."

I examined it carefully for any clue or sign that would help, but I could find nothing. The only conclusion I could reach was that someone had written a letter to Chris Reed and that they'd known to forward it to me. "Where have you been this past year?" I murmured.

"It hasn't been that long!"

"Christopher Reed! You scared me!"

He laughed before he reached out and took the letter. "Emma said I had a letter in here. But when I knocked, you ignored me and continued reading my mail!"

I gasped but his laughter drowned out anything I would have said.

"You are so easy to tease, Sorrel!" He turned the envelope over and over. "Mind if I take this with me?"

"Of course not. It's addressed to you."

"So you did notice!"

His laughter again covered my gasp. "Do you have anything I can put this in?"

"I have some plastic sandwich bags in the kitchen. Would that do?"

"Sure would. There's no reason to try to preserve prints. But it looks fragile. Mind if I come with you while you find the bag? Have something I'd like to have you consider."

He waited while I locked the office door and unlocked the connecting door, then followed me into the living quarters. "I'm not sure I like the sound of that," I threw back at him.

"You may not."

I turned to look into his solemn face.

"I think Coach had some serious secrets," he said.

Chapter 44

"So what do you think about our letter?"

Chris didn't immediately answer. Instead, he stared at the empty envelope a moment longer, then handed it to me.

"This doesn't seem anything more than strange," he finally said. "I wonder if it would be worthwhile to check with the postal service. Or maybe we should wait until after we get this mess solved here. I doubt it has any relation to our current situation. And this one demands our priority. We may never know what was in that envelope."

"It makes me curious, but I really don't have time for it just now either. Unless you want to keep it, I'll put it in a bag and store it in the file cabinet when I go back out to the shop."

"Sounds good to me. Sorrel, is it my imagination or is this the busiest day you've ever had here? Cars are everywhere out there."

"I think so. In fact, I was just—"

"Hold that thought!" Reed pulled out his phone. "Chris Reed here."

He paused and listened. "Are you sure? What channel?" He listened a bit more and then said, "Would you record that? I'd like to hear it. . . . Okay. Thanks, Jose." He punched the off button and looked at me. "You're never going to believe this!"

"What?"

"One of your television cronies has not only identified you as the former television anchor for her television station, but she also listed your current business."

"How could that be? I haven't talked with any of them yet. They were 'too busy.'"

"It seems that she called in to her station and during the transmission someone recognized the name of the place and eventually—"

"Figured it out."

"Great free publicity."

"You're right. Maybe that explains the packed parking lot."

Chris gathered me into a hug. "What do you want us to do?"

"Exactly what we're doing. It doesn't do anything more than give me more business."

"You'll need an extra helper in the shop for a bit. Want me to call Teri?"

I glanced around. "I have plenty of food and such. Maybe she could get one of her cousins to take care of the pets—just to see that they have plenty of food, etc. I'll pack an emergency bag in case I don't get home at night."

"You do that. I'll stay here and make the call, along with a couple of others."

Within a few minutes, I had a suitcase packed, checked to see I had plenty of supplies for the cats, and dug through the closet until I found the box where I'd stored a cheap cellphone. I'd kept it charged, just in case I needed it for anonymity. "It seems the time for anonymity has arrived," I muttered.

"It appears so."

I squealed as I whirled around. "Chris—"

"I see you've packed. Jose will be by to bring you something to wear."

"But—"

"You wouldn't happen to own a wig, would you?"

"Why ever—"

"Thankfully, Teri has enough aunts and cousins to fit every emergency. I'll tell you later."

Someone tapped on the connecting door from the store. I stepped toward it, but Chris motioned for me to go into the bedroom. I left it cracked enough to hear him say, "Hi, Emma. I was just about to come see you. Sorrel asked me to tell you that she has a family emergency and may be gone a day or two. She'll be keeping Teri informed about when she will return. She's packing now. Do you need help out here? Someone else will be arriving to help you."

I could hear Emma's exclamations and then the door finally closed.

I finished packing and then wrote out notes about the cat care. I'd just finished when Chris returned.

"Is everything all set?" I asked.

"It should be as long as you keep out of sight," he said. "Emma suggested she put signs up explaining that the shop will be open afternoons for a couple of weeks. You will be away on a photography shoot. She doesn't mind coming in a few minutes early to care for the cats. And she's already given Teri a 'heads up'."

"Sounds good to me."

"Good! Since your shoot starts tomorrow, I need your Jeep keys so I can load these things into it and take them to my place. Jose will meet me at my place and bring me back here after I've parked your Jeep in my barn. By then, it should be late enough that we can get you into my truck and out to the house."

The cats snuggled by me while I waited for the switch. I didn't mind that the news of my background had come out. Why the news team leader had brought it up wasn't clear. It—and I—were old news. A former celebrity held about as much interest as leftovers. In fact, this whole cloak and dagger thing seemed more ridiculous by the minute.

By the time Reed's truck pulled in front of the house, I threw open the door and stood on the step with my arms crossed. He glanced toward the shop.

"Everyone has gone—except me! And I'm staying!"

"Sorrel, just—"

"Don't come up here sweet talking me, Chris Reed! The longer I've thought about this, the sillier it seems. Why would it matter who I was? This is about Coach and his family, not a former television news anchor who decided to become a nature photographer. I appreciate the publicity for my photography, but I'm not hiding out unless I have a clear reason why it is necessary!"

"Well, I guess I'll have to go to plan B," he growled.

"What's—"

"This!" He scooped me up and threw me over his shoulder in a fireman's lift. "And if you kick and scream, it will only make me tired and you look silly." he growled.

He tossed me into the open passenger side of his truck, fastened the seatbelt, and pushed a hat into my hand. "Do something useful and cram that red hair into this thing while I lock up!"

He hurried around to the driver's side, hopped in, and backed out.

We'd traveled down the road—zoomed actually—for a few minutes before he said, "Well? You might as well spew all those thoughts out before your head explodes."

I took a deep breath and made myself speak as carefully and as calmly as I could manage, turning my face to look out the passenger side window as I spoke. "Some of us prefer rational behavior to cave man tactics."

Silence. I waited. And waited. When I saw the turn-off for Reed's place near, I heard a sigh.

"For some of us," he growled, almost biting each word, "only cave man tactics work." He pulled into the drive at his house. "Teri's waiting for you."

I stared straight ahead.

"Well?" he asked.

"I'm waiting for you to throw me over your shoulder again and haul me inside!" I snapped. "Saves my pretty feet."

I kept my arms crossed and continued to stare ahead. Reed climbed out of the truck and walked around to my side. I could see him from the corner of my eye, but I refused to look at him. He opened the door. I waited. I could hear his feet scrunching on the ground. Finally, I turned to see him squatting next to me. "Are you nuts? What in the world are you doing?"

"Looking at the pretty feet I'm going to break my back saving a second time!" he said. Before I could reply, he yanked me out of the truck and hoisted me over his shoulder a second time.

"You fool!" I muttered, laughter creeping into my voice. He strode toward his front door, his laughter echoing. I tried to hold out, but I joined him within seconds.

By the time he set me back on my feet in his kitchen, both of us were out of breath.

"You crazy fool!" I gasped before he kissed me.

Chapter 45

"I don't want to interrupt, but—"

We both jumped. "Mr. Byrd! I didn't . . . " I gasped but paused when I saw his face. Then I started again. "We—"

"Think people have decided Sorrel and I are officially a couple, as you suggested," Reed finished. I glared at him, then looked at Mr. Byrd.

Randall Byrd simply gestured toward the table and sat in the chair at one end. "I made a pot of coffee," he said. "Join me while I brief you."

Reed gently urged me toward a chair. "Coffee, Sorrel?" he asked. I nodded and he moved toward the counter.

My first thought, after I'd slid into the nearest chair opposite Mr. Byrd, was that he'd make a joke or comment on our obvious discomfort. But at a closer look, I erased that thought. Randall Byrd wasn't pretending to ignore our situation; he hadn't even noticed. Besides dark smudges beneath his eyes, his face had new lines etched on either side of his mouth. And he hadn't relaxed against the chair back. Instead, he leaned his elbows on the table, reached inside his jacket pocket, and pulled out his cell phone and a small notebook.

Reed sat beside me and took a long gulp from his cup while we waited for Mr. Byrd to begin. Finally, when I'd decided to break the silence with a question—or anything—Mr. Byrd reached for his cup, took a long drink, and cleared his throat. "We have a situation here."

Reed's phone buzzed. He pulled it out of his pocket and looked at the number. "Excuse me. I have to take this."

He rose and stepped toward the outside door. "Reed . . . Yes, I can talk."

Mr. Byrd waited until Reed had closed the door. Then he turned toward me with an apologetic look. "This is a real mess, Sorrel," he said. He reached for his cup again, and I noticed a slight tremor. He raised the cup to his lips, but he didn't drink. Instead, he put it back on the table and stared down into the cup. "Sometimes you think you've seen everything and then—"

"I'm here!" Teri announced as she came through the kitchen door. "What's the emergency? Chris and Jose have left. Chris said for you to not worry, Sorrel. Here's a wig I wore one Halloween, but I have no idea why you'd need it. He said he was in a hurry and didn't have time to explain. So I brought it. Sorry, but it's the best I could do with short notice. Have—"

"Teri, why don't you get coffee if you want it?" Mr. Byrd didn't even realize he had interrupted her. "I don't know what you know," he continued, "but I was just about to brief Sorrel, and you can add anything you want."

"No coffee, thank you, Mr. Byrd." Teri sank down into a chair on my left. Both of us looked at him. He didn't speak immediately. I could see the inner conflict only in the way he gripped his hands together. Finally, he cleared his voice and began to speak softly, staring down at his clenched hands.

"I've been given permission to speak in confidence with the two of you, which is totally against protocol on an ongoing investigation. But I'm not law enforcement. If anyone asks you, you know nothing. Am I clear?" He stared at each of us, almost fierce in his demeanor.

"We will never reveal our source," Teri promised. "But don't tell us something that could get you in trouble, sir!" She glanced sideways at me. "Jose tells me everything. He tries not to, but I get it out of him. I'll ask him."

"If that is how you want to play this," he sighed. "Sorrel, I'd like for you to head down to the police station with me. I'd appreciate your help with writing the articles about who murdered Coach and his family—and why."

"Wait!" Teri pushed back her chair so hard I thought she might fall backwards. "I thought you were talking about . . . well, Coach's funeral stuff or something. Murder! They were all murdered?" Tears had already run down her cheeks, and she brushed at them with shaking hands. "How? Why?"

Mr. Byrd interrupted her gently. "It's complicated, Teri. I can't go into it now, and I'm sorry for being so abrupt."

I reached over and gathered her into a hug. Mr. Byrd handed her a big, soft handkerchief. When she seemed calmer, he began. "We'll take you by your house—"

"No," she interrupted, blowing her nose into the handkerchief. "I can drive. The kids are at Mom's, and she expects me shortly anyway." She gave me a wobbly smile.

"How about letting Sorrel drive your van to your mom's," Mr. Byrd said. "I'll follow and take Sorrel with me."

"But—"

"No argument, Teri," he said. "It works out better for us anyway. Sorrel has been identified by a newswoman who seems determined to snoop. This just might be what we need to evade this woman!"

Teri sat quietly during out drive, and I didn't interrupt until we pulled into her mother's driveway.

"We're here," I told her when she didn't move. She glanced about in surprise, then reached for the handle.

We both climbed out of the van and headed toward Mr. Byrd's car as he pulled in behind us.

Teri gave me a hug when I reached for the door handle to Mr. Byrd's car. She stepped back to let me close the door, then grabbed the door and leaned into the car. "Wait! You said murder, Mr. Byrd."

"I guess I can be overly dramatic sometimes too," he said. "I meant to say 'deaths.' I guess this has flustered me too."

Teri gave me another hug and closed the door behind her before walking up the driveway where her mother waited at the door.

As he started the car, I said, "Now, how about you tell me the real story?"

He backed out of Teri's mother's driveway and turned down the street. "I still need to tie up some loose ends," he finally said when we'd stopped at the stoplight on Main. "Coach was involved in something that most likely caused his son's murder as well as that of his wife and himself. I don't have all of the details, but I know enough to suspect that this also involves others."

"Why would he involve his wife and child?" I exclaimed. "You can't be right!""

"He didn't involve them as such. At least, I don't think they knew about it. They were likely collateral damage."

He started through the intersection.

"Was it some sort of gambling scheme?" I asked.

He glanced at me quickly. "Why would you ask that?"

"Well, he was a topnotch coach and his teams consistently won their games."

Mr. Byrd drove in silence for a moment. "No," he finally said. "I think it is even more sinister than murders connected to gambling losses." He fell silent again. Then dropping his voice almost to a whisper said, "I never would have thought it."

Chapter 46

Mr. Byrd turned the car in the opposite direction of the station. "I thought we were heading to the police station," I said. "Are we dropping by for someone else?"

"I just said that for Teri's benefit," he said. "I have all of the information I need for the obituaries. But with the snoopy reporters here, I thought I'd take precautions. Haven't you ever been on the back route to Chris's place?"

"I don't think so."

As we rode, Mr. Byrd reminisced about Coach and football. He was a compelling storyteller, and I was soon caught up in the tales. When the car stopped, I asked, "Is anything wrong?"

He smiled. "We're here!"

I looked around. We had parked in front of Reed's house, but the dogs hadn't greeted us. "So we are. I hadn't even—"

When I saw his face, I didn't finish the sentence. "Hop out!" he said. "Chris is inside. I'll park in a less obvious spot."

I climbed out and he pulled out toward the barn. I made my way carefully to the porch.

"We've got visitors inside," someone whispered.

I jumped. "Chris Reed! You—"

"Ssh. I said we have visitors . . . company . . . in the house. So keep it down."

"What kind of visitors?"

"People whom we can trust to help figure out what really happened in that gym."

"Surely—"

"I've already reminded them that you are an investigative reporter with discretion."

"And your superiors—"

"Have been promised that your confidentiality is guaranteed," Randall Byrd murmured.

I jumped. "This cloak and dagger stuff—"

"Is more than just for effect." Reed opened the door, put his hand on my elbow, and guided me inside.

The first people I saw were a couple of police officers. They eyed me suspiciously, I thought, as they officially swore me, then Randall Byrd, to confidentiality. Chris guided us to a corner of the room near the kitchen.

It was a small gathering: a few locals and some dignified strangers. Mr. Byrd joined us shortly. "Quite an impressive task force," he whispered, eyeing the strangers.

"Task force? Why me?" I whispered. No one answered. Either I'd not spoken aloud, or they were too preoccupied with the business at hand to answer. My knowledge of task forces was minimal at best. It was time to listen and ask questions later.

A gentleman whom everyone seemed to know—and I later was introduced to—began with a short mention of the family who had passed so violently. The press—with a stern glare at both Mr. Byrd and me—was reminded once again that we would be given releases when they could be shared. He reminded everyone of the ramifications of sharing false information. We would be given information on a "need to know" basis.

I caught Mr. Byrd's eye and leaned over to whisper. "Why are we here?"

"I have a problem with a member of the press here," a loud voice boomed. I followed it to a vaguely familiar face, but I couldn't remember where I'd seen him. People close by turned their heads in Randall Byrd's and my direction.

"We can step outside," Mr. Byrd offered. "I—"

"Wait!" A well-dressed gentleman raised his arms and his voice. "I can explain that." He raised a badge. "I'm FBI. We need these familiar faces to help with this investigation."

"Don't we have enough law enforcement?" a big guy called.

"Certainly. But this is a small, insular community. People aren't as likely to open up to a group of strangers. Ms. Janes, here, operates a shop that handles many items the townspeople make. They know and trust her. The sheriff's deputy has grown up in this town and was a former athlete. He has a close connection to the coach and his family. And the newspaper editor is equally respected. Many residents won't trust a group of strangers like they'll trust these people."

Several people offered their own opinions. Many sent suspicious looks in our direction as they spit out "the press" as if it caused a bad taste in their mouths. It wasn't anything I'd not been subjected to before, and Randall Byrd had been in the business much longer than I.

Finally, a dignified man whom I later learned was the state police chief held up his hand. "I need to explain some things and then we need to disband. So please give me your attention." The shuffling stopped and the grumbling dropped to a whisper or two.

"This meeting is a bit unorthodox, I realize, but due to the isolation of the area, it seemed appropriate. First, we do not have official cause of death; the three deaths have been recently re-classified as suspicious. Therefore, there will be no announcement at the memorial services tomorrow. The bodies have already been transported to Santa Fe for autopsies, and cremation—which apparently is what the parents wished—will follow.

"Secondly, we ask that you refrain from passing speculation and gossip out of respect for the families and community. However, should you have information which you think might aid in solving these murders, please contact your local law enforcement."

He gave Mr. Byrd and me a longer look than necessary before adding, "Only official news releases will be published," he continued, "and they will be issued to news sources only when it is appropriate.

This meeting or the attendees will be forgotten completely when we leave this residence."

He nodded toward the row of state policemen whom I'd not noticed. They were standing along the back wall of the crowded living room. "Please hold everyone here until our dignified guests have departed," he told them

As he began to weave through the group, several called out questions: "Is it safe here?" "Who do you think is involved?" "Have you arrested anyone—at least a person of interest?" He appeared not to hear any of them. They waited until he'd closed the door before they began chatting. The policemen stepped forward and organized them into a line out the door.

While Mr. Byrd stood near the police line and nodded to people, Chris pulled me quietly out of sight and guided me into the tiny pantry off the kitchen.

"Wha—"

"Ssh!" he whispered. "Maybe we can avoid people and their barrage of questions. Mr. Byrd will say we left out the back door."

We waited as we listened to people walking out.

Finally, Reed pulled away and put his ear to the door.

"This is a nightmare," he whispered. "Coach . . ." Then he sort of sighed and leaned his forehead against mine.

I held him until I felt him relax a bit.

"I'm thinking everyone is out," I whispered. At that moment, we heard a tap on the door.

"All clear."

Reed opened the door and peeked out. "You first," he said.

Randall Byrd had extinguished all the lights except in the kitchen, then led us to the living room. "They're gone. I checked. I told them you two had left first to go to another call."

With only a pale light shining through the kitchen door, it felt almost ghostly. I shivered.

"Cold?" Reed asked.

"No." Then I remembered something I'd been waiting to ask. "Mr. Byrd, you said murdered, but tonight everyone kept saying the results weren't in."

The two men exchanged looks. Reed finally looked at me. "Strictly confidential, Sorrel. The boy was killed as you know. But Coach and his wife—they died of bullet wounds to the head. That's all we know now."

"Oh my!"

"Right," Mr. Byrd whispered. "Murder, murder . . . or murder–suicide."

"Why the natural causes that was being passed around only recently?"

Reed sighed. "Some thought that might stop the constant chatter. The announcement actually only said that their deaths were being considered natural causes until further investigation. People added their own interpretations . . . as people do."

Will came into the room, his face still lit up from the excitement. "Wow! That was a real distinguished group!"

"Will! I didn't know you were here!"

He grinned. "Neither did they. Since I'm just a cub reporter, I was kept out of sight in case they decided to clam up."

"But how—"

Randall Byrd reached up under his collar and removed a tiny, wireless microphone. "Please forget you saw this, else no one will ever trust me again."

Chapter 47

"Any coffee left?" Mr. Byrd asked. "It's going to be a long night."

I mentally agreed with that statement several times as the hours stretched to dawn. We had sifted through crime scene photos, reports, interviews, and other evidence searching for any small thing that may have been overlooked.

By 2:00 am, only Reed, Randall Byrd, and I remained. I began cleaning up the clutter, listening idly to the discussion.

Randall Byrd finally excused himself at 4:00 am to prepare for the eulogy he would be giving later that morning. Chris followed him out to his car as he wanted to follow Mr. Byrd back to the main road.

"I'm just going to rest my eyes here on the couch," I told Chris. I vaguely remember being covered with a blanket.

"Coffee?"

"When I wake up," I answered.

I heard a chuckle. I squinted, moved the hair from my eyes, and peered up at blue eyes that should have looked must less tired. "It's not morning yet."

"Good morning. And yes, it is morning. Ask the critters who are hollering outside . . . while you've been snoring."

"If you sing that stupid sunshine song—"

He pulled back the quilt and pulled me into a sitting position. "There's a cup for you in the kitchen."

"I need to shower first."

"Follow your nose to food after your shower," he said. "Towel's out for you. I'm heading out to feed critters."

"How can anyone be so cheerful this early when they didn't sleep?" I muttered.

I still didn't have an answer as I turned my face into the warm shower, but it ceased to irritate me—especially with the aroma of strong coffee drifting into the bathroom from the kitchen.

I finished showering, blew my hair dry, wrapped myself in Reed's oversized terrycloth robe, and padded into the kitchen.

"Breakfast on the stove," Chris greeted me, his nose buried in a sheaf of papers. "Coffee on the counter."

I grunted and headed in that direction. "What breakfast? This?" I squinted at the stove.

"Yep! I got even less sleep than you. Did you want me to set the house on fire frying bacon?"

He was right, of course, so I grunted again and poured a cup of strong coffee, decided against watering it down with water or milk, then grabbed a cooling bun with bacon and a thin square of pretend eggs. The cheese stuff squirted out at first bite.

"Watch the cheese stuff," he said, his eyes glued to a document.

I silently chewed and sipped coffee until he looked up and set the paper aside. "What?"

"Just waiting for the daily itinerary. You mentioned a memorial last night."

"Yeah. Randall Byrd is speaking at a memorial in the gym at ten. Nothing formal. I don't know if something more formal will be planned later."

"I see. I wondered. It was just too quick. Then what?"

"Then we locals are off the case—at least, we'll help if needed, but we're not in charge."

"And the task force?"

"Off the radar. We'll be eyes and noses locally."

We drank our coffee and ate the food. Finally, I asked, "What do you think? Honestly."

Reed stared into his cup a long time. "I think the gym and the nursing home—totally unlikely partners—are suspicious."

"They've both been prodded and probed. Don't forget the church. Why was his body dumped there? And the library? Why did the girl start off friendly and then run every time I approached? None of it connects, Reed. There are no real—"

"Except Coach . . . or his son. We're missing something. And it's right here in our faces."

I opened my mouth, only to hear a bellow from the barn. Chris smiled tiredly.

"Speaking of faces, I need to shave mine. You and I need to be at this thing today, watching faces and noting anything that seems odd or out of place."

"Is it formal? If it is, I'll need to go by my place."

"Like do you need to wear all that stuff—"

"Just be clean then," I said as I rose and headed to the guest bedroom.

"Be comfortable, Sorrel," he called. "It's in a gym, remember?"

Chapter 48

I asked Chris to stop by the shop on our way to the memorial service. Even though he reminded me that it was in a gymnasium and that people would likely be casual, I could hear my mother's voice imprinted in my memory: *There are a few times you should remember how to dress, Sorrel. Events like graduations, weddings, and funerals are the most important. A dress is still—in my mind—best for a lady. But if you insist on pants, at least don't wear jeans! Promise me!*

"I promised."

"What?"

"Sorry, Reed. I was talking to myself."

He grunted. "What were you telling yourself to be sorry about?"

When I explained, he grinned.

I made quick work of getting ready while Reed gave the cats some food to eat. When I came out, he whistled. "So I can thank your mom for my glimpses of your legs?"

I started to answer and then just sniffed.

We were quiet on the way to town, each in our own thoughts. I kept searching through the past few days, trying to find something I'd missed or forgotten. I glanced at Reed as we turned onto Main Street. "It's a pretty day," I murmured, looking at the blue sky.

"For a funeral service? Is there any such thing?"

"I'm sorry, Reed. Of course not."

"Jose was closest to Coach," he said. "But it is more than sad to me. It's hideous! Anyone who will wipe out an entire family is not only evil but a monster! I keep thinking we are looking right at the source of this hideous crime but not seeing it. I'm frustrated!"

"You're right, there. We're going around in circles. When I was standing in the shower, I tried to think of every clue, every interview, every discussion among ourselves—and I'm as confused as I was at the beginning."

He slowed and I realized we were already turning into the parking lot at the gym. "Just keep your ears open and your nose into everyone's conversations. Since you can't be overlooked, especially with that hair, try at least to be innocuous."

I grimaced. "The old fly-on-the-wall thing."

He laughed. "Impossible!" He parked in a spot reserved for official use and came around to open my door. "Be careful!" he whispered. "This person may be hiding in plain sight."

Teri waved and pointed to the spot on the bleachers that she'd saved for me. "Here goes the fly!" I whispered to Reed and began the journey of weaving through people toward Teri. She had a good spot. The fourth row up, near the back exit doors, facing the speaker's platform. Should I need to leave quickly, I could hop off the side onto the gym floor without climbing over people.

"Jose said this would be a good spot if we needed to escape," she whispered when I'd settled. She looked at my simple navy dress, belted at the waist above a full skirt. "Your mama too, huh?" she asked. She looked down at her own loose black dress. "I still haven't lost all the baby fat!"

"You look great, as always," I assured her, my eyes scanning the seats around us as I spoke. "I like the scarf at the neck. It looks—"

"Like a distraction? If they're looking there, they'll miss the little roll below." She smiled at an acquaintance who called out her name. "You'd think this was just a reunion."

"I guess funerals or memorial services are just that. A farewell to someone you will miss."

"Or a 'Whew! Not me this time!'" a deep voice added.

I jumped and turned toward the owner, just behind my right shoulder. "If you're going to eavesdrop, Will, at least have the courtesy not to do so at a time like this!"

"Then whisper and I won't be tempted."

Teri covered a smile. "Even Coach would have laughed," she said defensively when I frowned at him.

A line of distinguished men had begun lining up onstage, and a hush slowly descended upon the crowd. While we'd been talking, several students in their band uniforms had seated themselves against the back wall. A balding man with a noticeable paunch stood and walked up to the microphone. "Please rise as we pledge the flag and remain standing for the singing of the National Anthem and the school song," he said.

"The principal," Teri whispered and spelled his name for Will. I hadn't noticed his pad and pen. He also had his phone out to record the service.

When we sat again, the principal read the statistical information: Coach's birth and death dates, his educational background, his awards, his years of service, and his marriage and the birth of his son. He briefly gave the wife's and son's entrance and exit dates as well and sat down.

"Wouldn't want to lose focus on who's important," Will whispered.

"Ssh!" I hissed. But inwardly, I agreed with him.

The hour that followed featured several speakers: ex-players who now held seats in the state legislature, presidents of banks and other corporations, heads of various state charities, and the city's mayor. I'd nudged Will a couple of times to shush his whispered commentary, once just as the young priest approached the podium.

"I did not know this family well," he began, "as I am new to this community. When asked to speak today, I visited with people who did . . . and I am sad to have missed that opportunity." Then he continued to recount stories he'd been told about the countless charities Ms. Coach had helped, about the years Brent had volunteered at the senior home, and about how much they loved and missed him. He ended by acknowledging the places this family's deaths would leave in

247

the community. "I am sure there are many of you here who will step up to fill those places," he concluded.

The final speaker was Randall Byrd. He could not erase all emotion from his face, and the crowd grew quiet as he struggled with his own composure for a moment, staring down at his hands. At length, he lifted his head.

"I have loved Coach . . . and Mrs. Coach (a light chuckle came from the crowd) . . . and their son Brent as my own family. This is a huge loss. Mrs. Byrd and I would have expected them to be speaking at our memorials instead of—." He wrestled a moment, regained his composure, and continued, recounting stories about all three people who had been a family and were now only a memory.

"Look around you," he said at last, "and you will see Coach's legacy. He was much loved by so many. We will all miss him and his beautiful wife for who they were . . . and their son for whom he would become."

As he walked back to his seat, the band members rose and the football players gathered in a single line across the gym. I hadn't noticed until then that they were in uniform. Each removed his helmet and held it to his chest as the band played the school fight song. They remained there as the principal told the crowd that the burial would be private and thanked them for their attendance and dismissed everyone.

"Impressive!" Will breathed behind me. "By the way, someone has been signaling to you, I think."

He jerked his head toward our left and up to the top of the bleachers. I saw her, her eyes red, her face pale. When she saw my eyes turned to her, she glanced toward her hand. I did too. She had made a "D" shape with her fingers. I nodded only slightly, and she repeated the gesture. Then we both turned away.

"Mind if I catch a ride with you, Will?" I asked. "I rode with Reed and he looks sort of busy."

"It's your life," Will muttered.

"Are you sure?" Teri asked.

"Pray for us," I whispered.

"I've seen him drive," she said. Then she wiped her eyes again. "I need to mingle."

"Me too," I whispered. "But I'll take Will away from your route." I gave her a hug. "I'm so sorry, Teri."

She simply nodded.

"These things make me nervous," Will mumbled when I joined him. "I'm kinda glad you agreed to go with me."

We'll see if you still feel that way later, I thought.

Chapter 49

While Will kept a running commentary on the Big Shots (his nickname for the out-of-town attendees who held prestigious state positions or big jobs), I focused on the best way to approach my nervous friend from the library. I'd devised a way to dump Will by the time we pulled up.

But I'd wasted my time. Before either of us could open a door, Sara hurried to the car and hopped in the backseat.

"Could we go somewhere less public?" she asked.

"Sure! Hang onto your hats, ladies!" In only moments, we had backed out and were holding our breaths as Will zoomed down the street, turned into a residential area I'd not seen, and executed an elaborate series of turns down one street after another. I gasped when a small dog trotting along the sidewalk without a leash looked our way.

"Don't worry, Sorrel! I see him."

But, does he see you? I thought. Now I understood Reed's grin when I'd opted to ride with Will. What had I been thinking?

Moments later, Will careened down a side street and pulled up alongside a small house that looked vacant. "This should be okay," he said as he moved his gearshift to Park. "I'll leave the car running, in case we need to leave quickly."

"Great," I said. "The neighbors will think we're—"

"Casing the joint?" Will grinned. "I'll keep my eyes peeled. If I say 'duck,' I don't mean the bird!"

I opened my mouth, but a small giggle came from the back seat. Will caught my eye and winked. He'd been purposely distracting our nervous passenger . . . and it had worked! He reached in his pocket and pulled out a lollipop. He offered one to each of us and, when we refused, grinned. "Good thing! These are my last." Another giggle brought another wink my way.

I glanced around us but saw no one, so I quickly opened the door and slid into the back seat beside her. Her hands were balled up, a tattered tissue inside one. I reached over and squeezed her hands lightly. "Whatever you say will be kept confidential—unless it's a crime. Then I'll have to report it to Detective Reed. But my news sources are considered confidential, and I don't have to reveal them."

She looked at Will, who made a show of putting in earbuds and plugging them into the car radio.

Sara gave a nervous laugh, looked over at me, and blurted out, "I'm pregnant and my dad is going to kill me."

I squeezed her hand again. "He may be upset, but I doubt he'll kill you," I said. "And the father is?" I asked, although I knew, as well as answers to several other puzzling questions.

"Brent," she whispered. Then she burst into tears—great, heavy tears that created snuffling sounds she attempted to cover with her hand before leaning down and wiping with the tail of her blouse. Finally, she swallowed and tried to pull herself together. "Now my mom is telling me to go to my aunt's in Texas until the baby is born and give it away," she whispered. Then she put her face in her lap, bumping Will's seat.

He glanced back, then pulled a handkerchief from his pocket and handed it over to me. I put it into her hand.

"Wipe your nose and face with this," I said. "I'm so sorry, but you have a while to think about this decision. Don't do anything before you get some good advice."

"We were going to marry," she mumbled behind the handkerchief. Finally, she blew her nose and wadded the handkerchief in her fist.

No one spoke. She stared down at her hand and words gushed out. "We were going over to Mexico and get married . . . elope. They have places there where you can do it. He said he had a quick meeting with someone and he'd pick me up at the Quick Stop over near the church. So I drove there and waited but then he didn't come. I was about to leave when I saw this pick-up truck pass by. I couldn't be sure—it was raining hard—but I thought I saw him between two guys."

My heart raced. "Did you recognize them?"

"No. The driver had a hat on—one of those black ones with a big bill in front—and the other one looked pretty overweight. I think his head was shaved. They both looked, you know, older and tough. It was quick and I only saw that much because of the lights as they passed the store. When they turned at the road that goes to the church, I started my car and took after them."

"Did they see you?"

"I don't think so. It was a dumb thing to do, I guess, but I was only thinking of Brent. The rain got even harder and I could hardly see the road even with the wipers. Their taillights were growing smaller as they drove so fast. Something jumped out and I swerved to miss it and almost got stuck in the mud on the side of the road. By the time I looked again, the lights were gone."

Will asked. "Can you show me where the store is? We could go there and sort of look at the area. It might help you remember."

"I doubt it," she said. "But it would be okay." Then she drew a big breath and said, "I must look awful. But what if one of those guys lives on that road and sees or recognizes me?"

"I doubt it," Will said. "It was dark and rainy and they had other things on their minds. And speaking of that, Sorrel, I might need help finding my way around."

"I might not be much help," I said. "But I'll try."

I got back out and climbed into the front passenger seat again. "This way I can maybe help Will look as he drives," I explained over my shoulder. "Do you have a comb? You can tidy your face and hair while we drive."

That seemed to divert her for a moment. The sniffles slowed and gradually died.

When we arrived at the store, Will hopped out, strolled inside, and pulled three bottles of cold water from the cooler. He made idle conversation with the checker, but he wasn't getting answers. In fact, the checker, an older guy who looked like he was of Mexican descent, kept his eyes down as he stuffed the water in a bag and made change for Will. As Will turned to leave, the man glanced over his shoulder and said something, his hands busily tidying up the register area.

Will handed out bottled water as soon as he sat down then started the car and quickly drove back in the direction we'd traveled.

"What did he say?"

He glanced over his shoulder. "He didn't say much. He didn't remember any customers that evening because the rain was so bad. In fact, he locked the door and worked in the back with stocking supplies until the rain stopped." He shrugged. "Like I believe him! I'll bet he not only knows those guys but is either afraid to say anything or has been paid for his silence. My dad always says when people can't look you in the eye… "

He slowed, turned onto a side street that ran behind the store, and headed back in the direction we'd just come. "Figured I'd try to divert his suspicion," he explained. "We'll travel through the subdivision before turning back onto the main road."

When we drove past the church on the right, I noticed Reed's truck there. Will opened his mouth to say something, but I interrupted by turning toward the back seat. "Do you have a new plan for this baby?" I asked her.

"Kind of," she said. "I called my aunt in Las Cruces, and she wants me to go there. I can attend the state university and she will watch the baby. I've saved my salary from the library, and I have good enough grades to get a scholarship or a loan."

"That sounds like a sensible plan," Will said. "Did Coach or his wife have any input in this?"

"No. I was afraid to say anything after Brent was murdered. He hadn't told them yet. His dad was really controlling, and Brent said he

253

could never please him. I mean, Brent hated football. He loved drama and literature. His dad was disappointed in him since he wasn't a very good player, so he was grounded a lot. He sneaked out for Drama Club until they caught him."

"What happened?" I asked.

"He wouldn't tell it all to me. He was crying." She wrung her hands. "I promised not to tell."

"Well," Will interrupted, "since both he and his parents are dead, maybe it's time to tell. Maybe it will help to find out what happened. And your child may be entitled to money from them."

She wiped her eyes and nose again. "Brent had discovered something to do with his job at the senior center. He said he'd discovered a crime there and he wasn't letting anyone make him 'shut up.' He loved those people; and even though he didn't really get paid—it was volunteer—he worked hard and never missed. He didn't have any grandparents living, so he said they felt like they were taking that place for him."

She kept folding the damp handkerchief, and I noticed her hands trembling. "He'd found something out and he was angry," she continued. "He told his dad he was going to speak to the police. His dad told him to pack a bag and get out."

"When was that?" I asked.

"The night before he died," she whispered. "I begged him to not go home. I had pulled out enough money and he had some he'd been saving. We could just go to Mexico then instead of waiting until after graduation. But he wouldn't. He said he wanted to tell his mom and he wanted to get the money he'd been saving. That's the last time I spoke to him."

She broke into sobs. "I don't know what to do!" she finally said.

"Tell your parents that you aren't giving up your baby," I suggested. "Sometimes they react differently from what you expect. Explain your plans. They're upset that their plans for you have been changed, but I think they may change their minds now that you have a sensible plan of your own."

"Do you think so?"

"Yes. You're going to be a parent, and you need to make wise choices . . . just like they've made for you. You need to trust them— and yourself. Amid this sorrow, you have a great joy coming."

For the first time, I saw a small smile.

"Guess we need to take you back to your car," Will announced.

When I hugged her goodbye, I reminded Sara that she could talk any time she needed it.

"Please find out who did this to my Brent," she whispered. "Once he said Coach yelled at his mom that he didn't think Brent was his son."

As we drove away, Will glanced over at me. "You were great! But I'm at a dead end on this case."

I pulled out my phone. "I think we need to go back to the senior center. Let me give Reed a call first."

"That's a dead horse," Will groused, flipping his left turn blinker.

I didn't respond, my mind already working on a plan.

Chapter 50

"I think you're wasting your time!" Will said, reaching for one of my French fries and swallowing it without chewing. "We've been over there at that senior home and found nothing." He looked over at Reed for support. We'd met up at the truck stop located a few miles down the Interstate, hoping to avoid curious townspeople. When Reed called to tell us he'd be late, Will and I had ordered food for all of us. It arrived at the same time as Reed.

"What do you think, Reed?" Will asked.

"I agree with Sorrel," Reed said. He bit into his steak sandwich, chewed, and swallowed. "Brent had volunteered there for a long time and had a good relationship with the residents. Everyone I've spoken to, whether employees or residents, speak fondly of him. But I think you two shouldn't go on your own. After Sorrel's misadventure in the ladies' room, we can only conclude that someone isn't happy with the snooping. I'd go but from what you just learned this morning, I need to follow up that lead. The sighting of Brent that your witness described . . . it sounds like the Hombres del Diablo gang. Chatter from the gang units in Albuquerque and Las Cruces mentions an expansion and recruiting drive for them."

"You don't think he joined them?" I interrupted. I'd reached for my hamburger, but I'd lost my appetite for it. I put it back on my plate and pushed the whole thing over to Will, who immediately moved it in front of himself and gave me his empty plate.

"No, Sorrel, I don't think he joined them. But I suspect he may have been targeted to use as leverage—"

"Or blackmail." At least, that's what I thought Will said around another French fry that he'd stuffed in his mouth.

"Maybe, but doubtful. Blackmail is more sophisticated—and certainly risky. These gangs tend to intimidate their prey with violence. Plus, they're usually dealing with teens who wouldn't have big money. They want activity, not traceable cash."

"Do you think they threatened Coach?" I asked.

"Maybe. But I'd think they were more likely to threaten a weaker prey . . . possibly a woman. You know, they choose women because they're vulnerable."

"So what if they chose his—"

"Mother," Will suggested between bites.

"Or his girlfriend," I murmured. "They were being sneaky—they thought."

"In this little town?" Will rolled his eyes.

"In any town," Reed corrected him.

"The residents of the senior center! They are not only mostly women, but their age lends even more vulnerability." I could see all sorts of possibilities. "Or maybe even—"

"If you two keep finishing each other's sentences, I'm going to hear wedding bells." Will hummed the wedding march until Reed's glare stopped him.

Both men seemed to remember their food at that moment and reached an unspoken agreement to shelve the topic. I sipped my iced tea and watched the two plates of food disappear, idly wondering why men could do that and stay thin. Reed shoved his plate away first and nodded to the waitress passing by. She refilled his coffee and gathered up several of the dirty dishes.

Reed watched until she had moved on before turning back to Will.

"How—?" Reed reached inside his uniform pocket and pulled out his cell. "Reed!" He listened for a moment then pulled a small tablet from his other pocket. "Can you spell that . . . Right. I'm not familiar with that name in Saddle Gap. We need to check Cruces, Albuquerque, even Santa Fe." He listened for a moment. "If you find them, send them to my phone. I'm going to be out of the office most of the day, I think."

When he'd returned the phone and small pad to his pocket, he looked over at Will. "I think Sorrel and I should go to the senior center," he told Will.

"But I—"

"If we all three troop in there, we'll draw more attention than we need right now!"

"Then why not just—"

"I'll have some names emailed to you at the paper shortly. I need you to look them up, read the information, and then email it to me with your comments."

Will seemed flattered by that, which may or may not have been Reed's intent.

"Oh, and I have a text message from Randall Byrd," Reed added.

"Really?" Will rolled his eyes.

Reed looked at his cell and read:

If you come across Will, would you ask him when he plans to come to work—or am I looking for another reporter?

"Oops!" Will looked anything but sorry. "Reporters do not find news while sitting at their desks! And, by the way, what about other reporters?" He glared at me.

Will was working up to a full tantrum from his tone of voice. I wasn't looking forward to riding with him, so I was relieved to hear Reed continue as he slid out of the booth. "I'll give Sorrel a ride—"

"To my Jeep," I finished for him, gathering my things.

Will stalked across the restaurant ahead of both of us. I started toward Reed's truck when Will started the engine of his car.

"Wait!" I called, dumping my things in the truck's passenger seat and hurrying to Will's window. "Remember, Will, that what she told us was in confidence."

He rolled his eyes. "Really! I was planning to write a feature article about her!" he snapped.

We waited until he'd pulled out before we laughed.

"That will give him something to chew on until Randall gives him something to do," Reed mused. He opened the door for me, gave my elbow a small boost when I stepped up, and then walked around and slid into the truck. "Guess we're once more heading to the senior center. But we need a plan. We already know that someone, likely an employee, has something he or she doesn't want you to know."

"As a matter of fact, I have a plan . . . sort of."

His shout of laughter startled an older couple who were passing on their way inside. I gave a small wave. "What's so funny?" I growled.

"It would take too long to explain. Just tell me the plan while I drive."

By the time he pulled into the nursing home parking lot and parked, Chris was all business again. He turned off the key and turned to me. "It just might work. But you have to promise me one thing."

I sighed. "Anything."

"Save anything for another time. For now, just promise me that you'll listen to what I say and follow my plan."

I listened to the plan. *It might work*, I thought.

"It will work," he agreed.

When had he started reading minds?

Chapter 51

According to Reed's plan, we would enter the facility separately and act as if we were on two different missions.

I would check in with the activities director to discuss the success of the most recent sale at the shop. Since many of the residents had entered items on consignment, I would have an opportunity to roam from person to person and discuss successes and new ideas. I could also casually gather gossip and generally snoop.

"Keep your eyes, ears, and nose open for any clues about who may have attacked you," Reed urged. "Somehow, I think that incident has to be connected to all of this. Someone wanted to discourage you, not really hurt you. Why?"

"It just doesn't seem to go with Coach and these murders," I argued. "I think we're focusing on an insignificant incident that doesn't relate to anything else."

Reed, on the other hand, thought it might have been meant to discourage my discovering evidence of a crime. I finally agreed, but I wasn't convinced.

His plan of action would be to express condolences and remind the residents and employees about basic security measures without scaring them.

"Most of them will likely forget them by tomorrow," I told him.

He shrugged. "I won't," he said. "I'll feel better knowing I tried to protect them."

I entered first. Reed stayed in his truck and returned a couple of calls. Again, we hoped to appear as two separate entities—which we were—most of the time.

I noticed the empty rocking chairs on the big veranda in front. When I stopped at the front desk to sign the visitors' log, I asked, "Where is everybody? I didn't see anyone outside."

She continued studying her nails. "No one seems in the mood, I guess."

"Oh," I told the top of her head. "I don't believe we've met. I'm Sorrel Janes."

I hadn't seen this lady before. From a casual glance, I'd have guessed she'd be fiftyish. But when she raised her head, her makeup suggested an attempt to disguise another decade. The expensive hair color and boutique outfit hadn't worked so well either. I reached for the visitors' log and filled it in.

"I know," she said in a bored tone. "You have that little shop out on the highway." She handed me a badge to sign and stick to my blouse. Then she flipped through a calendar book. "I don't see your name in here."

"Oh . . . I don't—"

"Everyone is required to have one now," she said. "I notice you didn't specifically write the names of people you were visiting either."

"I visit several. Most of the time I go to the rec room and see who is there first." She added that after my name. "Then I stop by the lunchroom to catch whomever I have missed." I watched her write that as well.

"And your business?"

"Well, today I need to let them know how their items have sold. I'll also collect more items if they are ready."

"Don't you have a list?"

"No, I've never been asked for one. But I can make a list as I go and give it to you when I leave."

She might have continued to detain me, but she glanced over my shoulder and brightened, her whining tone turning to warm sugar.

"Well, hello!" she gushed, casually waving me on.

I snatched the moment and stepped away, hiding my smile when she continued to gush. "Now I feel safe with the sheriff's deputy here!"

I doubt he does, I thought, not bothering to erase my wicked grin as I turned and walked past Reed.

I first stopped by the activities office. It was vacant, but a clipboard on the wall beside the door displayed daily lists of residents who'd signed up for certain activities. Cards were currently being played in the lounge, a billiards tournament was in session in the rec room, a movie was playing in the TV room, and the Horticulture Club was meeting out in the back yard.

I decided to return to the office later; but before leaving, I glanced over the names of residents in each activity. One name on the horticulture group list, a nosy older resident who loved to pass on gossip, seemed a good starting place. Maybe he had gathered some information that would provide leads for me to follow. I wrote it down, as well as the next places I would visit.

A quick glance showed Reed had noted my actions. I winked and hurried on before the giggles erupted. He was trying—but not succeeding very well—to appear charmed.

Horticulture Club was an overly optimistic description of the group I met in the back yard. Two gentlemen slept in their wheelchairs by an outdoor table while their attendants gossiped about a party they'd attended the weekend before. "Hello," I said as I walked by. Neither looked my way or acknowledged my greeting.

"Nice security," I muttered and walked over to another small canopy.

A very old lady sat in her wheelchair and watched a young man pull weeds, calling out endless instructions that I doubt he even heard. I leaned over to admire the scraggly flowers. They looked a little sad after the weeds were gone.

"Did you plant these?" I asked her. She smiled but didn't answer, continuing with instructions for the young man.

When she finally paused, I leaned toward him. "Are you full time here or volunteer?"

He snatched another weed before he answered softly, his lips hardly moving. "I'm not supposed to talk to visitors."

"Did you know Brent, the young man who volunteered here?"

He pulled two more weeds and turned my direction to toss them. "No, and I don't want to know why it happened and get involved at all." He glanced right to left and lowered his voice. "There are aliens here, you know."

"Aliens? You mean—"

"Yep. Those green guys in suits." He glared at me. "Did you bring them?"

"No, I—"

"I'm too busy to notice much else." He pulled up a couple of flowers as well as weeds, grumbling under his breath.

I shrugged, smiled at the little lady, and moved on.

Farther down the walkway, I approached another pair of women sitting in lawn chairs pulled up to a picnic table. Each had a cluster of grapes. Occasionally one lady popped one in her mouth; the other dropped hers into a small purse she held open in her lap. "Hello," I called out. "I'm Sorrel."

The Purse Lady closed it quickly. "I'm not hungry just now," she said. "These are for tonight."

"Good idea," I told her.

"What are you doing here?" the other lady asked.

"Just visiting," I said. "I'm the one that has the little shop, and many people here make things to sell in it. I thought I'd stop by and see if anyone had started a new project."

"Can't!" Purse Lady grumbled. "My fingers don't work so well anymore."

I didn't mention that she'd managed to open and close the purse very well.

"It's quiet here," I said. "I miss the young man who volunteered here."

"Ssh!" the Eater said around a grape. "We're not supposed to talk about him."

"Why?"

She leaned forward and lowered her voice. "He was killed."

"Oh," I said. "Sad."

"We didn't do it," Purse Lady whispered. "He helped us."

I nodded encouragingly.

She waited a moment. "He said when I signed those papers, I'd never have to worry again."

"Hush!" her friend warned. "We're not supposed to talk about that."

"I hate signing papers," I murmured. "Did you?"

"No," Purse Lady said. "But a lot of people did."

"Why didn't you?"

"Because I don't own a house or anything."

"Bella!" her friend hissed. "Remember? Bad things happen to people who talk about it."

I noticed a uniformed worker heading our way. I leaned over and said loud enough for her to hear me, "Thank you for the grapes. I'll visit another time." The worker watched until I'd reached the porch. I didn't look back, but I could feel her eyes boring into my back.

The activities director had returned to her office when I stopped by a second time. "Thank you for encouraging our residents!" she sang out when I looked in. "They were so excited about the money they made. We have bus trips that some of them love to take and the extra cash helps." She leaned forward and lowered her voice. "The casinos."

We chatted for a few moments. But when I casually mentioned I was there to see any whom I might have missed because they'd gone to Brent's memorial service, her manner changed. "Sad," she murmured. Then she apologized. "I have some phone calls to make. But thanks for stopping by."

I mingled for another half hour among the residents but finally decided I wasn't going to find anything here. As I rose to leave, a man in a deep olive green suit entered through a side door. The older gentleman who'd been telling me all about how to cheat at dominoes without getting caught noticed and looked as well. He immediately looked down and whispered, "You need to leave."

"Why?"

"The Green men come and somebody dies." He began to move, his agitation evident. "Hurry!"

I rose and put my hand on his shoulder. "I'll be okay."

As I turned to walk away, he whispered one last warning. "Don't sign anything! When you do, you die!"

Chapter 52

When I stopped by Reception, no one was there. I glanced around while my hand casually pulled the sign-in list closer. By standing sideways, I could glance at the names without being too obvious. At least, I hoped so.

It wasn't a long list, sadly. I only recognized myself, Reed, and the young priest I'd interviewed a few days ago. It seemed much longer than that. I almost passed over the handwritten note someone watching the desk had added in the Etc. Column:

Please have these envelopes mailed to Detective
Reed and Ms. Sorrel Janes in the event of my death.

It was signed by—it couldn't be! I looked a second time. "Miss Eleanor Hoskins."

"The toughest, legendary Senior English teacher at Saddle Gap High School."

"Reed! Don't slip up on me! This is the name on the empty envelopes!" I gasped.

"Sorry." His tone and face didn't look sorry. "Where is the person who's always at this desk?"

"I don't know. I haven't been here long and no one has been by." I pushed the list back where it had been. "We're not supposed to be looking at it," I whispered.

Reed had just opened his mouth when an irritated voice snapped instead. "What are you two doing?"

We jumped guiltily. "Hello," I began. "I'm—

"I know who you are. You're that gal chasing after the deputy sheriff . . . and looks like you found him. What are you doing with this list?"

Reed spoke up. "We see a notation for some envelopes to be mailed to Ms. Janes and myself."

"And?"

"We received the envelopes, but they had been opened already and were empty. And you are?"

She drew herself up. "I'm Eleanor Biggs, president of the Helping Hearts Auxiliary. We volunteer here and at the hospital."

Reed smiled his smile he used when he wanted to be most charming. "Miss Hoskins was my Senior English teacher, bless her soul," he said. "I am most anxious to read that letter. If she's passed on . . . has she?"

The smitten president of the Helping Hearts Auxiliary nodded. She's already president of the Christopher Reed fan club, I thought.

Reed replaced the smile with his next most charming look, the only-you-can-help-me one.

It was working too. Ms. Biggs began opening drawers and searching through them. "I can't imagine why that would be," she said, her fingers rifling through several documents. She pulled the drawer out farther until it almost came loose. "Here they are!" she crowed. "They were added to the shredding folder, but it looks like they were wedged at the back of the drawer and were missed."

"You are a wizard, ma'am," Reed yelped. "I am so grateful!"

I may barf, I thought. Instead, I smiled happily and thanked her a couple of times.

"Anything else I can do?" she asked, handing them over with her eyes on Reed.

"No, we're fine," I answered quickly. "Sorry we can't help you."

We had almost turned to leave when she answered. "Well, I can think of one way."

"Blabbermouth," Reed muttered out of the side of his mouth. But he quickly adjusted to his dazzling smile. "Anything, if we can," he told her.

"One of Miss Hoskins's friends here is not doing well. He never has visitors and his health is dropping. Maybe if the two of you could just stop by? Room 319. Private." She wrote our names and the date and time onto the list before she deposited it on a shelf behind her. "And the one who signs up new visitors earns a heart!"

"And the one who earns the most hearts?" Reed asked.

Her smile lit up even brighter. "A weekend at the casinos and $100 for gambling money." She handed me a slip of paper. "Henry Stilton. He requested to see someone. He says he wants to tell his story, whatever that is. You two would be perfect."

We started toward room 319.

"Why are we always perfect for chores like this when we are under pressure to finish a hundred things?" Reed grumbled. "And then there's this letter from the person who despised me most. Miss Hoskins prayed for the day I was out of her class! And then there's you. You have a store that must be wilting under a load of unfinished chores, and you don't even know either of these people."

"What if it were you in this place, Chris Reed? You had this important thing—maybe even a secret—and no one to listen and you're staring at the Pearly Gates! Would you feel different then? We can't just leave him on the doorstep, Reed."

He was already talking softly into his cellphone, but I knew he'd heard me. I stopped outside room 319 and waited, my fingers itching to take out the letter and read it. But it was only fair that we read it together. And this old lonely guy wouldn't take long.

My phone vibrated. I had a text from Will. "U guys coming?"

Give us 30, I tapped back.

"Anything new?"

Surprise, I tapped, then told him we would be finished soon. He named a food place and signed off.

Well, the letter from Reed's English teacher was a surprise. Maybe we had others in store. Either way, I had waited long enough.

I squeezed Reed's elbow. When he glanced at me, I motioned toward the room. He clicked off and took my hand. "Lead on, Miss Wild Goose Chaser," he whispered.

Chapter 53

"You'll have to let yourself in!" a gruff voice called when I tapped at the door. "The butler is on vacation!"

Reed whispered, "Great! We have a comedian!"

"Better than a grouch," I murmured. "Behave. This shouldn't take long."

We'd been told that he had a private room, and the arched eyebrow had insinuated that it would be plush. Looking around at the beige walls, tiny metal clothes cupboard, single chair, and hospital bed, I hoped I never had to visit the economy rooms.

"Mr. Stilton?" I asked when I encountered the grumpy glare.

"Henry will do. And who are you? I'm not into religion. That the preacher with you?"

"Preacher?" Reed barked. "Deputy Sheriff is more like it." He turned so that the cranky old man in the hospital bed could see him. "Chris Reed is my name." His voice softened as he stepped forward with his hand out. "Pleased to meet you, Mr. Stilton."

"Henry." The old man reached out to shake his hand.

"My friend here is Sorrel Janes. She owns a shop on the edge of town, but she also works part time for the newspaper."

I smiled and reached out a hand. Instead of shaking it, he raised it to his lips in the manner of a courtly gentleman. "I can only offer one of you a seat."

Reed pulled it up near his bed. "Sorrel, you sit. I prefer the window." He moved over and leaned against the sill, removing his hat.

His actions had the immediate result he must have wanted. Henry Stilton straightened up and cleared his throat. "I'm not sure if anything I say will be of great value," he began, "but I have some concerns."

"May I record you?" I asked. "Should we want to write a story, I'd like to have my facts straight."

"Not this time," he said. "I'd like for you to write my story, young lady, but at this moment I am more concerned about someone else's story actually." He stopped to cough and wheezed. Finally, he cleared his throat enough to continue.

"I grew up on a ranch near here. In fact, I remember when Saddle Gap was just a couple of dirt streets and a few buildings along them. My Papa—Grandpa but he preferred Papa—owned a general store. Also was the undertaker and coffin maker too. People had to be versatile to survive. Dad was a blacksmith and rode horseback once a week over to Las Cruces for the mail. Ma was the schoolteacher. There weren't many kids in town then besides the six of us. I was the first of my family. We had eight of us, but one died of the fever and another died from a fall. Only two of us left in this world now, and my sister is in a place kind of like this, only has bars at the windows." He tapped his forehead and rolled his eyes.

He paused then to cough. Reed stood up and poured him a glass of cold water, which he accepted with a nod. I'd switched on the recorder on my phone in spite of his earlier comment, and I was glad that I had. This gentleman had already captured my interest, and I knew he'd make an interesting feature someday when he agreed to allow it.

He set the glass back on the bedside table. "I don't need sympathy," he grumbled, looking at Reed. "I wouldn't trade my childhood for anything. We learned right from wrong and good from bad. Nowadays, it's hard to tell them apart!" He took a deep breath.

"I took a while to learn it. I was hardheaded, Mama called it. One time I sneaked Dad's pistol out to play cowboys . . . and ended up shooting myself in the leg." He stopped to cough again then looked at me mischievously.

"Did you get in trouble?" I asked.

"Papa was there and he fixed me up. But it really did hurt. 'Men don't cry!' he scolded me as he wiped the blood running down my leg. 'Hold still and let me get the bullet out!'"

I shuddered. "Did you stop?"

Henry smiled. "I wasn't a big hero," he said. "'But it hurts,' I told my papa. He knelt beside me, his knees cracking, and cleaned the wound. Finally, he put a poultice he'd made on my leg and wrapped it up. I watched him hobble back to the kitchen and return with a bottle and spoon. 'Here,' he said. 'This will burn going down, but it will warm you up inside and take away the hurt. It's medicine that helps us men, but we only take it when we are sick.' I decided right then I'd try to never need it again!"

Henry was interrupted by a coughing fit just then. But he wiped his mouth and continued. "'Doesn't it hurt when you get old and your knees crack?' I asked. 'Nah,' Papa said. 'It isn't hurting then. Hurting is when you're too old for people to listen to you, when they think your mind is gone and they take advantage of you. That's not hurt—that's agony.' I asked him, 'Is that bad?'"

He stopped, emotion in his eyes. "My papa told me that it was the worst hurt of all. He said it was 'untold agony that nibbles on your soul until you disappear from sight.' I asked him if I had to grow up to be a man." This time he wiped his eyes. "He told me I'd be a man that he would always admire, even if he had to do it from above." He stopped again to cough.

I had to fight to keep my own eyes from misting, and Reed found something interesting to study out the window. Henry finally cleared his throat. "I told you this story because it is my time for speaking up. I'm not complaining for me. Understand that?"

Reed stepped closer and looked into his eyes. "I completely understand. You are handling what you must, but you are worried about others. How can I help, Mr. Stilton?"

It was that interaction between them—the trust and relief in Mr. Stilton's face as he stared into Reed's eyes—that made me swallow hard to stop tears of my own.

"I don't have much proof, Sheriff," he answered, lowering his voice until I had to strain to hear him. "But people are dying around here. I know, we came here to die. But people are dying unnaturally."

"What can you tell me about their deaths?" Reed asked. I could see Henry Stilton reach for Reed's hand again and lean forward to speak even softer.

"There are business people coming here. I don't think they're from here. They have leather cases, and they talk all secretive with people that run this place. Then they mostly visit the women." He stopped to catch his breath, then pushed on. "I saw one signing papers. She looked worried. The next morning she was dead."

Reed handed him his water glass. While he sipped, Reed glanced at me, then back to Henry. "You know—"

"That they're dying anyway. But only hours later? I nosed around—that was when I used a walker—and listened. They were mostly maiden ladies but some gents also—never married, no kids, maybe a distant nephew or niece." He grabbed Reed's arm. "These business people—mostly men in these green jackets—something's strange."

He leaned back onto his pillow, his face pale and his breathing labored. He motioned for Reed to lean close. "Coming here to me . . . soon. I loved once but no little ones, though we wanted them. She left me too soon—a feisty little lady like yours here."

We heard a tap at the door, and a nurse poked her head inside. "Visiting hours are over." She smiled distantly and pointed to a sign above the door. "Tell your guests goodbye, Henry." She stood aside and motioned for us to leave.

I stood and went to the side of the bed so that my back faced her. I leaned down and looked him in the eye. "See you later, Mr. Stilton," I said and winked. I squeezed his hand, and he gave me an answering squeeze back. I glanced over my shoulder to check the nurse, but she was focused on Reed. "Thank you," I mouthed.

As we walked out, I spoke to several people who had entered items in our sale at my store, encouraging them to get busy on new ones. Reed stepped outside when we reached the lobby area to answer his beeper. I stopped to let Ms. Biggs know we were leaving. She was on the phone, so I just waved. "Thank you!" she mouthed.

Lonna Enox

By the time I reached Reed's truck, he was finishing up his call with Will. "What do you think?" I asked as I climbed inside and closed the door.

He pulled out and flicked on his blinker. "Murkey waters here," he said. "Methinks we need to look closer. Time to check in with our co-conspirators."

Chapter 54

"The mystery of the aliens seems to have been solved," Will commented when we had finished our tale. "The men in green who visit the lady residents are crooks—maybe even murderers—from some planet far away." He hummed the tune from a popular science fiction movie.

"I don't think we should treat it as a joke, Will," I said. "Death rates are increasing. I checked the statistics, and they're above the state average."

"Neither do we know who they are or why they are visiting the ladies shortly before they die." Reed scowled. "They could be perfectly innocent—church people sharing information about the hereafter."

"Or volunteers listening to their parting ramblings," Mr. Byrd remarked. "The only sinister things about them may be the gossip created and passed along by the residents. I personally think this avenue is a dead end—no pun intended."

Will dipped a chip into the small bowl of salsa near him and poked it into his mouth. Immediately, he coughed and choked, and tears rolled down his cheeks. I grabbed his glass of iced water and put it in his hand. He promptly swallowed half the glass. Finally, he gasped. "I thought this stuff would be mild," he accused Reed. "You've been eating it like candy."

"That's the secret," Reed grinned. "You eat it fast until your tongue and throat are numb. I thought you said you're from Santa Fe! Surely—"

"I'm a pizza and burger guy! And I'm sticking to them from here on! This," he sputtered pointing to the salsa, "is liquid fire! You don't think those green men are after me too!"

"Shh!" Mr. Byrd leaned close and whispered. "This is our safe house, so we can't insult the proprietress."

"Okay, boys! Enough banter. We have business to discuss." I looked at Mr. Byrd. "It's your turn to share."

We could almost see the cloud return in his eyes, his momentary jocularity forgotten. "It was a sad morning, of course, but also weird. I was most confused by the people who had been invited to attend. Coach had been a huge figure in Saddle Gap for so many years, yet almost no local people were invited to the services. Only Mrs. Byrd and I, a few school officials, and some ladies from the social club were invited. Nor had family been included, apparently, and—"

"But surely their friends—" I interrupted.

"Weren't invited." He shook his head. "This just doesn't sound like either of them!"

"At least you were invited," Reed commented. "But I would have thought Jose and the other former athletes who were close to him would have attended. And the faculty. I've never heard of anything like this. Are you sure this was Coach's wishes?"

"Apparently it was written in the will, which was read at the end of services."

"Stranger yet. I guess you can't reveal anything?" Reed asked.

"I wasn't able to stay for the reading as I'm not a recipient." Randall Byrd could not hide the pain in his eyes. "So I was forced to do something highly unethical . . . maybe I shouldn't . . . "

"Did you plant a recording device?" Reed turned to me before Mr. Byrd could answer. "I need to step out to the restroom. Please don't tell me anything that is said while I'm out."

"You don't have to step out," Randall told him. "I didn't record anything and I'm not repeating anything I shouldn't. I didn't hear anything specific besides the names of the recipients. And I only heard their names because the door may have been a bit open. Besides, amounts left to them were not revealed orally, only in the envelopes handed to them." He paused. "Maybe I shouldn't—"

"Speak so loudly," Reed warned. "Or at all. But if you happen to give us a clue . . ."

"The recipients mainly seem to be people elected by the people of New Mexico or people who are working with or for them. It shocked me, as they weren't the sort of people I'd suspect a high school coach would interact with on a social or a personal basis." He paused, his eyes watering. "I would have also expected Mrs. Byrd and I before those people. Then I wondered if I was totally off track. Maybe he wasn't leaving them monetary gifts. He could have been leaving them personal notes . . . but did he know them personally?"

He shrugged and drew his hand across his eyes. "Now, I wonder if I'm just an old fool. So—"

"So, of course, you will not speak of this to anyone else," Reed finished for him. He looked at Will and me. "I'm trusting my life—and your lives—on the promise you give me that you will not breathe a word of what you've heard. This is too big for our group here."

He looked at Randall Byrd again. "I need to inform people who can handle this as it should be handled. The murders are our jurisdiction. This other is for the Big Boys!" He caught my eye. "And girls!" he added hastily.

He rose, his hand already reaching for his cell, and started toward the door. As he opened it, he turned back for a final word. "Mr. Byrd, let me find out if there is anything to this. Promise me you'll not breathe a word to anyone! Let us do our job." His last words came with a hard glance at me and a quick glance at Jose and Will. "Some of you are too dear for me to worry about what could happen."

After Reed had stepped into the hall and closed the door, Randall Byrd seemed to compose himself before he looked around at us. "I guess we have our orders—and they're good ones. We have helped as much as we should. Now we need to let those trained for this job finish it."

"But we still don't know—" Will sputtered.

"We know as much as we can at this moment." Randall Byrd looked at Will. "I need you at the paper, Will. You're the best one to write a human-interest article for Sunday's edition. Also, since Brent spent so much time volunteering at the senior center, I'd like you to write a tribute to him. Maybe when other teens hear of it, they'll—"

"Fill the vacancy his death has created," Will murmured. He hopped up, his eyes already filled with ideas. "Thank you, sir! I can do this!"

After he'd almost galloped out, Mr. Byrd turned to me. "That young man is going to be an outstanding news reporter someday!" he said.

"Thanks to you, sir."

He didn't reply but opened his briefcase and pulled out an envelope. "Sorrel, I found an envelope addressed to you in the mail tray at the paper. I don't know when it arrived. It had gotten pushed under a stack of papers on my desk. I'm embarrassed to say that it may have been there a while. My secretary said it didn't come in the mail . . . and there are no postmarks. She had never seen it, and she suspects it may have been intercepted. With all of the—"

"No need to apologize, sir," I said. "It's probably insignificant. You've had a horrific week."

As I reached for it, he took my hand first. "News is in your blood, young lady. I know photography is your love just now, but you'll always be a reporter first."

Maybe he has a point, I thought, as I carefully opened the envelope. *Or maybe he just doesn't have a replacement yet.*

I pulled out the folded paper and saw my name printed on the outside in a spidery hand. But when I opened it, I paused. It wasn't addressed to me at all. I looked back at the outside, then shrugged. *Your name is on the envelope*, my curious inner self urged. So I unfolded it and a note fell out. I reached inside, and pulled a letter with Reed's name printed on the outside.

"This letter is for Reed," I said. "Maybe he's still outside." I hurried to the door and looked out. He was leaving the men's restroom down the hall. When he saw me, he must have seen my upset. We met halfway between the restroom and Mr. Byrd's office.

"Reed," I said, waving the letter at him. "I think this is the long-lost letter we expected to find in the envelopes. Mine is still missing, but a note here addressed to me explains it."

When we re-entered Mr. Byrd's office, he was finishing up a phone call. We sat and waited as patiently as we could. When he hung up, I explained to him what I thought had happened. "I want to read my note first, and then Reed can read his if he wants." I handed it over to Reed, but he turned it away.

"You can read it, Sorrel. I trust you."

I felt tears gather for a moment, but my curiosity overrode them. "My note first then."

Dear Ms. Janes,

I know that you are a journalist as well as owner of the little shop where people send their handmade items. I have attempted to contact the sheriff's deputy, Christopher Reed, to whom this letter belongs. I have heard nice things about you, as well as gossip that you and Deputy Reed are close. I sent you both copies of this letter, but as I've heard nothing from either of you, I am hoping it is because you did not receive it . . . instead of ignoring it. I've sent copies to your shop as the gossip around here links the two of you together. Did you receive it?

I doubt that you did. So I am sending a copy of the letter—via the young gardener—for Christopher Reed to the newspaper where I've heard that you work. It is a risk, I know, as I fear the others copies of this letter have landed in the wrong hands. I may not save myself, but I hope to help others. Please be cautious with whom you and Christopher share this.

Eleanor Hoskins

I hadn't noticed that the tears had returned until one dropped onto my hand. I pulled out the other letter. "Why would those envelopes sent to my shop be empty?" I asked. "They must have been the ones she sent first! Why—"

"Let's find out," Reed said. "Read us the letter addressed to me."

Dear Christopher Reed,

This letter may not be welcome. I can remember the number of times you served detention for not writing an essay for my class, which angered not only you but the football team as well. Should you choose to ignore this letter, I will accept your decision. Still, I'm counting on your sense of fairness and your sharp mind—in every other area besides English—to investigate my murder.

Yes, I said murder, even though I know my death will be reported as natural causes. (I wonder who coined that term *natural causes*. Death is an unnatural—although inevitable—state.) But I doubt I have much time left to ponder the subject, so I'll try to present my case as quickly and efficiently as possible.

Near my 80th birthday, my banker advised me to secure a guardian to oversee my last days as I am a spinster with no blood relatives surviving me. I agreed and actually welcomed the help with interpreting the healthcare and legal issues that inevitably arise. And I must also admit, in the spirit of honesty, that I enjoyed the attention I received from the appointed guardian. After retiring from teaching, I'd felt myself growing invisible . . . and insignificant. Suddenly, someone listened again and appreciated my dry sense of humor. But you know the adage: "Beware what seems too good to be true."

Immediately, a caregiver moved into my house to cook, clean, and launder my clothes. I agreed to the addition and flourished for a few weeks. Then, I became nauseated after eating, and once I emptied my stomach as I slept. My medicine made me ill—and I noticed the pills had changed their shapes. So I stopped swallowing them. For a short time, I felt better. Yet, still I grew weaker and I slept more.

Visitors and phone calls stopped, but I excused this at first as my friends being older and infirm. However, I'd expected someone from church to miss my presence. Had I angered everyone? I glimpsed a neighbor passing along our adjoining fence and tapped the window glass. She heard, glanced, and waved, her face a study in confusion . . . sympathy . . . horror?

My bills had been rerouted to my guardian, but I no longer received notes from church, friends, notifications of teacher retirement group activities, or even sales flyers. When I mentioned this to my guardian, he seemed surprised. "I'll check into it," he promised.

Things are missing—heirlooms left from my parents and siblings. My caregiver explained that she wished to safeguard them, so they were stored safely. I told her that no one came to the house, so how would they be broken or stolen? She tutted pityingly and gave me hot tea. I poured it in the potted plant. That night, I heard soft voices and peeked out. Strangers were carrying boxes and talking in hushed tones.

I could continue, but time is short. I grow weaker each day. This morning, I noticed a young teen mowing my yard. When he came near my window, I managed to open it a crack and called a cautious, "Hello? Can you help me?"

"I need to get a letter to the sheriff," I told him. "I will pay you, but you must bring me proof that you delivered it. Give it to Officer Chris Reed. Ask him to come by here."

He looked around and started to turn away.

"Come to this window tomorrow at this time. I have a ten-dollar bill that is yours when you do." I'd tucked one into a book of Frost poems—the only cash I had.

I pray he returns and delivers this letter and that you no longer harbor any resentment from those aforementioned detention sessions. I fear you may be my last hope—not only for me but also for the other poor souls who follow me.

Hopefully,
Eleanor Hoskins

No one spoke for a bit. Finally, Reed folded the letter and brushed his eyes. "She was the reason I graduated," he whispered. "I'd decided to drop out and get a job and help Mom as soon as football season was over. But she gave me such a talking-to and then dared me to see if I was brave enough to finish. She made me so mad, so I did it to prove to her that I could. I wish I could have been here for her when she asked."

I reached over and covered his hand with mine. "You are . . . and you will. She trusted you, and she was right."

Mr. Byrd casually wiped a corner of his own eye and told Chris, "Tell us what to do to help!"

Chapter 55

Just as we were about to leave, Will opened the door and came back in. "I noticed you hadn't left yet, so what else is going on?" he asked.

"I'll leave you two to fill him in," Mr. Byrd said, rising from his seat. "I've got to get back to the paper. Keep me informed—and be safe."

"So what's—"

"Sit down, Will. Reed and I both received envelopes from someone at the senior center," I said, "but the letters were missing. Mr. Byrd just gave me a copy that had been sent to me in care of the paper."

"The letters may have an impact on our investigation," Reed explained before Will could interrupt. "You should read them to be aware of what seems to be going on."

Will nodded as he took my note and Reed's letter in hand and began to read.

"Miss Hoskins! A voice from the past." Chris murmured. "To think, she terrified Senior English students for years. We were fully convinced that she was more powerful than the president, the pope . . . you name it! She sure had me convinced that she could control my fate as far as graduation was concerned. But her class was interesting, even some of that poetry. She was so hard . . . but fair. We weren't very kind to her, I'm ashamed to admit, although most of the unkind things we said were behind her back." He grinned. "We were scared to do it to her face! Still, I hate to think that she ended her life scared and powerless."

"She doesn't sound very scared to me," Will said, laying the letters on the table. "She just doesn't want these guys to get away with what they're doing."

"And she knew who could take care of it," I added. "She was likely ready to leave this earth and confident that you would clean up the wickedness she couldn't."

"Where has this letter been?" Chris mused. "And how did it appear now? She's been gone for a while now."

I thought of the empty envelopes. "Someone has had it. Maybe he—or she—promised to mail it and didn't. Remember back in the fall when we got the envelopes with no letters inside? But how did she know to send one to me?"

"This letter is clearly addressed to me, Chris Reed. You were already making a name for yourself at the newspaper. And you'd also started recruiting craft items for the senior center. I don't know if she was still home or at the center then, but she would have heard friends speaking of it. She would have read the newspaper."

"She mentioned a young man," Will interjected. "Remember? Maybe it was Coach's son. He volunteered at the senior center. But he also did yard work."

"Could be," Reed mused. "This letter clearly reinforces the things we've just heard. The little-green-men tale grows more sinister."

"How would this tie in to Coach? I mean, his kid may have been a delivery boy, but there's no real connection to Coach!"

"There could be, Will. Think about it. Coach may have needed money. At this point, we can only speculate why he would, but he was living very well on a Coach's salary. His wife was involved in several charities but didn't work. He had a son entering college. That would be another big budget bust coming up."

Reed stared at his hands for a moment. "Brent's death could be explained easier: maybe a drug deal gone wrong, some cheating or stealing he'd gotten involved with, or even something to do with his girlfriend. I could maybe see the gang involvement in any of those, but it feels unlikely. He seemed like one of those kids who sort of fade into the background . . . don't make waves, never draw attention to themselves . . . more of a loner. But Coach? His reeks of money, power—"

"Gambling?" I watched Reed's incredulity. "What if Brent, who seemed to be the errand boy for some of the people at the senior center, either overheard too much or was taken into confidence by some of the people or snooped into the letters?"

He shook his head. "Coach would never kill his own son!"

"Someone else did it." Will's voice grew more confident as he continued. "It fits! The green men were stealing money and property from these people. They are con men! When these people die, they've already signed over their worldly goods to these guys, thinking it will pay for their care. I mean, most of them probably didn't read the documents, just trusted what they were being told."

"Or didn't even know!" I exclaimed.

"No, Sorrel." Reed shook his head. "Miss Hoskins seems to have been as bright as ever here. She wouldn't sign something she didn't read. Unless she totally trusted the person. She might have trusted Coach. But I can't believe that Coach would get involved in this."

"Reed, he might have been desperate. People sometimes get involved in things that draw them into desperate situations. Maybe he'd gambled or misspent money that his wife and son expected would pay for college. Their lifestyle doesn't sound cheap." I could see the doubt entering his own eyes.

"But he wouldn't have ordered his son's death," I continued. "Something must have gone terribly wrong, and while he was trying to find a way out of it—maybe Coach even thought he had—someone raised the stakes. Maybe it was someone he trusted. Maybe he felt—"

"He had to take his and his wife's lives to spare her further grief," he whispered. "Or maybe she was complicit since her only child had died."

Will opened his mouth, but I caught his eye and shook my head.

Reed's momentary horror quickly turned to a steely resolve. He pulled out his cellphone and started out the door. "I need to make a call," he said over his shoulder as he strode out.

We watched him leave before Will spoke. "An operation of this size would need several people."

"I agree," I murmured. "How deep does the corruption go? Even worse, does it stop here? Maybe this scheme is being played out in other cities as well."

"I would think it would be difficult to control unless the facilities belonged to the same people."

"Will," I cried, "you're a genius! You need to check that out! If some conglomerate owns this center as well as several others, this operation is much more complicated—and lucrative—than we can imagine."

He nodded and rose, but he was stopped by the steely voice from the door.

"I told you two to wait. And, yes, it is owned by a group called Progressive Living. And Coach had a large number of shares." Reed stepped inside and closed the door.

"I will be meeting with my chief and several others shortly. From this moment, it will be in the hands of law enforcement." He noticed Will's fallen expression. "But you two—and Randall Byrd—will have advance notice to scoop the story." He addressed Will. "Mr. Byrd intends you to have the by-line . . . unless, Sorrel—"

"Happily! I have a gift shop and photography business to run."

"Let's meet at the bed and breakfast for a meal this evening and a complete debriefing."

Reed glanced at his watch. "I have things to handle at the station. Will, Mr. Byrd wants you at the paper. Pronto! Sorrel? A young lady has been trying to reach you." He handed me a note. "And would you mind stopping by my place on your way home? Those pups may have broken into the barn and eaten themselves into a coma or something!

I'll be tied up all afternoon." He leaned over and dropped a quick kiss on my cheek.

"I didn't even say yes or no," I muttered.

"You two are acting more like a married couple every day." Will held the door for me and followed me out.

"Marriage has never been even mentioned with us," I corrected him. "We don't have time."

"Right. You can continue to protest too much at dinner. I have a story to write!"

I waited until I turned the car toward Reed's place before I turned on my cell. I had several messages. "Call soon!" she begged. I'd been so involved, I'd not even checked it. I hoped she was all right.

Lonna Enox

Chapter 56

Some days fly by—a cliché, I know, but a true one. The cats glared when I entered my little house, only warming enough to stroll over to the food dishes when I headed to the shower.

I showered in spite of being short of time. I'd been much loved by Chris's pups. They were so cute and awkward. Past the puppy waddly-toddly stage, but still innocent and naughty. I probably stunk like dogs, explaining the cats' irritation.

With minutes to spare, I swept my hair up into a sort of emergency up-do thing, stepped into a denim ankle-length dress with a straight skirt (to hide legs I'd not shaved), and fastened gold loop earrings into my ears. Mascara, lip gloss, and a dab of perfume would have to do their magic.

"I'll be back!" I called to the neglected cats as I left. They didn't answer.

On the short drive to the bed and breakfast, I mentally replayed my phone conversation with the expectant mother just after I'd stepped out of the shower. After our gloomy chat earlier in the week, I hadn't expected her excited chatter. "My aunt and my mom hashed it all out," she'd said. "I'm going to college and staying with my aunt in Phoenix. After the baby comes, she'll help. There are programs for women like me, so I'll have help there also. I can do this!"

"Of course, you can," I told her. "I'm excited for you! I'd hoped you wouldn't—"

"Give it up? I was just mad and sad and scared. But moms don't have time for that. I need to educate myself so my baby will be proud of me. Plus, babies use so many diapers!"

"You can do it!" I repeated. "I'm sorry to be quick, but I have a dinner meeting. When are you leaving?"

"Tomorrow! But I'll keep in touch!"

As I parked the Jeep, I pictured Coach and his wife with their grandchild. I wished this young mother the very best. She'd promised to keep in touch. I hoped she would.

In spite of my rush, I was still the last to enter the private dining room. Randall Byrd stopped talking until I'd closed the door. I glanced around and noticed a seat by Reed. So I slid into it, ignoring Will's grin across the table.

"I ordered iced tea for you," Mr. Byrd said, "unless you want a cocktail or—"

"This is fine." I glanced at Will and Reed. "Sorry to be late. I had a phone call. Where are Teri and Jose?"

"I'll explain later. First, can you tell us about the phone call?" Mr. Byrd asked.

When I explained what I'd learned from Sara, everyone smiled and the atmosphere in the room warmed. *Babies do that*, I thought.

Chris turned and winked. His eyes told me he'd heard my thoughts.

"We have a lot to share," Mr. Byrd began, finally. "I wish we could keep this happy mood, but we can at least be relieved that justice has again prevailed. What a mess!"

Then, for the next half hour, he and Reed outlined what they had learned—or at least what they could share.

"Jose is finishing up the front page for tomorrow's paper," Mr. Byrd told me. "I'll be writing my editorial after I leave here. I wish my friends could have been here for this."

"I can't believe our green men are actually the good guys!" I said. "Reed, why didn't you tell me?"

"He didn't know," Randall answered. "None of us did."

Then a thought jumped in my mind and I grabbed Reed's arm. "Why didn't you tell me? I was terrified in that bathroom and—"

"He didn't know," Randall repeated. Then, "Did you?"

Reed grinned. "Nope. I was as mad as the rest of you."

"Why did they do that?"

"Because they didn't want you to ruin their sting! You had helped convince everyone else that there was something going on, with you the focus. Since you weren't really the focus, it diverted the attention from the criminals."

"And the green men?" Will repeated for at least the third time.

"Undercover agents," Mr. Byrd answered. "That's all you or I or any of us besides law enforcement need to know. That's how they will be addressed for the public."

"How long has this investigation been going on?" Will persisted.

"Apparently, it began a couple of years ago," Reed spoke up. "Brent told his dad that he was concerned about some of the things the older people had told him. Coach knew some people—whom I can't name just now—and shared Brent's concerns. They finally agreed to investigate, after swearing Coach to secrecy. When their initial investigation uncovered questionable practices, they began the undercover investigation."

"The letter?" I interrupted.

"They intercepted it." Reed met my glare with his hands in the air. "I was as dumb—uninformed—as you, Sorrel."

I ignored Will's smothered laugh. Instead, I maintained my stony glare at Reed.

"So, if the green men are the good guys, who are the criminals?" Will asked. "And what were the green men doing there?"

Reed ignored the first question. "The green men were law enforcement officers who posed as volunteer estate planners. They approached residents of the senior center with a proposition that would entice them to talk."

"To talk about their abuse?" Will asked.

"Of course not. At least, not so the residents noticed. Instead, the estate planners—our undercover officers—approached the residents about securing their estates for whomever would inherit them. Soon a pattern developed. The ones who'd already turned their powers of attorney over to the crooks would say so. They'd relate wonderful tales of huge interest rates and other impossible rewards. When our people followed up, researching legal records, they found court rulings declaring these people in the senior center incompetent, a legal guardian for medical and financial—one of the scoundrels— appointed, and their land and bank accounts stolen." Reed sighed. "Relatives or other guardians who took the matter to court found themselves overridden."

"How could this escape the public's attention?" Will asked. "When did this whole scam begin?"

"We don't know all of the details yet," Randall Byrd interrupted. "Reed is outlining the offenses, but there is only so much he can say. And we can't write about police activities—beyond what they have approved—at this point."

"Why not? Has freedom of speech vanished from our country? Has—"

"Jose is working on the front page right now, Will," Randall Byrd explained. He managed to keep his voice soothing yet stern. "I have written the story—front page headlines—and included information for the public. This isn't a cover-up. We're telling all of you now because arrests are being made and suits being filed as we speak. Relatives are being notified if they hadn't been already."

"Remember," Reed interrupted, "even people being arrested in this scam are considered innocent until proven guilty."

"I don't consider them innocent," Will grumbled.

"Of course not, but think about it. You can think of times when people looked completely guilty and later were exonerated. And whether they were really guilty or not, if a court finds them innocent, they are set free. It's our justice system, Will. Wouldn't you want the same careful scrutiny if you were accused of something that could send you to prison and possibly ruin the lives of your family?" Reed waited, leaving the question hanging in the air, until Will reluctantly nodded.

"I see your logic." He sighed. "But how can they do it? Some of these people must have just stood by and let this kid be murdered!"

Reed looked around the table. "What actually sped up the whole thing was Brent's death. The task force had found no indications that Brent was in danger. In fact, we in local law enforcement still do not know if his murder had anything to do with this illegal scheme at the senior center."

"Of course, it does!" Will looked around the table, seeking support. "Who else could it have been?"

"It could have been anyone." I didn't realize I'd spoken my thoughts aloud until everyone looked at me. "Will, Brent could have unknowingly crossed a gang either at school or—"

"He wasn't in high school, remember, Sorrel?" Will burst out. "So now gang members are attending college? Or residents of senior centers? Or—"

"Or even had their eye on his girl?"

We all turned to Reed.

"Seriously?" Will asked.

Reed shrugged. "Investigations are early yet, Will. Justice may be slow, but it is the best tool we have. To jump to a conclusion right now . . . we will get there. Some crimes take much longer in reality than they do on television."

A quick rap at the door startled us. Reed tensed beside me as Randall Byrd called, "Come."

A cute waitress poked her head inside the door. "Excuse me," she said, "but the . . . people over me have sent me with a message." She glanced nervously at Randall Byrd. "I've been told to ask a question." Again she paused, then continued, her eyes on the floor. "If you people plan to eat . . . uh, I'm quoting . . . you need to place your orders before the cook leaves to watch her television show."

Randall Byrd smiled. "I'm sorry to have made you wait. Would you bring enchiladas, chili rellenos, tacos, refried beans, and rice? Just bring them in platters and we'll all share." He paused only briefly. "We're honoring a family that I hold dear—true heroes—with their favorite dishes."

"*Si*," she replied, her eyes bright. "A wake." She backed out of the room.

Immediately, we heard a familiar laugh outside the door, and then Jose and Teri poked their heads in. "We're done. Are we too late for the food?"

"Are you ever?" Reed drawled. "Pull up a chair!"

Chapter 57

He was sleeping. I couldn't disturb that as I knew it must be hard enough to sleep in a place like this. I turned to go, but a whisper made me stop. "Aren't you even going to say hello?"

I whirled back around. "You startled me!"

"Really! It's my room, you know." The smile lighting up his face delighted me. "What time is it, anyway?"

"A little after ten. I'm sorry but we had a dinner I had to attend and . . . "

"How did you get past the guards? They have eyes in the back of their heads! We prisoners can't . . . er . . . expel gas without their hearing us."

In spite of the grouchy voice, he looked pleased to see me. "I wanted to let you know that we have solved our mystery."

"About the aliens?"

"Well, they're not—"

"Aliens?" He grinned and continued in a stage whisper. "Some of these people around here have left their brains in the closet! I knew they weren't aliens."

I grinned back. "They're the good guys!"

"Really."

"Yes. They were following complaints of relatives about some of you residents being—"

"Robbed? I knew something like that was going on. I told that young boy that he needed to alert the authorities. He was the only one I trusted not to have been pulled into it. Then the next thing I knew, he'd been killed. They said he died, but I know he was killed. I shouldn't have told him—since he was just a kid—but he already suspected something. When he asked, I told him."

"It wasn't your fault. I can't share much—and I don't know much, really—but I think it was some sort of scheme. We get more vulnerable as we age. You may need to check—"

"Mine is in trust. We did that early. Just in case. Do they know who it is?"

"Probably . . . or they will know soon. I think it may go very high up."

He grinned. "They always want more, don't they? Anyone who starts every sentence with 'trust me' can't be trusted. Like I told that Coach feller—"

"Coach? You met him?"

"Sure. He came out here, visiting. Selling fundraiser tickets—"

"Fundraiser tickets? For the team? I wouldn't think you would have much change."

"We don't. It's for our own safety. So he'd bring a document and a lady who could notarize—"

"What did she look like?"

"Blonde. Younger than him. They were friendly. Everyone liked them."

"Did you buy any fundraisers?"

He grinned. "I'm old but I'm all here. I didn't sign anything. Pretended I couldn't remember anything. Thought he might be one of those little green men." He laughed out loud. "You should have seen how fast they got out of here!"

"Did you tell anyone?"

"Who'd believe me? They think we're all nuts." He leaned closer and lowered his voice. "My nephew is an attorney. I told him. He said he'd make them wish they'd never come out here trying to rob us seniors!"

"I see."

His grin slowly slid away. "I didn't want the guy or the young lady to die. I'd never wish that. But people all around here were dying. As I said, we know that's how we'll leave, but we don't expect a mass exodus, you know? So what if that couple and their crooked friends think they're so important? Why steal money from those of us who worked all our lives? Just because their friends have big positions in government, do they have the right to steal? I asked that coach guy that. I told him he should show his boy how to be honest. He said he owed money. He looked scared. A big guy like that. He almost begged me not to say anything. I told him it was too late. Do you think I was wrong?"

I felt a chill. This thing was bigger than even I had suspected. I smiled at him and answered as calmly as I could. "No, I don't. Stealing is wrong for anyone. Everyone should be able to die in dignity, no matter how young or how old. You're very brave."

"Not really. I heard he killed his wife and then himself." He looked away, toward the window. "I didn't want them to die. I just didn't want to hold their secrets in my heart. I have ones of my own."

"I guess we all have secrets . . . good and bad."

He nodded, still gazing toward the window. "Some are good," he finally murmured, "and some are pure agony. It's those—the untold agony—that grieves us."

I wasn't quite sure how to respond. Before I decided to change the topic, he'd turned back and smiled slightly. "Don't pay attention to me, young lady. I'm old. When we get old, we tend to look back on our lives and regret things we did—and didn't—do. Some nestle in our hearts, and others haunt us in the dark. But it's the things we don't regret—loving, happiness, hard work, family—those are the ones that push the agony into the darkness where it belongs."

His last words were mumbled. For a reason I hadn't quite put words to, I waited there while he dozed off to sleep.

Epilogue

"I love this shop!" The lady handed over her third armload of items and motioned for her husband to add his items to the counter.

"So you found several items you liked?" I asked, smiling.

"We only have a large motorhome," her husband grumbled. "At this rate, I'll be sleeping in the driver's seat!"

His wife caught my eye and grinned as she pulled the items from his arms and placed them on the overloaded counter. "Early Christmas shopping!" she sang out. "I'd never find these in Twin Falls."

"If we can get them there," he groused, but he pulled out his wallet and handed me a card. Then he picked up a framed photograph he'd leaned against the counter and added it to the lot.

"I didn't get that," his wife said. She squinted at it. "What kind of birds are those?"

"Sandhill Cranes," I told her. "I photographed them during the Festival of the Cranes at Bosque Wildlife Refuge."

"Where's that?" she asked.

"Remember when we stopped at that place and you didn't want to miss your soap opera so you stayed in the motorhome?" her husband asked.

"Oh. And those are?"

"Cranes," he answered patiently.

I ran his card and handed him the slip to sign.

"Oh," she said. "The ones that bring the babies."

Her husband sighed and shook his head.

I boxed the ceramic tea sets she'd chosen and packed the embroidered tea towels and several boxes of Teri's homemade soaps into sturdy bags. "You're going to love this soap," I told her as I handed them over to her. "My friend makes it herself."

"Oh," she said, "I forgot! I want a dozen of those picture postcards!"

Her husband sighed. "We need to get started if we're—"

"I'm hurrying!"

A few moments later, I watched him struggle out the door with the bags and boxes while she stopped and eyed other items. Finally, he called, "I can't open the door!" and she hurried to do so. "I'll try to close it."

"I'll get it," I called. "I need to lock up anyway."

He nodded and followed her out as I grabbed my keys and started toward the door.

A deep voice murmured over my shoulder, "Twenty bucks says he's going to be sleeping in the driver's seat before he gets that motorhome back to Idaho."

I jumped and spun around. "Chris Reed! How do you always sneak up on me? I might have whacked you or . . . something."

His grin stretched across his face. "I'm shaking in my boots! I just thought, with all the money you're raking in, you'd appreciate a lawman to guard the doors."

I groaned. "Lame."

"I see that grin trying to escape," he teased.

"What are you doing here? Don't you have to be chasing down criminals or feeding dogs or something?"

"Can't a guy bum a glass of tea without being hounded about his other responsibilities? Doesn't he get anything for rescuing a maiden in distress?"

"I'm not in distress and I don't need rescuing," I said as I handed my keys to him. "But since you're here, you can lock up."

I heard his naughty laugh as I straightened the counter and put things away underneath it.

"And if you want a glass of tea, you can help me shut the store down," I said when he returned to the counter.

He raised his eyebrows and I snapped, "Don't lawmen know how to escort the cash drawer to the lock-up?"

He didn't answer but started closing out the cash, that sassy grin that I . . . liked? . . . on his mouth. I walked on into the office and tidied up my desk. When I glanced out through the small window into the store, I couldn't see Reed. Had I made him mad enough to leave? I stepped back and heard a yelp.

"That was my foot!"

I pretended to swoon. "Finally, my prince. What happened to the shining armor?"

He didn't answer.

"Follow me and I'll revive you with that iced tea!"

He nodded and followed me into my living quarters. "I won't be a minute. I have some already made in the fridge."

He didn't answer. When I looked around, he was standing very close, his face so serious I feared more bad news.

"What—"

He leaned forward and kissed me, then pulled me into his arms and hugged me gently. Finally, he pulled back a little, keeping me in his arms, and rested his forehead against mine.

"We're not kids," he said.

"I know—"

He kissed me again. "I like doing this, but I need to say something while I still can."

He sounded serious. "You're not sick or—"

He sighed. "Would you come out to the truck?"

"What? Chris Reed, if you're trying to prepare me for the worst—"

"This is getting more and more jumbled. You just wait here," he said. "I think I forgot something."

Something was seriously wrong with Reed. As I watched him walk out the front door, a dozen scenarios flashed through my mind. I wasn't waiting. Something was wrong and Chris Reed was going to tell me. I opened the front door and bumped into a solid chest.

"Whoa! Did anyone ever tell you you'd make a great linebacker?"

I jumped and stepped back inside the door as he followed me, his arms holding my favorite of Madonna's pups.

"Ohhhh!" I squealed. Then I stopped and glared at him. "Are you giving this one away?"

"Yep."

"I'm never speaking to you again!" I turned away and stomped to the counter. "I promised you a glass of tea, and then I'm never saying another word!"

"Promise?"

I ignored him and continued to fill the glasses with ice and pour the tea. I could hear the puppy grunting and yipping. I didn't want iced tea! I filled one for him and whirled around.

Reed wasn't grinning. In fact, he looked a little scared. "Promise?" he asked again.

Then I noticed the hand not holding the squirming puppy was extended toward me.

"What's that?" I asked cautiously.

"We—Madonna and this wiggly pup—wonder if . . . "

The puppy chose that moment to break out of his arms and promptly raced after Flash. She whacked him on the nose and he yipped. Then he waddled back to Reed's foot and yipped.

"What?"

"We wonder if you'd be interested in—"

"What are you trying to say?"

Reed picked the puppy up in one arm and wrapped the other around me.

"I'm trying to tell you that there must be thirty lottery pots going around Saddle Gap about us. I'm sick and tired of people asking me when!"

"Are you okay? When what? You're not—"

He bent and kissed me again. This time, I felt the tingle run down to my toes. "My toes," I murmured.

He understood that one. "Finally! I'm trying to tell you that I want us to officially date!"

"Okay."

"Well, aren't you going to let me finish before you interrupt me again?"

I shook my head.

He stepped back, took my hand, and he and the pup led me to the overstuffed chair. He gently nudged me into the seat and then handed me the pup. I wasn't sure what he was leading up to. I'd been teasing, but he looked serious suddenly. Had I misread this whole thing?

He squatted down in front of me and looked into my eyes. "This whole thing—Coach . . . his family . . . the grandchild he'll never see . . . the poor people cheated out of their life's work—has made me reconsider some things."

"And?"

"I'm not ready just yet to settle down. My place isn't ready. I—"

"What? What are you rambling on about, Chris?"

"A man should be ready. And he shouldn't have a crazy job like mine. Look at all of the times you've been in danger!"

"I was in danger in Houston, Reed. But why are you worrying about me being in danger? You're not making sense!" I tried to pull away. The puppy yipped.

"This is absolutely the stupidest thing I've ever done!" he muttered, thrusting the puppy at me and walking to the door.

I stared at the door for a bit after he slammed it. The squirming puppy finally got my attention. He was chewing on something. It was . . . a small envelope.

I grabbed it out of the puppy's mouth, yelping when his sharp teeth nipped my fingers. Where had he gotten it? I tore it open. Had Reed gone berserk? He'd never written notes to me unless . . . I pulled out a small card and read: Mama told me to give this to the girl who won my heart.

Sitting there, a squirming puppy in my arms, I felt the tears running down my face.

"I didn't mean to insult you!"

I looked up. Chris, an uncertain look on his face I didn't recognize, pulled the puppy out of my arms and soothed him.

"You didn't insult me," I finally said, wiping the tears with the back of my hand. "He's a sweet gift. But I don't have a place for him here."

"Wait here. Hold the thought." Chris took the pup back out the door and put it in his truck. When he came back, he reached for my hand and pulled me into his arms. "I didn't mean to make you cry. I— you didn't like it?"

"It was a sweet note, Reed."

"No, I mean—" He walked back and looked at the chair. "Here it is!" He picked up the note. "So it's a no?"

"What's a no?" I asked.

He held the note toward me. "Mama told me to give this to the girl who won my heart," I read aloud. "So?" Then I felt something glued to the back. I turned it over. Taped to the back was a dainty gold chain necklace. I removed the tape and let it drop before me. On the chain was a heart-shaped stone.

"Oh, Reed," I breathed. "This is the most beautiful necklace I've ever seen! But it's not my birthday!"

"No, it isn't . . . nor mine," he said. He fastened the delicate necklace around my neck, his fingers lingering against my throat. "My dad gave it to Mama when I was born. He loved sapphires but could only afford this very tiny one. He said he should have chosen a ruby because of the Bible quote about a virtuous woman having a price above rubies."

He leaned down and kissed my cheek. "I'm giving this to you because you have won my heart. I'm not naïve. I know I have a dangerous job, and I'm short tempered sometimes, and I'm stubborn, and my house isn't ready for anyone yet. Besides, I believe people should be old-fashioned and court. What do you think?"

I snuggled against his chest. "I think this is the most romantic thing anyone has ever said or done. But it's too soon—"

"For marriage," he finished. "I'm asking if you'll enter an old-fashioned courtship with me. We know we're attracted to each other. Right?"

I nodded.

"So I think we need to step things up a bit. I don't want to move in with you. I want to savor this time, get to know you, fall head over heels—if I haven't already—and give you time to do the same. I wouldn't give you this—and it is yours, by the way, no matter what—I wouldn't give you this if I already wasn't loving you as a person. Now,

I'd like to see if we love each other as soulmates and future parents maybe, even if it's only mutt parents."

He pulled back and wiped my cheeks with his finger. "I don't want to rush us. But you haven't said how you feel. Is this too crazy? I promise you we will always be friends if you can't—"

"I can!"

We didn't talk for a while after that.

When Chris's phone buzzed, we parted reluctantly. The conversation was brief.

"You have to go," I whispered. "Be safe!"

He gave me another hug and turned to go.

"Wait!" I cried. "My pup! I'll take him home and feed the rest of the critters."

Chris grinned. "If I wasn't already convinced, I know now I've made the smartest decision of my life!"

Teri's Simple Posole

INGREDIENTS

- 2-3 cans Hominy drained
- 2 large cans Hatch green chiles (Mild to Hot depending on taste)
- 2 pounds fresh pork belly, cut into 11/2 inch cubes
- 2 pounds pork shoulder, not too lean, cut in 2-inch chunks
- Salt and pepper
- 2 cloves garlic (chopped) (approximately 1/4 cup)
- 1 bay leaf
- 2 cups finely diced white onion

PREPARATION

Place Hominy into a large soup pot. Cover with water and bring to a boil. Let simmer briskly for 1 hour. Season pork belly and pork shoulder generously with salt and pepper. After posole has cooked 1 hour, add pork shoulder, pork belly, onion, bay leaf, garlic, and cumin. Add enough water to cover by 2 inches, then return to a brisk simmer. While adding water occasionally and tasting broth for salt, simmer for about 2 1/2 hours more, until meat is tender and posole grains have softened and burst. Skim fat from surface of broth. Stir in 1-2 cups green chile and simmer for 10 minutes. Taste and correct seasoning.

Author Biography

Lonna Enox is the award winning author of three previous mystery novels. Her first book, *The Last Dance*, was selected Best First Novel by Chanticleer Book Reviews. Her second book, *Blood Relations*, won First Place for Mystery and Thriller and First Place and Grand Prize for the Clue Awards from Chanticleer Book Reviews. Her third book, *Striking Blind*, won First Place in the Clue Awards and Mystery and Thrillers from Chanticleer Book Reviews. Her books have been likened by *Readers Favorites* to Marci Muller, longtime cozy mystery author. You can visit Lonna's website at lonnaenox.org or join her on Facebook at www.facebook.com/lonnaenoxauthor.